Otis

Scott Hildreth

DEDICATION

My first introduction to a motorcycle club was over a decade ago. In a short period of time riding with them, it was apparent why men chose to become members of such clubs. The camaraderie within the ranks of the MC was indescribable. To call the men *brothers* would be an understatement at best.

A young man who was a Prospect for the club was denied his patch when his probationary period was over. Immediately following the denial of his patch, he committed suicide at home in front of his wife.

Ranger, this one's for you.

PROLOGUE

A man dressed in a dark blue well-fitted suit walked methodically toward the edge of the conference table. After exchanging glances with the ATF agents seated on the opposite side of the room, he hesitated. As he adjusted his tie, he exhaled an audible sigh. Filled with hatred for all Outlaw Motorcycle Gangs, his hands began to shake from anticipation of the pending arrests he believed his branch was certain to make. Eventually, to stabilize his hands and disguise the shaking, he placed them flat on the surface of the table as he leaned forward.

After clearing his throat, he spoke.

"Special Agent Pintler, the Grand Jury testimony is paramount to the prosecution of this case. How much additional time is necessary?" he asked.

Pintler, dressed in jeans, boots, and a leather vest adorned with a *Selected Sinners* patch, straightened his posture as he raised his hands to the sides of his face. Now rubbing his temples nervously with the tips of his fingers, he inhaled a deep breath, sighed, and fixed his gaze on the Director of Operations.

"A few more weeks, a month at most," Pintler said under his breath as he lowered his hands to the thighs of his faded denim jeans.

The Director of Operations released the edge of the table from his grasp and took a step rearward. Clearly frustrated, he placed his hands into the pockets of his slacks. As he fumbled to find his 1 year sobriety coin he had recently received from his Alcoholics Anonymous group, he bit into his lower lip slightly.

"I want this OMG, the *Selected Shitheads* - or whatever they're called - out of the picture, Pintler. These sons-of-bitches are an up-and-coming group of outlaws that is certain to be a huge threat if left to their own devices. Need I remind you of your responsibility not only to the bureau, but to the branch, and to the citizens of the United States of America?" he asked as he nervously rubbed the coin between his thumb and forefinger.

Pintler stood from his seat as he continued to press the palms of his hands against his thighs.

"I don't need a reminder. I'm well fucking aware of my responsibilities, *Sir.* You know as well as I do, as well as everyone else in this room, and everyone in the God damned division for that fucking matter, that *not* having all of the facts of the case in order will lead to a jury finding a *not guilty* verdict. Hell, a judge would throw this fucking case out of court if we tried to prosecute it right now. I'm currently putting pieces together for the murder of one of their own by the current Sergeant-At-Arms and the President, Todelli and Bishop. I didn't directly witness the killing, but there have been inferences made that lead me to believe..." Pintler paused as he tugged at the bottom of his leather vest.

As he released his vest he crossed his massive arms in front of his chest and continued.

"The local LEA declared it a suicide, but there's been some discussion it was tied to the sale of the firearms to the Hispanic gang listed in my report earlier this spring; April or May, I don't remember. I believe it was possibly retaliation for an insider - a Sinner - setting up a robbery during the sale."

"This field investigation is currently the longest in ATF history,

Pintler. It's becoming painfully obvious your mind and judgement are clouded. You're acting as if a murder is…" he paused and shook his head as he continued to rub his thumb against the coin.

The director pulled his hands from his pockets and narrowed his gaze, "You're acting as if murdering someone is just another day in the life of agent Pintler. You're becoming one of *them*. You've been inside this group too damned long. I'm afraid your vision has become blurred. Your allegiance and alliance are with the men and women of the United States, the ATF, and the Department of Justice. Remember that."

It bothered Pintler how the director spoke of the group as if the Selected Sinners weren't members of the United States, but outsiders. Frustrated, and without consciously deciding to do so, Special Agent Pintler began walking toward the exit. As the director continued to speak, he slowly walked toward the door, uncertain of the closing remarks the director made.

As Special Agent Pintler reached for the door, he glanced over his shoulder, "Is that all?"

"I want arrests, not excuses," the director barked.

Pintler opened the door, hesitated, and turned to face the director. After studying him for a short moment, he turned and walked through the door. As the resentment within him mounted, he silently walked to the elevator, inserted his key into the switch located beside the button pad, and turned it to the right a quarter of a turn. He pressed the button leading to the basement parking and stared down at his boots. In a matter of thirty minutes he was expected to be in attendance for an emergency meeting with the Selected Sinners MC. The ride to the clubhouse would normally take him forty-five minutes. As the elevator door opened, he methodically checked the basement for any onlookers. After a quick survey of the parking floor reserved for US Marshals and ATF agents revealed nothing out of place, he sighed and walked to his motorcycle.

While the sound of the motorcycle's exhaust echoed through the concrete basement, Special Agent Pintler checked his watch.

Eighteen minutes until two o'clock.

As he squeezed the clutch lever in his hand, the pit of his stomach filled with worry. In each and every meeting he attended with the Selected Sinners MC, he was at risk. He knew if the group of men ever determined he was an Agent with the ATF, or even suspected it for that matter, he would be killed.

It was a risk, at least initially, he was willing to take. Considering the time he had been in the field, and his ever growing understanding of the depth of the brotherhood of the MC, he was beginning to second guess if he would be able to testify against the men who had accepted him as a brother.

Pintler released the clutch and sped out of the parking garage. His mind filled with wonder over who his loyalties were currently aligned with. Over the years, he had become two separate people with two clearly different agendas. He was an agent with the ATF who had taken a vow to protect the United States from certain types of criminals, *and* he was a fully patched member of the Selected Sinners MC. When push came to shove, he would be required to take a stand on one side or the other.

Time, he decided, would tell. For now he knew, as soon as he rode from the confines of the garage, he became a Sinner. And a Sinner he would remain until he returned to the ATF offices.

OTIS

Axton crossed his arms, flexed his biceps, and clenched his jaw muscles as he surveyed the group of men. He was as predictable to me as any man could be. His telltale signs were clear - at least to me. He was aggravated with something, and wanted everyone in attendance to realize his level of disgust. A much more emotional man than me, Axton believed in the value of intimidation. Personally, I was more reserved than most of the Selected Sinners, and preferred to *act* over speaking in an authoritative manner. To me, Axton was easy to read. To the other members of the club, he was an unpredictable God. The fact he was president of the MC elevated him by everyone's standards, and his intimidating nature placed him even higher in the eyes of some men. I stood quietly with my arms crossed and waited for him to speak.

"Well fellas, we've got a clear fucking mess on our hands. The *Bandidos* and the *Cossacks* are at war, and the ATF is coming down on MC's hard all over the country. Right now, they've got 200 men in jail on charges of conspiracy to commit capital murder, and I suspect they'll arrest many more. As I've said over and over," he paused, uncrossed his arms, and rolled his shoulders rearward.

"We need to keep our shit wired tight. These sons-of-bitches will make any connection they can to tie us up and charge us under the RICO act. As long as we're not dealing in *illegal* arms, we've got nothing to worry about. Now I'm not trying to get into your business as individuals, but if you've got illegal firearms in your *personal* arsenal; unregistered machine guns, short barreled rifles, silenced weapons, sawed-off shotguns, or fucking rocket propelled grenades, leave those fuckers at home. I don't want 'em here or on your bikes, and I don't want the club exposed to the problems they create. Understood?"

Most in attendance either nodded or gave an audible acknowledgement of some sort. After he glanced over his shoulders and slowly studied the group, his eyes became fixed on Pete, who began to grumble expletives under his breath from the rear of the group.

Axton craned his neck and gazed toward the rear of the group.

"There a problem back there I need to know about, Pete?" Axton growled.

Pete pulled against his long beard with his right hand as he seemed to consider his response.

"I ain't saying I do, and I ain't saying I don't, but let's say a fella has a couple of illegal firearms like you're talkin' about. As long As they're *his* property, and not *club* property, what's the problem?" Pete grunted as he released his beard from his grasp.

"Listen up, fellas," Axton shouted as he raised his hands in the air.

"Pete asked a question. He wants to know how a fella having illegal weapons becomes a *club* issue, and why it doesn't remain one of *personal* nature. Here's the thing. If you get in a pinch with the law, and you've got illegal weapons when they search your house, they can't make a tie between what you've got at home and the club. But, if you're with the club, or on club property, and you're in a position to be searched and the weapons are found, you immediately put the club at risk. They'll be able to say you possessed the weapons while acting as a club member, and they'll say the weapons were going to be sold by the club, or that they were club property. They call it *constructive possession*. It's different than *active possession*, which is actually having physical possession. Believe me, I don't like it any more than you do, but all I'm asking is that you leave your *illegal* weapons at home. If they're legitimate, do as you please. I'm asking that regardless of whether or not you think you're going to get caught, to leave your bad boy toys at home, out of respect for the club. Am I making fucking sense?" Axton asked.

"Fucking cops," Pete grunted.

Axton nodded his head, "That's right, Pete. *Fucking cops*."

Axton looked around the room. All members in attendance nodded their heads.

"So what exactly happened in Waco, Texas? We alright down there?" Mike asked.

Axton sighed as he crossed his arms in front of his chest. "The Texas Sinners are fine. As you know, we have permission to wear our Texas rocker, and we pay our dues faithfully. I'm not here trying to knock another club, and this is mostly rumor, but it's a pretty *solid* rumor. We all know Texas is a Bandido state. The Cossacks were initially paying their dues to the Bandidos to wear the Texas rocker, but either out of pride or sheer stupidity they stopped. They thought they were big enough and bad enough to go up against the Bandidos. A few weeks later, a group of Bandido's saw a Cossack riding through town and forced him off the road. They hit the fucker in the head with a hammer and took his cut. A few weeks after that, six Cossacks saw a lone Bandido, forced him to the side of the road and stole his fuckin' bike. After a few more weeks, a quarterly coalition meeting was scheduled to discuss legislative issues, and they rented the outside portion of the Twin Peaks restaurant to have the meeting."

"Having a quarterly meeting at a *breastaurant*. Now that's what I'm talking about. Titties, beer, and brotherhood," Biscuit chuckled.

Axton raised his hand to silence Biscuit.

"So, on the day before the meeting, Cossacks started posting pictures of their colors on Facebook, showing the Texas rockers they'd sewn on their cuts. Without a doubt they had called the Bandidos out by flying the rocker, and the Bandidos had to act. When the Cossacks showed up at the meeting with the Texas rocker sewn to their cut, the war began," Axton explained.

"Disrespectful pricks," Biscuit sighed.

"That's right," Axton nodded, "It's about respect. People don't understand it, but that's what it boils down to. It was blatant disrespect toward the Bandidos. Cops are trying to make it sound like MC's are waging war on cops or even on society, but we know better. Hell, you don't go into a gay bar and scream *I hate fags* without expecting a fight," he paused and turned toward Toad.

"And you don't walk into a room full of Marines and call 'em *dumb fucking jarheads*. Nor do you ride in Texas, a Bandido owned state, wearing a *Texas* rocker without either paying your tax or having Bandido permission. It's all about respect. That's as much as I know. Are there any other questions about that?"

"How many dead?" Fancy asked.

"Nine, most are probably dead at the hands of the returned fire from the cops. Ballistics aren't in, but mark my words, when it's over, it'll be the cops that killed most of 'em. Roughly 200 are in jail, and charged under RICO on capital murder charges," Axton responded in an authoritative tone.

Toad turned toward Axton and shrugged his shoulders, "Talked to A-Train yesterday. He said Ripp and Dekk got pulled over and questioned yesterday morning when they were riding to the gym, and they're not even 1%ers."

Axton nodded his head in agreement, "That's what I'm talking about. Most city cops don't know the difference, and the news is saying MC's are waging war on cops in retaliation. It's just more proof of how the media uses the news against *all* of us. Hell, they love this shit. Now, if there aren't any other questions on *that*, I have one other issue we need to discuss."

Axton looked around the room. After absorbing the few seconds of the silence, he inhaled a shallow breath and continued.

"As you know, the trial for your Sergeant-At-Arms' future brother-in-law is coming up next week. He's been in prison for quite some time, and has been awarded a new trial on appeal. I've got mixed emotions about how to handle this. It's a case with the ATF, and there will be ATF agents in court testifying, observing, and just being the assholes that they are. We need to show support to this man and have a presence, but I'm wondering just how many of us need to attend the trial?"

"Fuck them pussies with the ATF. I say every available man needs to show up. It's my God given right to attend," Biscuit howled.

Axton nodded his head, "It certainly is. But we don't want to sway the jury one way or another. A large presence, considering what happened in Waco with the Bandidos, just might work against him."

Biscuit shook his head, "And having just a couple of the fellas there makes it look like nobody gives a shit about him. Hell, if the court room's empty, the jury will think he's a piece of shit. I say we have every available body in attendance, and we *do* intimidate the jury. Intimidate them into thinking if they don't find him *not* guilty, we'll do right here in Wichita what the Bandidos did in Texas. Shoot the courtroom into a big piece of Swiss fuckin' cheese. Let 'em think whatever they want to. Hell, they can wonder if we're going to show up at their houses afterward and burn them to the fuckin' ground for that matter."

I considered what Biscuit said about intimidating the jury. There was no doubt if the jury saw a *tremendous* presence, they'd be intimidated. Hell, anyone seeing a huge presence of 1%ers in their cuts was intimidated. Subconsciously, they would probably lean toward a not guilty verdict for fear of retaliation alone.

"Slice, I've got to agree with Biscuit on this one," I breathed.

"If we're in the courtroom thirty or so deep, the jury is going to be as nervous as a bunch of whores in church. They may find him not guilty for fear of retaliation alone. Let's use the massacre in Texas to our advantage."

Axton stared down at the floor for a long moment. As he looked up, he crossed his arms and gazed blankly into the crowd.

"Trial starts Monday, and begins with jury selection. How many can attend? I understand if you've got to work, but we're talking about that case with the ATF setting this fella up on murder, and he's the brother of the Sergeant-At-Arms Ol' Lady. Jackson Shephard with Hells' Fury, road name is *Killer*. Now, by a show of hands, who can attend?" Axton asked.

Arms shot into the air. I gazed around the room. Every man I could see had his arm raised. I glanced toward Toad and patted him on the shoulder.

"Well fuck. If we're going to show up, I say we *show up*. I'll call the other chapters and see who else can attend. I hope the courtroom is a big fucker," Axton chuckled.

Toad smiled and nodded in apparent appreciation as he glanced around the room. Sydney's brother was the only family she had, and having him taken away had taken a toll on her emotionally, and left her feeling alone for the majority of her adult life. If he could be freed from prison, not only would it allow her to have her family back in place, it would set a legal precedent regarding the ATF and entrapment of members of a MC. A win in this case would be huge for MC's across the nation.

Axton sighed as he studied the group, "Avery's going to be there, and Sydney will be as well, so if for some reason you want to bring your Ol' Ladies, that'll be fine. And remember, we're not only there for Killer, we're there to show support for Sydney. This is going to be a tough one for her if he's found guilty *again*."

I viewed Avery and Sydney as if they were my younger sisters. Seeing harm come to them in any way was beyond comprehension, regardless of whether or not it was physical or emotional. A large showing in court would not only show support Sydney's brother, but Sydney and Avery as well. Avery spent long hours assembling the paperwork to receive a new trial for him, and obtaining it was a victory in itself. Citing law and recent applicable federal cases to the appellate court, she was instrumental in the trial being awarded. Sitting in the courtroom would not only be interesting, it would pay respect to her for all the hard work she did in requesting a new trial.

Personally, attending the trial wasn't something I felt I *needed* to do; it was something I had to do.

As a matter of respect.

OTIS

Having a woman *fit* me was near impossible, as I had some pretty serious issues trusting people. I would never describe myself as paranoid, and in fact, I was quite the opposite. I was more of a realist, and realistically speaking, people seemed to always press their noses into cracks and crevices of a person's life where they just didn't belong. For me to *get to know* a woman would require exposing myself to her, and in doing so, I took a tremendous risk. My life, lifestyle, and day to day activities weren't something I could trust anyone with, male or female. Even spending *short* periods of time with people I didn't know exposed me, the club, and my club brothers to potential scrutiny. And, for the Selected Sinners, something as simple as a very shallow examination would certainly reveal more than we were prepared to allow outsiders to see or attempt to try and understand. Placing me under a microscope was one thing, but potentially placing my MC Brothers in harm's way was something I wasn't ever willing to ever jeopardize.

Taking the risk to even *meet* a woman was difficult for me. Meeting a woman would potentially cause me to want to naturally know more about her. Knowing more would require more exposure. More exposure equaled more risk, and the risk grew with everything she learned about me. In time, if I found out she either couldn't be trusted or she wasn't what I was looking for, the damage, so to speak, was already done. The life of a 1%er was a difficult one, and many outsiders didn't understand what they perceived as arrogance or conceit within the ranks of outlaw bikers when in fact it was nothing more than a façade used to preserve what it was we believed in.

Freedom.

When I was young, long before I became a Sinner, life was different. In high school, and for several years following my graduation, there was a woman in my life; a woman I loved dearly. She was everything I needed, almost everything I wanted, and we fit each other perfectly. One thing kept me from spending the rest of my life with her.

My selfishness.

She wanted a family, and I yearned for freedom. At the time, I perceived children as an annoyance and an obstacle between me and a world which was otherwise free of confinement and restriction. We separated when I was twenty-one years old, and I had spent a lifetime regretting it. Since then, I had been with very few women, but each one I met reminded me of the same thing – just how extraordinary Sam was.

After having experienced the love she and I shared, attempting to accept someone else as anywhere close to her equal was to admit I had a special procedure for shoving a square peg into a round hole. There would never be a soul on earth to completely fill the hole she left inside of me, and admitting it allowed me to accept a life of solitude as being not only what I needed, but without a doubt what I deserved.

Living in my self-imposed womanless hell had some benefits. The freedom I once yearned for was now well within my grasp. My life had no restrictions and very few regulations I was required to adhere to. I had the ability to do whatever I wanted, whenever I pleased, without answering to anyone.

Well, *almost* anyone.

As my mother bent down and opened the oven, she turned her head to the side and widened her eyes slightly, "They're saying on the news the police were threatened by some of the motorcycle clubs, Steve. They threatened those poor officers with retaliation. I don't like that at all. People are supposed to respect law enforcement officers. For heaven's sake, your father was a police officer."

"Ma, they're full of shit, no one threatened the cops. If for some reason one of those clubs wanted to do something, they'd just do it, they damned sure wouldn't announce it or warn the cops. And it's pretty tough for me to respect some city cop when every time I turn around they're shooting another unarmed citizen for having a taillight that doesn't work or for arguing with them about a traffic ticket. *Serve and protect.* That's their job. It's damned sure not what we get from them anymore, is it?" I shrugged.

"They said they recovered a hundred and fifty weapons, it's pretty obvious to me those men came with killing on their minds. It makes me nervous having you and your friends out there riding anywhere near those thugs," she said over her shoulder as she situated the casserole dish on the countertop.

"They're not thugs, ma. And it was in Texas. *Everyone* is armed in Texas. They're trying to make it sound like it was an all-out war, but it was nothing more than a bar fight and the cops came and shot everyone up. Hell, if you went to Wal-Mart in Texas and rounded up everyone in it and searched them, I'd be willing to bet more than seventy-five percent of them would be *armed*. I'm tired of talking about it," I complained.

She turned to face me and placed her hands on her hips, "Well, it makes me nervous. I don't want you or any of your friends hurt if you go to one of those get-togethers."

My mother was fifty-nine years old, and appeared to be much younger. She was a small woman, standing barely over five feet tall, and weighed roughly one hundred pounds. I attributed the majority of her preserved appearance and youthful looks to the fact she rarely left the house, and spent most of her time either cleaning or preparing meals for my father, who was a mirror image of me.

"We're not going to get hurt, ma. Not unless some cop decides to shoot one of us," I chuckled.

As I heard my father's footsteps coming into the kitchen, I turned to face him, hoping he had heard at least a portion of what we were talking about. His opinion mattered to my mother, and he was not much different than me in his judgement of today's police officers and their poor decisions.

"Ken, talk to your son," my mother sighed as she folded the towel that dangled from her fingers.

"My son? He's *our* son, Marge. What are we talking about?" he chuckled as he slapped his hand against my back.

"Game's over and the Royals won. Best team in the league," he bragged as he rubbed his hands together.

"It's about time," I laughed, making reference to the fact the Kansas City Royals hadn't done anything good in baseball since the 1980's.

I glanced at my mother for a second, and shifted my gaze toward my father, "We were talking about the biker shoot-out in Texas. Ma's afraid the fellas and I are gonna get hurt if we're hanging around the *thugs* who were at the bar in Texas. I told her the only way any of us would get hurt is if one of those trigger-happy cops decided to shoot at us for getting in a fist fight."

As far as my mother and father were concerned, I was part of a group of men that loved riding motorcycles together. They either didn't want to accept or were afraid to admit that I was the Vice President of a 1%er MC. I didn't press the issue or try to explain anything, and they didn't ask. For them to understand just what it was the club offered me or to learn of and comprehend our day-to-day activities would be nothing short of impossible.

"That's the damned truth Marge. That whole thing stinks. They said the other day the shooting was *inside* the bar. Now they're saying it was *outside*. The officer in charge originally said the police returned fire when the bikers shot at them. Now the film from the security system of the bar has been reviewed, and it looks like the only shooting was from the police officers. The whole thing makes me sick. Cops today are too damned trigger happy. Hell, I made hundreds of arrests, and never pulled my service revolver once," my father explained as he walked toward the casserole dish and peered down at the concoction my mother had cooked.

My father worked for thirty years as a police officer, and had retired unharmed. He now attempted to maintain his sanity by working part-time at a local hardware store, which seemed to work well for him. Still standing six foot five at sixty-two years old, he was in good physical and mental condition. His job kept him busy enough that he continued to feel his life was worthwhile, and it allowed a little physical separation from my mother during the day, which, according to him, was necessary.

"I just don't want him to get hurt," my mother sighed.

"He's a big boy, Marge. He'll be fine. Hell, he's got that Marine by his side half the time, nobody's going to mess with him," my father said under his breath as he walked toward the dish my mother had placed on the countertop.

"What have we got here, Marge?" my father asked as he poked the top of the casserole with his fingertip.

"It's a recipe I got off of Pinterest," my mother responded, "Enchilada casserole."

"You know, we ate for thirty years without Pinterest. Now it seems every time I turn around, we're trying something new that some shit-head in San Francisco cooked, took a few pictures of, and posted a recipe. They're probably sitting back there now laughing at all the people trying to cook that shit. Just because they took a pretty picture of it doesn't mean it tastes good," my father growled as he shook his head.

"What are we going to eat with it?" he asked as he glanced around the kitchen.

"I'll slice up an avocado and a few tomatoes. It's supposed to be a complete meal," my mother shrugged as she turned toward the refrigerator.

My father glanced at the casserole dish, turned toward me, and shrugged his shoulders.

"It's any wonder I haven't starved to death since she joined that damned web site. You still not messing with any of that internet stuff?" he asked over his shoulder as he walked toward the refrigerator.

"Nope. Facebook, Pinterest, Twitter, I don't have any of 'em. Can't see any need. I don't want people who don't know me digging through my life. As far as I'm concerned, it's like leaving your front door open for anyone to come into your house and dig through your shit," I responded.

"Amen," he said as he held a bottle of beer at arm's length.

I accepted the beer, twisted off the lid, and took a drink. My father was a very understanding man, and rarely pried in my personal business.

I believed he understood far more than my mother what me, the club, and my MC Brothers were all about, but he never asked, and I never offered.

"Sit down," my mother said as she arranged the plates around the table.

As I slowly walked toward the table, I peered down at the plate of sliced avocadoes and tomatoes and eventually shifted my eyes toward the enchilada casserole. My father was right. I was surprised we both hadn't starved to death since my mother found Pinterest. Trying new things was fun for her, but it seemed she was constantly searching the site for an easier way to prepare a meal. An entire meal in one dish was her obvious desire and my father and I were the test subjects. For me, it was one day a week eating with my parents. For my father, it was a daily occurrence.

Sunday dinner at my parent's house wasn't necessarily a requirement, but I was always *expected* to attend. Although I was thirty-six years old, I was still a little boy in the eyes of my mother, and I always would be. I looked forward to the dinners, and enjoyed the conversations we had. For me, it was a way to unwind, become normal, and mentally exhaust myself from all of the atrocities from the previous week of being a *Selected Sinner.* It allowed me to begin each week with a new start, a fresh mind, and the reminder that family is more important than anything else this world has to offer us.

Drinking beer and Sunday dinners were a guilty pleasure. Any other day of the week, my strict diet excluded foods which would cause me to forfeit my form, muscle tone, or physical condition. Setting Sunday dinners aside, drinking beer was my only vice, and I tried to keep my drinking to no more than five or six beers a day. My daily physical conditioning not only allowed me to maintain a sound mind and body, but did a pretty good job of working off the beers I typically drank throughout the course of any given day.

"So, your father tells me the Marine friend of yours is engaged to be married. Said he's with that cute little blonde waitress down at the barbeque joint," my mother said as we sat down.

Here we go.

"Yeah, ma. He's engaged to the girl at the barbeque joint. Her name's Sydney," I sighed as I scooped half of the casserole dish onto my plate.

"And your other friend Ashton is living with a girl and they're just as good as married. Is that right?" she asked as my father turned toward me and wagged his eyebrows jokingly.

"Axton, ma. With an X. His name's *Axton*, not Ashton. And yeah, he's got a girlfriend or whatever. And her name's Avery," I responded as I raised my beer bottle to my lips.

"Talk down at the store is that the tall brown haired girl is an attorney. They said she filed an appeal to get a new trial for the other girl's brother, who was set up by the ATF years back. Is that all true?" my father asked as he shoved a forkful of enchiladas into his mouth.

I shook my head as I placed my bottle of beer onto the table, "Who told you all that?"

"Common knowledge down at the store," my father said as he finished chewing his food.

"Well, it's partially true," I sighed as I pressed my fork into the casserole.

"Avery is the brown haired girl, Axton's girlfriend. She's a paralegal or whatever. Works downtown with one of those powerful defense attorneys. She filed an appeal for Sydney's brother, who was railroaded by the ATF for agreeing he didn't like some other club. They granted it, and trial is next week," I explained as I raised the forkful of food to my mouth.

"A man don't get tossed in prison for saying you don't like someone. There's got to be more to it," my father shrugged as he reached for his beer.

I nodded my head as I alternated glances between my mother and father, eventually fixing my gaze on my father, "There is. He said if push came to shove, he'd kill 'em if they messed with him. But only after getting drunk and harassed by the ATF for two years."

"Oh lord," my mother said under her breath as she raised her hands to her face.

"Ma…" I breathed as I shook my head.

"Hell, if anyone messed with me, I'd kill 'em Marge," my father grunted as he cut another chunk of casserole off of the slab sitting on his plate.

"Ken!" my mother gasped.

"Well, I would. I'm sure the court will decide who's right and who's wrong. It'll be interesting to see how that pans out," my father said.

I nodded my head and glanced down at my plate. Conversations at my parent's dinner table seemed to not only have no boundaries, but they typically had no limits. It wasn't uncommon for us to begin talking about my father's tomato crop, and eventually end up in a heated discussion about the benefits of legalizing prostitution. Personally, I believed my father often changed the subjects until the conversation took a course that he believed would irritate my mother.

"Speaking of attorneys, did you hear about that doctor that sewed a pecker on that Asian stripper in Wichita? She's dancing down at the strip club by Boeing now with a chunk of meat between her legs. Clyde says he's seen her over there and she's hung like a horse. Said she draws the biggest crowd out of all those girls. Rumor has it they're getting up a petition to have her tossed out, saying now she's not a girl, but a guy. What do you think about that?" my father asked as he reached for his beer.

"Ken!" my mother breathed.

"Well, it's the damned truth, Marge. Sewed it right on there. Now, what I'm wondering about is this…" he paused and lowered his bottle of beer to the table.

"Where'd they get the pecker?" he shrugged.

I shook my head in disgust, "Hard saying."

"Well, someone had to give it up. Maybe it was one of those fellas who wanted to be switched into a girl. I'm thinking they must keep a running tally, and when there's a guy who wants it whacked off and a hole drilled down there, they add him to the chart. And later, when they find a girl who wants a pecker, as long as there's some dip-shit on the chart who wants his cut off, they got a match. People are just plain weird these days. Anyway Clyde seen him. Or her. Said she was pretty, well 'cept for the bulge in her pants," he chuckled.

"Let's change the subject," my mother sighed.

Disgusted at the thought of an Asian stripper with a cock swinging between her legs, I shook my head.

"Enchiladas are pretty good, ma," I sighed.

She smiled and nodded her head, "Thank you."

"Maybe next time, *if there is a next time*, we should have some tacos or something with this shit. You took a little piece, and Steve and I took what was left. Either that or make a double helping," my father

22

complained as he gazed down at his plate and pierced a tomato slice with the tip of his fork.

My mother gazed down at her plate and began to speak without looking up.

"It worked out just fine, and we don't have to worry about leftovers. Now what I was trying to talk about earlier was that all of your friends have girlfriends or fiancées, and you haven't had a girlfriend since I don't know when. Maybe it's time you get one. You know we all have to grow up some time."

Half pissed off that she'd mentioned the subject, I grabbed my bottle of beer and pushed myself away from the table slightly. As the bottle dangled beside my hip from between my thumb and forefinger, I studied her until she looked up from her plate.

"Ma, I don't have a girlfriend because I haven't found one yet that suits me. They're all too damned nosey or far too controlling. As soon as I find one good enough for me, you'll be the first to know," I said as I raised my beer bottle in the air and tilted the neck toward her.

"I liked Samantha. I can't see why she had to up and move away. A girl like her would be perfect for you," my mother said as she glanced toward her plate.

"I liked Sam too, but that was fifteen years ago, ma. Fifteen. Not yesterday, but fifteen damned years," I said as I stood from my seat.

I walked to the refrigerator and grabbed two more beers. After finishing what little was left in my bottle, I dropped it into the trash and twisted the lid off the other. As I walked to the table, I studied my mother and waited for her response as I handed my father a beer.

She sat silently and picked at her food.

"Why you bringing up Sam after all this time?" I asked as I sat down.

As she looked up from her plate, my father gazed down at his.

"Her mother passed," my mother said as she shifted her gaze to meet mine.

My heart sank. Short of Sam's husband, and what I was certain to be a house full of kids, her mother was all she had. Her father, who was considerably older than her mother, passed away when she was twelve after a short battle with colon cancer. Her mother, to the best of my knowledge, never remarried. Sam had no brothers or sisters, and longed for a large family, one I wasn't willing to provide.

I took a long swallow of beer and washed the lump from my throat.

"When's the funeral?" I asked flatly.

"Tomorrow," my mother said as she looked up from her plate.

I shrugged my shoulders, "Well, I've got the trial tomorrow or I'd go. Probably best that I don't see her anyway. She's married and has a family. Her husband doesn't need a reminder of who her high school sweetheart was."

"Your father and I argued about going, you know how he is about funerals. We decided to send flowers instead. I just found out yesterday when your father told me. He heard it at work from Clyde," my mother said.

"What happened?" I asked.

My mother lowered her fork to the side of her plate and shook her head from side-to-side, "Well, that's the sad part. Apparently, she was cooking, and was pulled some aluminum foil off the roll. She cut her wrist on the little strip or the foil…I don't know…and she bled to death before the ambulance arrived."

An aluminum foil death didn't immediately make sense to me. I sat and stared blankly at my mother and waited for her to say it was a big joke. After a few minutes of silence, I realized what she said was reality and a part of Sam's life she would be required to accept.

I shook my head, "Aluminum foil? Jesus, how does someone prepare for that?"

Frustrated, I shrugged my shoulders, "I guess they don't. That's a damned shame."

My father looked up from his plate and nodded his head, "Sure is. Just goes to show you, you never know…"

I stared at the bottle of beer for what seemed like an unreasonable amount of time. The thought of Sam's mother dying, and dying from something no one would or could make any plans or concessions to prepare for caused me to feel a deeper sorrow for the entire family. Even a car wreck would allow a person to eventually accept it as God's will.

But aluminum foil?

I began to worry about Sam, and wondered how she'd accept the death. I attempted to consider myself in the same circumstance, and decided I'd probably never accept it as being part of life's big plan for me or my family. Trying to make sense of it was beginning to make me feel uneasy. Although I was raised by a God fearing family, I in no way struggled with God as much as Axton or Toad, but still struggled nonetheless. I did, however, believe I lived in God's world; and that all things happened for a reason.

I sat and stared at the amber bottle, wondering if my lifetime would produce enough time for me to come up with a good reason for the mother of the only woman I ever loved dying from such an unfortunate incident.

I eventually lifted the bottle and drank the remaining beer with the understanding that although some things in life are unavoidable, we may never accept them as being necessary.

OTIS

A two hour long workout provided little relief, and my tension was still at a level I wasn't comfortable with. Obviously having a difficult time accepting the death of Sam's mother as being necessary, I stepped into the shower with the hope it would wash away the remaining discomfort I was feeling.

After showering until there was no remaining hot water, I dried off, took a precursory glance in the mirror, and walked to my bedroom. Although I should have climbed into bed and retired for the night, I felt falling asleep would prove impossible.

A quick text message to the Sinners I reserved as friends revealed Biscuit as the only one available to have a drink. Eager to attempt to rid myself of what was bothering me, I got dressed, hopped on my bike, and rode to Wichita to meet him at the bar.

I parked my bike beside his and surveyed the parking lot. A few cars littered the otherwise empty lot. Sunday night at most bars in Wichita was a slow night, and considering the problems in Waco, Texas with the shooting, several of the bars had made new rules regarding bikers wearing their cuts inside the bar. It came as no surprise, and although most bars prevented gangs such as the Crips and Bloods from wearing their colors, none had taken the chance at attempting to prevent MC's from doing so. This bar was one who was still *biker friendly* and had made no such rule, leaving it as one of our available options. As I walked through the door I recalled the night I met Axton's Ol' Lady, Avery.

"Big O, what's shakin'," Biscuit said as he stood from his bar stool.

I shook my head and grinned, "Just needing to unwind. Let's go over and sit in one of those booths, I don't need the bartender listening to what we're talking about."

"No argument from me, that stool is as hard as a wedding day cock," he said as he wrapped his arms around me and slapped me on the back.

"Place don't seem the same without Avery and that other chick workin', does it?" Biscuit sighed as we walked toward an open booth.

I shook my head, "Sure doesn't."

Biscuit sat down and placed his Red Bull and glass of vodka in front of him. As he sat and studied me for a short moment, he rubbed his beard with his right hand, and eventually drug his fingers through his thick brown hair.

"Sure you heard about Corndog and that poor girl who worked here, huh?" he asked as he leaned onto the edge of the table.

I nodded my head, "I've heard some, yeah."

He pressed his forearms onto the table, clasped his hands together, and leaned forward, "They're inseparable now. He's been fuckin' that poor girl six ways from Sunday. Talked to him after the meeting the other day. Said he's been schooling her on sucking cock, and it sounds like she's got quite the sexual appetite. Anyway, He's making up for the five years of lost time he spent in the joint."

"I'm sure he is," I said as I raised my hand to get the waitress' attention.

He turned his palms up, and widened his eyes slightly.

"You know, every one of the fellas is fascinated by that girl's big fucking titties. But me? I'm fascinated with the fact Toad wrapped her head in God damned Saran Wrap, fucked her until she was damned near dead, and then took her to the Dog's house, dropped her off, and she ain't fuckin' left yet. Hell, until the Toad dropped her off, she'd never met Corn Dog."

As I noticed the waitress walking toward the table, I raised my hand to silence Biscuit.

"I'll take a couple of Michelob Ultras and bring him another can of Red Bull and a few iced double vodkas," I said as the waitress approached the table.

"Sounds good. You guys aren't going to shoot the place up, are you?" she chuckled playfully.

Biscuit grinned as he turned to face her, "We might after we get a few drinks in us."

Probably no more than twenty-one years old, and more than likely one of Avery's old college friends, the waitress was cute, but young. Tall and thin with athletic legs, I wondered if she played volleyball with Avery and Sloan, but decided not to ask. Having a conversation with her wasn't at the top of my current list of priorities.

"God damn…" Biscuit said after studying her for a short moment, drawing the word *damn* out for five seconds or so.

She shifted her gaze to meet his and grinned, "What?"

"Your eyes. That's the craziest blue I ever seen," he said as he twisted his body to face her.

"Contacts," she shrugged.

"Figures," he said under his breath as he turned around.

"Be back in a minute," she grinned as she turned away.

Biscuit took a drink of his vodka, chased it with a swallow of Red

Bull, and immediately pressed his chest into the edge of the table as if preparing to tell me a secret.

"Nothin' against the Dog, but I wonder about that fuckin' girl, Sloan. Damned thing can't have a lick of proper upbringing in her. Personally, I wouldn't fuck her with Pete's cock, and he's a nasty fucker. Corn Dog's pounding that shit like each day's his last, so I guess I'll say good for him; and from what he was sayin' she's become mighty fine at sucking cock. Oh, shit, I almost forgot, I got a story to tell ya," he said as he sat up and rubbed his hands together.

If Biscuit ever decided he no longer wanted to be a Sinner, he could immediately seek employment as a stand-up comic. His ability to tell a story was only matched by his willingness, and he was always willing. The problem was trying to decide if what you were hearing was the truth or another one of his wild made up fables. Either way, hearing him talk was entertaining, and probably exactly what I needed.

He pressed his forearms into the edge of the table and began to almost whisper, "So, speaking of suckin' cock, there was this girl; she gave the best fuckin' head ever. Damned thing was like a trained professional, and probably should have had a college course on how to properly suck a cock. She could take my meat all the way to the balls, stick out her God damned tongue, and curl it around my nut sack without missin' a beat."

I grinned and nodded my head, waiting to hear more about this professor of oral pleasure.

"So, this bitch had the most beautiful blue eyes. And, because she had no gag reflex, I could fuck this girl's mouth just like I was fuckin' a pussy. Anyway, when I'd pound her throat with my cock, I'd look down into her eyes, and after she bat those long lashes and revealed those damned eyes a few times, I'd just explode. She knew her eyes were my biggest weakness, and she was right," he paused and rubbed his beard with his hand.

"So one night, she's down on her knees, and she's going to town on my cock. Just a slurpin' and a suckin' like this one's her last. Hell, I'm lookin' up at the ceiling like I got no interest in watchin' her, which couldn't be any further from the truth. My problem was this," he paused as the waitress walked up with a tray of drinks.

"Here you go, two iced vodka doubles, a can of Red Bull, and two Ultras. Anything else?" the waitress asked as she placed the drinks onto the table.

I smiled and shook my head as I reached for a beer.

"Other than being like super big, you don't look like a biker, I mean not *really*," the waitress said.

"Never thought I was *like super big*, but thanks, I guess," Biscuit chuckled as he tugged on his cut.

"I uhhm, I was meaning him," she giggled as she tossed her head toward me.

"Oh," Biscuit said as he turned toward me and raised his eyebrows in wait for my response.

"I don't know that bikers look *any* certain way to be quite honest. I look the way I look and I'm a biker. One has nothing to do with the other," I sighed as I lifted my beer and tilted it toward her.

"Oh, I didn't really mean anything by it, I was just. I don't know. You know, trying to make conversation. Do you know Avery?" she asked as she tossed her hair over her shoulder.

I lowered my chin slightly, rested my elbow on the table, and dangled the beer bottle from my hand, "Sure do, she's a good friend."

"Well, we're not *close*, but I played volleyball with her. I'm a senior this year and she's a year older than me. I just heard she was like dating one of the guys in your gang," she said as she attempted to force her fingertips into to the extremely small pockets of her overly tight jean shorts.

"Club. We're a *club*, not a gang. A motorcycle club," I said as I lifted the bottle of beer to my lips.

"Oh, I thought you were a motorcycle *gang*. What's the difference?" she asked as she gave up on shoving her hands into her pockets and allowed her arms to dangle at her sides.

"There isn't one," I shrugged, "But gang sounds bad, and club sounds more professional and less criminal, so we all call ourselves clubs now."

She tilted her head to the side, seemingly slightly confused, "So you *are* a gang?"

Biscuit turned to face her and raised his index finger to his lips, "Shhh. Don't tell anybody."

"Oh, I won't. You can trust me," she grinned, "I'm Kat."

"Like a pussy cat?" Biscuit chuckled.

"Kind of, but with a K. Katrina, Kat for short," she said.

"I'm Biscuit, that's Otis," Biscuit said as he motioned toward me.

"Biscuit? Why Biscuit?" she shrugged.

"Why not?" Biscuit snapped back.

She shrugged her shoulders as she shifted her gaze to meet mine. As our eyes met, she grinned.

"Nice to meet you guys. I'll leave you two alone for a while. If you need me, just holler. We're not real busy, I'll probably stop by in a few and see if you're doing alright," she said as she turned away.

32

I nodded my head as she turned away. She seemed nice enough, but from what little I could see, had nothing to offer me. Although Avery proved to be as solid of a woman as I had ever met, I had my doubts that other college students would be as mature and trustworthy as she was. After Biscuit watched her walk away over his shoulder he turned toward the table and grinned.

"Meeefuckingyow. Kat, huh? She's a hot little number," he sighed.

I lifted my chin slightly before taking a long drink of my beer, "Where were we?"

"Hold up a minute, I've got to clear my mind of evil thoughts," he said as he grabbed a glass of vodka.

After taking a drink and chasing it with Red Bull, he shook his head and narrowed his gaze.

"I was face fucking my blue eyed girl," he said as he placed the can of Red Bull beside the glass of vodka.

I tilted my beer toward him and nodded my head, "The professor of oral pleasure."

"She damned sure was. Could have given a course on it for sure," he said as he glanced over each shoulder.

"Okay. So I've got my cock down her throat, and she's staring up at me, knowing if I look into those beautiful blue eyes for more than a few seconds I'm gonna shoot my load. Me? I'm lookin' up at the ceiling, countin' them little popcorn dealios they spray on up there. Now she's suckin' away, and I'm at about two thousand five hundred and fifty-three, knowing I can't last much longer. I glance down just for a quick second, and luckily her eyes are closed," he paused and reached for the vodka.

After a drink of vodka and a red Bull chaser, he leaned forward

33

and continued, "So, I reach down and grab blue eyes by the ears. Now, I got her ears in my hands, and I start pounding my cock in and out of her throat like I'm gettin' paid. Hell, I'm watchin' that fucker disappear in her mouth, amazed by the sheer talent of this girl, and I pull it out and shove it back in. Then, I pull out, and shove it back in balls deep. She don't gag or whimper or nothin'. Hell, this is turning me on like a motherfucker, so I turn it up a notch."

He pushed himself away from the table, stood, and held his hands in front of his thighs as he began to buck his hips violently back and forth. As he continued to thrust his hips no differently than a male stripper hoping for a tip, he began the remainder of his story. I shook my head and grinned at the fact Biscuit could care not what anyone in the bar thought about his little charade.

"So I'm shoving my cock balls deep into her throat, pulling it out, and shoving it right back in, and it builds up that throat snot like a motherfucker," he said as he continued to thrust his hips back and forth.

"Throat snot?" I shrugged.

"Yeah," he sighed, his hips still gyrating back and forth, "That goop down deep in their throats. Hell, you probably ain't got a cock big enough to find it, but ole Biscuit does."

I rolled my eyes and shook my head as I took a drink of beer.

"So anyway, I'm pounding away and things get kind of slippery. So I pull back..." he pulled his hips rearward and paused.

"And I don't realize it at that exact minute, but my cock slides all the way out of her mouth. So I go to shove it back in, thinkin' the tip is still in her mouth, and the head hits her top lip, and the fucker's all covered in slobber and throat snot, so it shoots up the side of her face and sticks her in the eye," he said as thrust his hips forward and held them there.

"Now, initially, I don't think nothing of it, other than the fact I just poked her in the eye with my cock. So I pull my hips back and prepare to shove her throat full one more time," he paused and pulled his hips rearward.

"And she looks up and opened her eyes…"

His eyes widened significantly as he continued to speak, "And she's starin' back at me smiling', ready for the cock, and she's got one brown eye and one fuckin' blue one. I got my cock in my hand, starin' back at her, and I blink my eyes, not sure if what I'm seein' is what I'm seein'. Nope, she's still crouched down there, with her mouth open, starin' back at me with one brown and one fuckin' blue one – ain't got a fuckin' clue of what's happened. Now this freaks me the fuck out, because the entire reason I like this girl, other'n the fact she can suck a golf ball through a garden hose, is that she's got them crazy blue eyes. And I glance down, blink one more time, and my eyes focus on my big fat cock. And the tip of my rod's got a little transparent blue dot on the end of it."

"Contacts?" I shrugged as I began to laugh.

He nodded his head, "Yep. That's when I learned about 'em. Fucked it right out of her God damned eye."

I shook my head as he slid into the seat.

"That's a hell of a story," I chuckled as I finished my beer.

"Damndest thing I ever seen," he laughed as he reached for his vodka.

"So what was all *that* about?" the waitress asked as she walked up to table.

"What?" Biscuit asked over his shoulder.

The waitress thrust her hips back and forth, more in a fluid motion that Biscuit's jerky haphazard method. She placed her hands on her hips and smiled as she gyrated a few more times, appearing to be perfecting a dance move more than imitating Biscuit. As much as I hated to admit it, seeing her do it was not only quite sensual, but rather erotic. It was evident she had at least some experience at dancing and did so quite well.

"God dayumm," Biscuit said as he turned in his seat to face her.

As she stopped gyrating, she grinned and slapped her hand against her thigh.

"I just thought it was funny when you were doing it. I'm sorry, I'm just bored," she shrugged.

"You can come over here and fuck the air anytime," Biscuit chuckled.

"Is that what you were doing, *fucking the air*?" she asked.

"Here? Yeah, I was fucking the air. But in the story I was tellin', I was fuckin' a girl's mouth," Biscuit responded.

Here we go.

"Sounds fun," she said with a smile.

"I probably ought to go clean some tables before I get myself in trouble," she shrugged.

I grinned and tilted my head her direction as I reached for my full bottle of beer. Oddly, as she turned to walk away, her eyes remained fixed on Biscuit until her body was completely turned around. As she walked toward the bar, she glanced over her shoulder once and grinned.

"Damn, Biscuit. Looks like she likes ya," I chuckled as I slapped my left hand against the table.

"Sooner or later, they all do," he grinned as he glanced over his shoulder.

I rolled my eyes as I lifted my bottle of beer.

"So what'd you want to talk about?" Biscuit asked as he reached for his can Red Bull.

As I shook my head, he reached for his vodka and drank the remaining liquor from the glass.

"Nothing, just needed to unwind. I'm good now," I said.

"You sure you're alright, Brother?" he asked.

I nodded my head, "Positive."

"How long you want to stick around?" he asked.

"Drink this and go?" I responded as I raised my beer in the air.

"I might stick around until she gets off," Biscuit said as he tilted his head toward the bar.

"Trial's tomorrow," I said under my breath.

"You see that girl's legs?" he asked.

I nodded my head, grinned, and drank the remaining beer from my bottle. Biscuit's decision to stay and try his luck with the waitress provided very little guidance to my current situation, but did provide some comfort in the form of reassurance.

Reassurance the woman I would end up with, if I ever did end up with a woman in my life, would come from a far more grueling application process than thrusting my hips in the air.

"You sure you're alright?" Biscuit asked as I finished my beer.

I nodded my head, "My old girlfriend, Sam. Her mother died. Just wanted to try and let it all settle. Just trying to make sense of it."

"Oh shit, your sweetheart? Damn, Brother, I'm sorry. What happened, if I might ask?" he asked as he shook his head from side-to-side.

"Aluminum foil. It was an accident," I shrugged, realizing my poorly executed explanation would raise an eyebrow as I finished speaking.

"Damn, did she work at the Reynold's Wrap factory or something?" he asked

I shook my head as I reached for my keys, "No, she was cooking and went to pull some aluminum foil off the roll, and it cut her wrist. She bled to death before the ambulance arrived."

He shook his head as he stood from his seat.

"Well, when a deal like that happens, you just got to stand back and realize that this world we're living in ain't ours, it's His; and things like that are just proof of it. His plan's much bigger'n this," he said as he pointed his finger back and forth between us.

"Agreed," I said as I slapped my hand against his back.

"See you in the morning," I said as I turned away.

"Long as I'm done with her," he grinned.

"Just don't fuck her in the eye, and everything'll be fine," I laughed.

And just like that, everything made a little more sense. Sometimes, having a friend or loved one confirm our already one-sided beliefs provided all the reassurance necessary for us to continue believing our way of thinking was just what it needed to be.

As I walked to the bike I realized although I didn't believe the death of Sam's mother was necessary, I was able to accept it as being out of my control, and part of a plan I did not understand *today*, but one day may.

OTIS

The courtroom smelled like money. The judge was seated on an elevated platform in front of where we were seated, but on the far side of the courtroom. In the center of the floor was an ornate lectern used by the attorney as he presented his case. On the immediate left was the jury, seated in comfortable leather seats as they studied the witness. Directly in front of us were two tables, one occupied by the defense attorney, and one by the prosecution and defendant. As they presented their cases to the judge, the attorneys faced away from us, making their facial expressions impossible to read.

Sitting in the courtroom amidst the ATF agents made me feel uneasy. Seeing roughly sixty Selected Sinners supporting Sydney's brother was enough to allow me to believe Jackson had all the backing necessary to ensure he at least *felt* he had sufficient support. The fact none of his club, *Hell's Fury*, attended the trial caused me to lose what little respect I had for the MC he represented when he was arrested.

Jury selection began, and took very little time. After each attorney throwing a few potential jurors out *for cause* or *peremptory challenges*, the jury was selected. Much to my surprise, the twelve men and women of the jury included three men who rode motorcycles. Hopefully, even if they weren't in a club, they'd have a better understanding of what was being discussed.

After several hours of questioning several ATF agents and Sydney's brother Jackson, the prosecutor seemed to run out of gas. His tone of voice changed, and he became far less aggressive. Not sure if it was a tactic or a dose of reality, I sat back in my seat and watched the show continue.

"During your time as a member of Hell's Fury MC, were you known by any other names than your God given name?" the prosecutor asked.

Kurt, Jackson's attorney and Avery's employer, immediately stood from his seat.

"Your honor, I object," he barked in a very matter of fact tone.

The judge raised his finger in the air, attempting to silence the witness before he responded.

"Grounds?" the judge asked.

Still standing behind the table, Kurt spread his arms apart and tilted his head slightly to the side. He was a very large man, standing almost 6'-5" and weighing probably 250 pounds. His military style haircut, well-defined features, and the tone of his voice made him rather intimidating in the courtroom.

"Your honor, it asks the jury to prejudice the evidence. You, your honor, me, the prosecutor, and the witness know what the defendant's club name was during his tenure with the club in question. Other than using the name to prejudice the jury, I see no value in providing it in testimony," Kurt argued.

The judge raised his hand to his chin and clenched his fist as he considered ruling on the objection.

"Your honor, the former President of the United States, Lyndon Johnson, was nicknamed *Bullshit Johnson*. The boxer, Thomas Hearns, was nicknamed *The Hitman*. Richard Hill, the English Rugby player, was nicknamed *The Silent Assassin*. And Pete Sampras, the tennis player, was nicknamed *Pistol Pete*. I doubt any of the nicknames provided an accurate depiction of who the people were or what they represented," Kurt explained as he continued to stand behind the large ornate table where Jackson was seated.

"*Granted*. I'll instruct you not to answer the question," the judge said as he gazed toward Jackson.

Wow, Kurt came prepared. Hell, he even had a list of names mentally prepared.

The prosecuting attorney turned away from the lectern, stared at the floor for a moment, and eventually turned to face the witness.

"The club you were a fully patched in member of, *Hell's Fury*, would it suffice to say this was an Outlaw Motorcycle Gang, or OMG as the Justice Department labels them?" the prosecutor asked.

Kurt stood from his seat.

"I object your honor; on the same grounds. The club in mention is not on trial, and now that the ever so gracious prosecutor has opened the gate, I'll step through it," he growled.

"The *witness* is not on trial your honor, as a matter of law, the prosecution's team of ATF agents are. This trial was awarded on the grounds of potential entrapment by ATF agents. As a matter of law, the witness sits before us a *guilty* man not an innocent one. His *guilt* is not in question. What *is* in question is whether or not the ATF entrapped him to commit the crime he was charged with in the indictment. And, with all due respect, as a matter of law, when the issue of entrapment is raised, the burden of proof switches to the prosecution to prove the defendant was *not* entrapped," Kurt explained in a very clearly spoken tone.

"And, as a matter of law, he is to be considered entrapped until the prosecution proves otherwise. In *Sorrells versus the United States* the entrapment doctrine was covered in detail, and the Supreme Court responded to the issue of entrapment more recently - and quite clearly - in *Jacobson versus the United States*, your honor," he continued.

The prosecutor threw his hands into the air comically.

"Your honor, now that entrapment seems to be the subject in question, and certainly defense counsel's only hope at winning this case, I will ask that the court reconsider allowing me to question the witness in regard to his club name. Predisposition is required to prove the defendant was *not* entrapped, and his club name, in itself, is *proof* of predisposition," the prosecutor bellowed.

"Your honor, a *name* is proof of very little, and a predisposition to commit murder coming from a name is a line that cannot be drawn, no matter who draws it," Kurt said sternly.

"Counsel," the judge said sternly while facing the prosecutor.

"And counsel," he said as he turned his head to face Kurt.

"I ask you both to approach. I will not allow a battle of wits in my courtroom," he said firmly.

"What the fuck's going on?" I whispered to Avery.

"Kurt's pissed. This case is about entrapment," she whispered, "When the entrapment defense is raised, it changes the case *completely*. The burden of proof shifts to the prosecution to prove the defendant *wasn't* entrapped; it's no longer a requirement for the defendant to do anything to prove his innocence, or to try and prove he was entrapped. It's assumed as soon as the subject is raised on the record that he *was* entrapped."

"I think I understand," I said through my teeth.

She placed her hand on my shoulder and leaned closer to my ear as she whispered, "It's simple. The appeals court saw enough evidence to believe the possibility existed that the government entrapped Syd's brother to commit the crime. If it's possible that he was entrapped, and the judge agrees, all of a sudden he's guilty of the crime. But, his guilt is a result of the government coercing, inducing, or enticing him to commit the crime. So now, the government must prove they didn't coerce, induce, or entice him. If they can't prove they didn't, then the jury must see it as they did. And, if they see it that way, he's not guilty."

"Okay, that makes a little more sense. What's the judge doing?" I asked as I leaned toward her.

"He's chewing their asses out for going at each other in his courtroom. Federal court is a far more formal approach than state or city court. Federal judges don't take shit, and they don't allow any disrespect in their courtroom. He probably saw their little tirade as disrespectful. He'll set them straight and they'll loosen up a little bit. I'm going to guess the prosecutor is about done. He's frustrated," she said.

I nodded my head and sat up straight in the seat. As Kurt walked away from the judge and toward his seat, the prosecutor walked to the lectern, gripped the sides in his hands, and sighed.

"On the date of the instant offense, did you state your willingness to kill a member or members of a rival club, namely the *Shovelheads MC*?" the prosecutor asked.

"Yes, but…" Jackson began.

"Yes or no?" the prosecutor interrupted.

"Yes, I did. But…" Jackson continued.

The judge turned toward Jackson and spoke quietly.

Jackson lowered his head shamefully. After a short pause, he looked up and answered.

"Yes I did," Jackson responded.

"No further questions," the prosecutor hissed as he released his grip on the lectern.

The prosecutor crossed his arms, studied Jackson for a moment, and sighed.

"Your witness," the judge said as he turned toward Kurt.

Kurt stood, walked to the lectern, and sighed loudly as he shook his head.

"On the day of the instant offense, had you been drinking?" he asked.

"Yes Sir," Jackson responded.

"Prior to your taking the first drink, did ATF agent Blackburn, acting in the capacity as one of your MC brethren, ask you what you'd do if the Shovelheads tried to claim your territory?" he asked.

"Yes Sir," Jackson responded.

"And your response was what?" he asked.

"I said I didn't know," he responded.

Kurt nodded his head.

"And did he then ask you if you'd kill them?" he asked.

"He did, yes. I don't know, maybe thirty minutes later," Jackson responded.

"And your response?" Kurt asked.

"I said no," he responded.

"Did he continue to ask you the same question or types of questions?" Kurt asked.

Jackson nodded his head, "Yes he did."

"So, you testified a moment ago that you'd been drinking. How many drinks would you say you consumed over the course of the night?" Kurt asked.

"I don't know, maybe six shots of whiskey and ten or twelve beers," Jackson responded.

"Wow, quite a night," Kurt chuckled.

Jackson nodded his head.

"Were you intoxicated?" Kurt asked.

The prosecutor stood from his seat and tossed his hands in the air. "I object your honor. The witness is not a specialist on intoxication, nor was he able at the time to perform a blood alcohol level test or a breathalyzer test. To testify as to his toxicity level would be nothing more than a sheer guess at best."

"Rephrase the question or change your line of questioning," the judge warned.

Kurt nodded his head.

"How many times would you say the undercover ATF agent, who you believed to be a brother in your MC, asked you if you'd kill a member of the Shovelheads?" Kurt asked.

"Six or eight," Jackson responded.

"No less than six?" Kurt asked.

Jackson shook his head.

"You know, I've had several years to think about this. It's really bothered me. I can count six times in my head for sure. For *absolute* sure. And I know there were others, but the more I drank, the drunker I became. So for me to testify under oath to an exact number would be a lie. He asked no less than six times," Jackson nodded.

"Did you know agent Blackburn was an ATF agent at this time?" Kurt asked.

"No Sir."

"Did you view the members of your club as brothers?" Kurt asked.

Jackson nodded, "Yes Sir. I sure did."

"Family?" Kurt asked.

"Yes Sir, I did. They were my family," Jackson responded.

"Mr. Shephard, where is your mother today?" Kurt asked.

Jackson shook his head, "She's dead, Sir. She passed away when I was a very young boy."

"I'm sorry to hear that. And your father?" Kurt asked.

"The same, Sir. He passed at the same time. I grew up in orphanages and eventually in a foster home with my only sibling, my sister," Jackson responded.

"I'm sorry for your losses," Kurt paused and appeared to wipe his eyes with the tips of his fingers.

"Would it suffice to say the club and your MC brothers were the only family you had?" Kurt asked.

"Yes Sir. Them and my sister," Jackson nodded.

"And you perceived agent Blackburn as a brother?" Kurt asked.

Jackson shifted his gaze toward the prosecution's table, where the agent was seated. After shaking his head from side-to-side slightly, he responded, "Yes Sir, I *did*."

"To the best of your knowledge, are the Shovelheads MC a 1%er club?" Kurt asked.

Jackson nodded his head, "Yes Sir, they are."

Kurt nodded his head as he released the lectern. He stepped to the side slightly and rubbed his jaw with his thumb and forefingers.

"And Hell's Fury was also a 1%er club?" Kurt asked.

"Yes Sir, we were," Jackson responded.

"When a 1% club who has claimed territory - for this sake I'll call them the parent club -has another club ride into the territory without permission, wearing their colors including a lower rocker claiming the *same* territory, how does the parent club perceive this trespass?" Kurt asked.

Avery slapped her hand against my bicep.

"You see what he's doing?" she whispered.

I nodded my head. "Shhh."

"As disrespectful. As a threat," Jackson responded.

"A threat?" Kurt asked as if he were shocked.

Avery slapped my arm again.

"Yes Sir."

"And when a 1% club makes a threat, what might that threat include, generally speaking?" Kurt asked.

"Violence," Jackson shrugged.

"Violence. I see. Let me back up a little bit, to where we were before. This club, the Hell's Fury, these fellas were your *family*, is that correct?" Kurt asked.

"Yes Sir," Jackson nodded.

"I see. And when agent Blackburn asked you what you'd do if they came into your territory, wearing a lower rocker claiming your state of residence as if their own, what was your fear, if any?" Kurt asked.

Avery slapped her hand against my arm again. I glanced toward Sydney, who was seated on my right side. She sat between Toad and I staring straight ahead, waiting for her brother's response. As Avery gripped my left arm in her hand, Sydney's brother responded.

"They were a rival club, always causing problems and talking…" Jackson paused and turned toward the judge.

The judge looked down at Jackson and nodded his head.

"Talking shit. Saying they were going to do this, and do that. If they rode in wearing their colors and claiming territory, I guess my fear was that they'd probably kill us, or at least try," Jackson responded.

"So, your eventual response to ATF agent Blackburn was one more of protection than of aggression, was it not?" Kurt asked.

"Objection, your honor. He's leading the witness," the prosecutor hollered.

"Granted. Rephrase your question," the judge said.

Avery squeezed my arm.

"Why did you eventually respond in the manner you did to the ATF agent? Agreeing that you'd kill members of the Shovelheads if they came to town?" Kurt asked.

Jackson grinned slightly.

"I didn't realize he was an agent. At the time, he was a brother, part of my family. And my fear was that the Shovelheads MC might hurt him or some of my other brothers. My thoughts at the time were that I needed to protect my family," Jackson responded.

"Your *only* family?" Kurt asked.

"Yes Sir, my only family," Jackson responded.

Avery released my arm from her grip.

"Fuck yes," she whispered as she slapped her hand against my thigh.

"No further questions for this witness, your honor," Kurt said flatly.

I turned toward the prosecutor, who slowly stood from his seat.

"The prosecution rests, your honor," the prosecutor stated.

"Your honor, I have only one witness to question. In lieu of a recess, and in an effort to please the court, may I call my witness and possibly wrap this up?" Kurt asked.

"One?" the judge asked.

"Yes Sir," Kurt responded.

The judge turned toward the prosecutor. The prosecutor shrugged his shoulders.

"I have no objections," the prosecutor sighed.

"Very well. My time, the court's time, is precious. In an effort to expedite this trial, we will continue. Call your witness," the judge stated.

"Your honor, I call Special Agent Randall Blackburn," Kurt said as he turned to face the agent.

"Oh yeah. This is going to be *good*," Avery whispered.

Personally, I couldn't imagine it being any better than it was. I realized I didn't fully understand all of the intricacies of the law the way Avery did, but from what I'd seen, Kurt was butchering the prosecution. His way of obtaining the answers he wanted from the witnesses was without much fault.

"Let's take a ten minute recess for the bathroom," the judge said as he looked up at the clock.

"2:13. I ask that everyone return to my courtroom no later than 2:13," the judge said as he studied the clock.

"I just want this to be over," Sydney sighed as the US Marshall led the jury from the room.

"It'll be over pretty soon," I responded.

"Those fucking ATF agents," Axton whispered.

I turned to my left to face Axton and leaned forward, resting my hands on my thighs.

"Rotten pricks. I'd like to line every one of them up, and do the world a favor by killing each and every one of 'em," he hissed.

"Be careful," I whispered as I raised one eyebrow and glanced along the ranks of Sinners seated in the courtroom, "there might be one

49

amongst us."

"Not in *my* club," he said as he shook his head, "I guarantee it."

OTIS

With a shaved head, a twelve inch long beard, and his arms covered in tattoos, Special Agent Blackburn appeared to be a biker, not an ATF agent. Sitting on the witness stand, he looked like he was pulled from the yard in prison, fitted with some fancy dress clothes, and placed in the court room. Studying him caused me to realize how little a person *really* knows about who it is at his side.

"Agent Blackburn, how many years have you been with the ATF, as an agent?" Kurt asked.

"Eighteen," Blackburn responded.

In your eighteen years, have you worked in the field in an undercover capacity?" Kurt asked.

"Yes, most of my career has been undercover," Blackburn nodded.

"Generally speaking, when you work undercover, do you wear some form of electronic listening device - *a wire*?" Kurt asked.

"We try to. It isn't something that can always be done, but if possible, yes," Blackburn responded as he adjusted himself in the seat.

Kurt nodded his head, "Is it done to preserve, or more accurately, to support your investigation?"

Blackburn sat up straight in his seat and spoke directly into the microphone, "Yes. The recordings support the agent's testimony, and provide corroboration in court of the events described in the investigation and in the daily reports."

"So wearing a wire sounds like it's a procedural matter. Is that correct?" Kurt asked as he stepped to the side of the lectern.

"Yes Sir, it is," Blackburn responded.

"Thank you for clearing that up, Special Agent Blackburn," Kurt said in a somewhat sarcastic tone as he took a step toward the witness stand.

Kurt stepped to the side of the lectern and placed his hands on his hips. "How many times did you ask the defendant if he would retaliate against the Hell's Fury before he responded in a manner contrary to law?"

"Two," Blackburn responded in a matter of fact tone.

"Two?" Kurt asked, the tone of his voice filled with annoyance.

"Yes, two," Blackburn nodded.

Kurt slowly raised his hands in the air and turned his palms outward, "Not six or eight?"

"No Sir. Two," Blackburn said flatly.

Kurt shrugged his shoulders slightly and took another step toward the witness stand, "Are you certain?"

"Very," Blackburn responded.

Kurt nodded his head as if accepting Blackburn's response as accurate.

"I've read the transcripts from the original trial. Have you made reference to them?" Kurt asked.

"Yes, yes I have," Blackburn stated.

"Your initial testimony was the same? Two?" Kurt asked as if he knew the answer, but simply sought confirmation.

"Yes Sir," Blackburn responded as he reached for the glass of water sitting in front of him.

Kurt turned away from the witness stand, and slowly began to take the two or three steps toward the lectern, facing the jury as he spoke, "As an ATF agent, you receive training in regard to law, do you not?"

Blackburn nodded his head, "Some, yes."

"Training to assure you will follow policies and procedures in accordance with law, and not contrary to it, correct?" he asked as he reached the lectern.

"That is correct," Blackburn responded as he lowered the glass of water to the platform in front of him.

"Would two requests, with the second response by the defendant being contrary to law, in your professional trained opinion, legally define coercion, inducement, or enticement?" Kurt asked.

Blackburn shook his head and chuckled, "No Sir, it sure wouldn't. Absolutely not. Asking him twice is not coercion or inducement."

"Out of curiosity, if that number was six or eight, would it define coercion?" Kurt asked.

After a short hesitation, Blackburn responded as he leaned toward the microphone, "It may."

"And your lengthy training with the ATF included instructions and training *not* to badger, coerce, induce, or entice a law abiding citizen to commit a crime, correct?" Kurt asked.

"That is correct," Blackburn nodded.

"Under oath, the defendant stated he was asked no less than six times. You have stated you asked him twice. According to your earlier testimony, six would define coercion, inducement, and or entrapment, and you merely asked him twice. I'm wondering, are you telling the truth or is he?" Kurt asked flatly.

"Objection!" the prosecutor howled.

"Counsel…" the judge said flatly.

"I'll advise you not to answer the question," the judge stated as he turned toward the witness.

The judge turned toward the jury.

"Be it known the witness is under oath and sworn to tell the truth," the judge said.

"How long was your investigation of the Hell's Fury?" Kurt asked.

"Two years and one month," Blackburn responded.

"And in that time, twenty-five months, how many arrests were made?" Kurt asked.

"One," Blackburn sighed.

"One? A twenty-five month long investigation of an Outlaw Motorcycle Gang, and it only produced *one* arrest?" Kurt asked.

"Yes," Blackburn responded as he crossed his arms in front of his chest.

"Did the ATF make a decision not to prosecute the other cases?" Kurt asked.

"There were no other cases," Blackburn said under his breath.

"You successfully infiltrated an outlaw gang of motorcycle thugs for twenty-five months, and produced this as your only case? Seems more like they were a group of good old boys, not an OMG," Kurt said flatly.

"Your honor, I object. It appears the defense counsel has chosen to provide his own testimony," the prosecutor snapped.

"I'll ask the jury to strike the last statement made by the prosecutor. Counsel, you have been warned," the judge said as he raised his index finger in the air.

Kurt leaned onto the lectern and pressed his chest onto the platform. Now staring at the ATF agent, he cleared his throat.

Avery slapped my arm and whispered into my ear, "He's going to make a point. He wants the jury's attention."

"In discovery, I requested the voice recording of the conversation on the night of the instant offence. I was advised it did not exist in legible format. Are you aware of the lack of availability of said recording?" Kurt asked.

"Yes Sir, I am. Unfortunately, the recording device did not work properly on that evening, and background noise made the recording worthless," Blackburn responded.

"I was provided recorded conversations before and after the date in question. In fact, I have a few hundred hours of recorded conversations. Almost four hundred hours if memory serves me correctly. Now, my question to you is as follows…" Kurt paused and turned to face the jury.

"Agent Blackburn, how many conversations through the course of the investigation were unintelligible, to the best of your knowledge, that is?" Kurt asked as he continued to face the jury.

"One," Blackburn breathed.

Kurt turned toward the witness stand, "I'm sorry, I didn't hear your response. Can you speak into the microphone?"

Blackburn leaned forward and breathed into the microphone, "One."

Kurt nodded his head and chuckled lightly.

"I'm curious. During your infiltration of the group of outlaw bikers, did you give them your *actual* name?" he asked.

"No," Blackburn chuckled.

"Did you make one up?" Kurt asked.

"Yes, I did," Blackburn responded.

"Did you give them an accurate history of who you were?" Kurt asked.

"No Sir, I provided fictitious information. Information believed to be more acceptable to the type of people I was investigating," Blackburn said.

"So you lied. You told lies to the bikers to get them to either like you or accept you, is that correct?" Kurt asked.

"I object!" the prosecutor bellowed as he stood from his seat.

"Your honor," Kurt sighed, "The witness stated he provided inaccurate information to the group during his investigation. I'm simply..."

"I'll rephrase the question," Kurt said as he gripped the edges of the lectern in his massive hands.

"Was the information you provided the bikers regarding your background and or name the truth?" Kurt asked.

"No," Blackburn sighed.

"Was it a lie?" Kurt asked.

"Objection, your honor," the prosecutor said as he stood.

"I'll allow it, but you shall make your point in a timely manner, counsel," the judge said.

"Yes," Blackburn said as he leaned into the back of his seat.

"Explain your thought process to me on lying to these men during the investigation. Why would you feel compelled to tell them lies?" Kurt said as he stepped to the side of the lectern and raised his hand to his chin.

Blackburn turned to face the judge. The judge in turn nodded his head. Blackburn then turned toward Kurt, who was now studying the jury.

"To preserve the investigation, we are taught to give either limited information, or false information. It provides protection to the bureau and to the agent," Blackburn responded.

"You're taught to *lie* during your investigations?" Kurt asked.

Blackburn glanced toward the judge. The judge nodded his head.

"Yes," Blackburn grunted.

"So, through the course of your work, you may tell a lie, but it's not necessarily a lie in a conventional sense, because you're *working*, correct?" Kurt asked.

"Objection, your honor, asked and answered," the prosecutor hollered.

"I'll allow it," the judge said.

Kurt turned toward the jury and spoke as he continued to stare at the jury.

"I'll ask the question again. Through the course of your work, you may tell a lie, but it's not necessarily a lie in a conventional sense, because you're *working*, correct?" he asked without turning away from the jury.

"Correct, we're often required to lie, as you say, to preserve the investigation," Blackburn responded.

"Are you being paid for your testimony today, agent Blackburn?" Kurt asked.

Blackburn sat stone faced and didn't answer.

"You must not have heard me," Kurt said as he turned from facing the jury to facing Blackburn.

"You testified that you told lies through the course of your work to preserve the investigation. My question was this: Are you being paid for your testimony today? Are you *working*?" Kurt asked.

"Yes, I am," Blackburn grunted.

"No further questions," Kurt said as he turned away.

"Boom!" Avery whispered as she slapped my knee.

After two short closing arguments, and the judge providing the jury with an instruction booklet, the jury was released to their deliberation room. After they were carefully tucked away, we were dismissed. As we filtered into the hall amidst the ATF agents and US Marshals, Axton stepped to my side.

"Pretty good trial, that attorney's on the fucking ball," Axton said.

"God damned right he is," Avery snapped back.

"So what now?" Sydney asked.

I reached over and patted Sydney on the shoulder. She looked exhausted, and I suspected she probably didn't sleep at all the previous night. Toad also looked as if he hadn't slept for a few days, and appeared to be on an entirely different planet.

"The jury deliberates. They read the instructions, and they decide guilt or innocence. The court will call Kurt when a decision is made, and he'll call us. It's 3:30 now, so he'll probably dismiss the jury at 4:45. There's really nothing that will happen tonight. Sometimes it takes six or eight hours, and other times it takes two or three days. You never know," Avery explained as she walked around me and toward Sydney.

"I just. I want this to be over. I feel so sorry for him. I hate for him to get his hopes up and then, you know..." Sydney shrugged.

I watched as Sinners got on the elevator eight or ten at a time, and went down to what I assumed was the ground floor. Several others took the stairs, talking quietly as they did so. I turned to Axton and shrugged my shoulders.

"Slice, I feel like *I've* been on trial; that was fucking exhausting. What's the plan, boss?" I asked.

"Hell, I had no idea when we'd get out of here, looks like we've got the afternoon to ourselves. Hell, the suns shining and it's a beautiful fucking day. What do you say we gather up the fellas and go terrorize a bar?" he said.

"We go rolling in sixty deep, everyone wearing their cuts, and they'll think we're gonna shoot the place to pieces," I laughed.

"Let 'em think what they want," Axton shrugged.

"Sounds good to me," I nodded.

"Up for a beer, Toad?" I asked as I slapped Toad on the shoulder.

"I'm up for whatever. I'm just fucking tired, brother. Haven't been sleeping for shit, been worried about Syd's brother and all," Toad nodded.

We hadn't been in the hallway ten or fifteen minutes, and Kurt stepped into the corridor, holding his phone in his hand.

"Jury's reached a verdict," Kurt said.

"What?" Avery snapped as she spun around.

Kurt nodded his head, "They'll be bringing them back in."

"Holy shit," Avery said under her breath.

Sydney covered her mouth with her hands and spoke between her fingers, "Avery, what's this mean?"

"Well, they say a verdict like this means only one thing. The jury decided the case long before they trial was over. Just take a deep breath, either way, it'll be fine, Syd," Avery said as she leaned over and hugged Sydney.

The few of us who remained in the hallway walked back into the courtroom and sat down while we waited for the judge to enter the room. After about a ten minute wait, the judge entered, and we stood and after he was seated, we all sat down. Instead of sixty Sinners, there was maybe fifteen or so seated. The ATF agents watching the trial, however, remained in full force. As I glanced down the row of Sinners, I watched as Axton gave one bearded ATF agent the shittiest stink eye I've ever witnessed. Only after the ATF agent broke the stare did Axton lean into the back of his seat and exhale.

"Counsel, please stand," the judge instructed.

The prosecution and defense attorneys stood.

"I want it understood there will be no outbursts in the courtroom, regardless of the verdict," the judge said firmly as he studied the group.

I nodded my head.

The judge turned toward the jury.

"Has the jury reached a verdict?" the judge asked.

"Yes, your honor, we have," the foreman responded.

I reached to my left and right, and after a moment of fumbling, grabbed both Sydney's and Avery's hands and held them firmly.

"In the matter of Jackson Shephard versus the United States of America, what say you?" the judge asked.

"In the matter of Jackson Shephard versus the United States, we the jury, find him *not guilty*; as he was entrapped by the ATF to commit the crime listed in the indictment, your honor," the foreperson responded.

Holy fucking shit.

Kurt reached down and patted Jackson on the shoulder. As the judge questioned each juror regarding their finding, Sydney leaned forward. Tears streamed from her face as she made a few attempts to speak. After collecting herself, she began to whisper to Avery, who was bouncing her right leg a hundred miles an hour.

"What now?" Sydney blubbered, "How long…uhhm…how long does he….uhhm…go back to prison for?"

"He doesn't go back to prison," Avery responded, "He goes home.

He's free."

"He doesn't have…" Sydney sobbed, "He doesn't…uhhm, he doesn't *have* a home."

"The hell he doesn't. We've got two extra rooms. He's got a home," Toad said.

And he's got a family.

Most of them are out in the street, and the rest are right here.

OTIS

Feeling somewhat frustrated Axton and Toad had women in their lives, and Biscuit was arguably close behind with Kat - while I continued to live a life of solitude - I sat at my kitchen table sipping a cup of coffee.

Wondering if my way of living life and the precautions I took regarding outsiders was possibly a little stricter than it should be, I stared blankly through window and into my back yard. Attempted to count the possibilities I had over the years of women I felt *comfortable* allowing into my life - but didn't - I searched my mind for those who had escaped me. After an entire cup of coffee worth of consideration, I came up with one woman in fifteen years.

Avery.

Avery's participation during our botched gun deal with the MS-13, along with her quick thinking, reacting, and accuracy with a handgun not only saved my life, but provided me with all the reassurance I needed to understand she was a woman who I could trust. Looking at Avery with a broader field of vision provided a view of a woman who was confident, intelligent, brave, beautiful, and responsible. Prior to Axton's acceptance of her into his life, I considered inviting her into mine. After Axton's claimed her as his Ol' Lady, she became off limits, and now remained nothing more than a close friend.

Realizing there was one woman through the course of fifteen years who provided me with a level of comfort great enough to allow me to let my guard down was nowhere near reassuring. In fact, the more I thought about it, the clearer it became.

My life was one I was living not for me, but for the betterment and the security of the Selected Sinners MC.

I had been in the club since the beginning, and although I wasn't close friends with *every* member, I viewed each and every one of the Sinners as a brother. After moving me from Sergeant-At-Arms to Vice President, I fully understood I was no longer responsible for their protection as far as the *club* was concerned, but releasing me from the responsibility completely was impossible.

The club was family to me no differently than my father and mother were, and I was naturally a protector of what I loved and cherished. Living the life of a Sinner allowed me to understand the camaraderie shared by military members who had spent time in combat together. Being a member of the club was not much different. Knowing a brother had my back was reassuring, comforting, and provided an odd sense of balance to an otherwise askew life I seemed to live.

I gazed down into the empty cup of coffee and began to wonder if forfeiting a conventional way of life was something I was willing to do. The answer was as clear as the blue sky outside - I had already done it. Consciously or not, I had cast aside anything conventional to protect the lives and preserve the rights of my beloved brothers. The Sinners were my family, and more than likely the only love I would ever know.

I stood from my seat and walked to the kitchen sink. After rinsing the cup of coffee and placing it in the dishwasher, I walked to my bedroom and grabbed my cut. My thoughts of Sam and the untimely death of her mother had begun to fade, but the event opened my eyes and allowed me to have a better understanding of myself, my life, and my true love.

The Selected Sinners.

I opened the door to the garage and pressed the button on the wall to open the door leading to the driveway. I stood on the steps and glanced around. An obvious extension of me and my beliefs, the garage was filled with tools and equipment for working on bikes, my two motorcycles, and my 1969 Z-28 Camaro. No second car, no flower pots or planters, and no indication of any interests other than the car and bikes. Satisfied my life was what it was meant to be, I grinned and fired up the bike. As the motor warmed up to operating temp, the low rumble of the exhaust filled me with pleasure. Riding a motorcycle wasn't something I merely enjoyed, it was part of my being. Each time I rode was as exciting as the first, and for that I was extremely grateful. If riding a motorcycle ever became boring, I suspected my life would become the same.

I rode to the clubhouse, enjoying the sunset against the few clouds that had developed along the western sky. With the warm summer air against my face, I gazed ahead at the slight curve in the highway leading into town. The empty highway invited me to twist back the throttle, and I did so without reservation. Now heading into the curve at eighty miles per hour, I leaned the bike to my left, dragging the toe of my boot against the passing pavement as I did so. The tips of my boots acted as a measuring stick of sorts for how far to lean my bike, and doing so until my boots drug against the road provided me a sense of worth. As the curve straightened into open road, I leaned right, bringing the bike back to upright.

In the distance, a tractor crossing the highway reminded me of the summer soon coming to a close, a farmer obviously spending as many daylight hours as possible harvesting his crops, he attempted to cross the road before I arrived at the intersection. I downshifted, released the clutch and grinned at the sound bellowing from the exhaust. As the distance between me and the tractor quickly decreased, I downshifted again, then again, almost coming to a stop before the tractor completely crossed the road. As my bike slowed to an almost stop, the farmer reached out the side window of the tractor and waved, obviously realizing his poor judgement in crossing the road in front of me.

I lifted my left hand, waved, and twisted the throttle. As the bike quickly accelerated, I shifted through the gears until once again reaching the eighty mile per hour mark. A quick glance in my rearview mirror revealed a dust cloud following the farmer's tractor down the county road he traveled along.

As I considered that he was probably going home to a late dinner, thoughts of having a woman in my life began to run through my head and filled my mind until I rode into town. Struggling with whether or not I'd ever be able to come home to a prepared dinner, under another person's expectation of doing so, I slowed down for the first traffic light.

I sat at the light, gazing blankly into the road ahead, as an old school Harley approached the light in the oncoming lane. A late 1960's Shovelhead Springer with a face I recognized as being one of the local Patriot Guard came to a stop in the lane immediately to my left. Bill was a Vietnam Vet, rode with the Guard, and often attended the funerals of veterans who were being protested by Pastor Fred Phelps' Westboro Baptist Church; providing a line of separation between the protestors and the families of the vet.

As the light turned green, Bill lowered his left hand to his side as he rode by. I did the same. Something as simple as lowering one's left hand had become the universal biker wave over the years; and as easy as it was to do, not *everyone* did it. The few who did stood for one thing and one thing only, realizing it was as big a part of being a biker as anything else. In recognizing this, I felt I had my answer to my ability to come home to dinner on a nightly basis.

The answer was *no*.

And the wave stood for freedom.

OTIS

Axton held his hands in the air as he studied the group of men assembled in the office. An uneducated glance at my brothers led me to believe if not all of the men were in attendance, almost all of them were. As the crowd quieted down from a dull roar to complete silence, Axton lowered his hands and sighed.

"As you know from the announcement, we're going to have a special vote. Those in attendance tonight will be considered the *entire* club, regardless of whether or not all patched members are in attendance. Be it known that any member not in attendance will forfeit their vote in said matter. I cannot vote, nor will I attempt to prejudice your thoughts on this, but we need to decide on something that's been brought to my attention as a motion by a member of the Executive Committee, and was seconded by another member of the committee. All records of said conversation and motion were recorded by yours truly," Axton extended his arm toward Fancy, who grinned and raised his hand as Axton pointed at him.

"Here's what we've got, fellas," Axton said as he turned and surveyed the group.

"Jackson Shephard, your Sergeant-At-Arms future brother-in-law, and the man we all supported in trial the other day, has been released from his former club at his request. He now is a local resident, and lives with Toad. The bylaws allow for the transfer of a fully patched member of another club into our club without prospecting, but it requires a vote of one hundred percent in agreement. Personally, I can't vouch for this man, but I can say I've spoken to the President of Hell's Fury. According to him, Jackson was not only a patched in member, but was solid as a rock throughout his legal battle and incarceration. When many men would have dropped a dime on their brothers, he kept his mouth shut. The vote tonight will be whether or not to allow him to come into the Sinners as a fully patched member. This will be a private vote, and as I said earlier, this will require a one hundred percent vote, fellas. Any questions?"

"I ain't saying I agree or disagree, and I know it's in the bylaws, but just out of curiosity, why wouldn't we have him be a Prospect?" Pete asked.

"Respect," Axton responded, "Toad and I discussed this at the meeting when the motion was made to allow the vote. Let me have Toad explain the analogy we discussed."

Axton turned to face Toad and nodded his head.

After clearing his throat, Toad began, "If a man's in the Army, Navy, or Air Force, and he wants to transfer to be a Marine, he must go through basic training all over again. It's humbling, and although he may be a Sergeant or whatever in the Army, the Marine Corps won't allow him to come in until he completes *their* basic training. But, if a Marine wants to transfer into any other branch, he can do so without any restrictions or going through the basic training of the branch he's transferring into again. Basic training, for those who don't understand, is basically being a Prospect for the military. The Marines are viewed by the other branches of the military as being trained in a superior fashion, and once a Marine has completed his Prospecting, and received his patch so to speak, he can transfer to any other military branch. Our bylaws are no different than any other 1% clubs bylaws in this regard. We view anyone as being in a 1% club as being trained in a superior fashion, and asking him to complete the process again is not only disrespectful to him, but disrespectful to the club he originally prospected for. And this bylaw only applies to members who were released in good standing."

Pete, as well as many other men in attendance, nodded their heads. Gunner, a former Army machine gunner, pointed at Toad and nodded his head as Toad finished his speech.

"He's right," Gunner nodded, "A Marine can walk in wherever he wants, but no one can walk into the Corps."

Toad glanced at Gunner and stared for a moment before nodding his head. For some reason, there always seemed to be a little military tension between the two, and I always dismissed it to being the difference between being a Marine and being an Army soldier. That, and the fact Toad didn't particularly open up to just everyone.

I patted Toad on the back and grinned.

"Good fucking speech," I chuckled.

"Appreciate it, Toad. So," Axton sighed, "Fancy will pass around slips of paper. There's about ten pens on the table to share, and to save any confusion, a *yes* vote means you agree to allow him in, and a *no* vote means you don't agree. If there's one no vote, the answer is *no*. If the answer is yes, it was agreed by the entire club, and I won't allow any future bitching or complaining about him being a fully patched member. He's paid his dues and then some, he just didn't pay 'em *here*."

Fancy began to pass slips of paper through the crowd. After everyone had a slip of paper, the pens began to float through the room. After roughly five minutes it was over, and the slips of folded paper were provided to Fancy.

"Official count for the attendance?" Axton asked.

Fancy glanced down at his notepad, "Thirty-four, including you."

"Count the slips as you read 'em off, we'll need thirty-three for a *yes* decision. You can stop counting as soon as you read off a *no*," Axton explained, "And hand the slips to the V.P. for confirmation after you read them if you will."

Fancy nodded his head in my direction.

"One yes. Two yes. Three yes. Four yes. Five yes…" Fancy said as he unfolded and read each vote individually.

After reading each slip, he handed them to Toad, who in turn handed them to me. I confirmed each slip was marked as Fancy indicated, and then placed them on the table in a helmet sitting in the center of the table.

"Thirty-two yes, and the last. Thirty three," Fancy grinned as he unfolded the last piece of paper.

"Thirty-three's a yes," he said as he handed the slip to Toad.

I nodded in agreement as Toad handed the slip to me.

"Well fellas, it's unanimous. Toad, send him a text or call him and have him get his ass up here," Axton paused and glanced around the group.

"Now, all we've got to do is name this poor fucker. His former club name was *Killer*, and that damned near got him life in prison. He doesn't have any recommendations from what Brother Toad has said, so I'm open for suggestions," Axton shrugged.

"I say we call him *Meathead*. He looks like one of those meat-headed fuckers from the gym. He's all swole up," Pete said as he raised his arms and flexed his biceps.

"We already got a *Jack* and a *Government Jack*," Knucklelhead hollered, "I say we either call him *Meathead* or *Big Jack*. He's a big fucker for sure."

"Anyone else?" Axton asked.

"Meathead reminds me of that dumb fucker on the Archie Bunker T.V. show, I don't like it. Big Jack sounds good, but Meathead just reminds me of that bald-headed fucker on the show," Tater said.

"Well, not everyone's as old as you, Tater," Axton chuckled, "Anyone else?"

"Second Chance," Gunner chuckled, "Let's call him *Second Chance*."

Axton shook his head and grinned, "Anyone else?"

"Big Jack is a good one," Mike nodded.

"Well, when he gets here, we'll see," Axton nodded, "Anyone else?"

After a few seconds of silence, Axton raised his hands, "Feel free to wander your asses around until he gets here. You don't have to stay, but if you do, feel free to drink your beers or whatever. And remember, don't toss your empties in *my* shit can. Toss 'em in the shop."

As the crowd diminished and members either left or wandered into the shop, Toad and I were left in the office with a few other lingering members.

"You're looking good. Look like you've slept since I saw you last," I said.

Toad sighed, "I tell you what, I don't think I slept good on even one night for the two weeks before the trial. Bet I lost ten pounds. It's all good now, and other than Jack being a little skittish just coming out of prison and all, he's a damned good guy. I thought Corn Dog was bad

73

when he got out, but Jack's pretty damned nervous about people getting up close to him or walking behind him."

"Yeah, probably the difference between being in state prison and a maximum security fed joint. I'm gonna guess him being a 1%er and all, he probably had quite a few people who tried to challenge his willingness to stand up against them," I shrugged.

Toad nodded his head, "So far, he hasn't offered to talk about it much, and Sydney and I decided not to ask, so I'm not sure. He seems pretty quiet, really. Sydney's sure happy to have him back, that's for sure."

I nodded my head, thinking about the day Sydney ran out to my bike at the bank. When she asked me to take her to Biscuit's house, making the statement *devil looks after his own*, I knew something was up, I just didn't know what. Later, when I found out the bank had been robbed, and Toad had single handedly apprehended the robber, I knew she was *somehow* involved with the robbery. Her reluctance to provide any information on the robbery, Toad, or anything to do with the person who robbed the bank caused me to immediately develop a feeling of appreciation for her and her ability to keep her mouth shut.

The explanation that followed of her brother and his involvement with Hell's Fury explained a lot about her knowledge of clubs, club procedures, and the importance of *not* talking before thinking long and hard about whether or not it was necessary. Sydney, no different than Avery, was a great addition to my extended family.

"I'm glad he's back. It's good for her, that's for sure. I'm sure he'll make as good of a brother for us as he has for her," I said.

The sound of a bike pulling into the lot echoed through the shop and into the office. I wondered as the tone of the exhaust increased if it might be Jack.

"Imagine so. Well, that sounds like my Softail, maybe we ought to walk out to the shop and greet him. He's liable to smack the shit out of someone if they bump into him," Toad said as he tilted his head to the side.

As we walked out into the shop, I immediately noticed Jack sitting on Toad's Softail in the drive. In boots, jeans, and a wife beater, he sure looked the part. Roughly the size of Toad from the waist down, it was apparent he wasn't *naturally* a big man, and all of his size came from hard work on the weight bench.

And size was something he did not lack. As he recognized Toad, he stood from the bike and stretched his back. His slim torso made his already massive upper body appear to be twice the size it already was. His short blonde hair and tan from all of the time he'd spent on the yard at prison made him look like the meathead Pete had joked about. If I didn't know him, I'd certainly think twice about going one round in the ring with him, and I'd fight just about anyone.

"Well, Jackson. We voted," Axton said as he stepped into the drive.

Jack stood stone faced and waited for Axton to finish his thought.

Axton spread his arms wide, "Welcome to the Sinners."

Jack grinned as he embraced Axton. After a few slaps on the back, Axton and Jack separated, and Jack took a few steps in our direction, stopping a few feet from where Toad and I stood.

"Come into the office in a few and I'll get you fitted for a cut. I make my own, so it'll be tomorrow before it's done. The fellas all spoke, and it looks like they want to call you *Big Jack*. We've got a few; *Jack* and *Government Jack*, but don't have a Big Jack. Your thoughts?" Axton asked.

"Big Jack sounds good," Jack nodded.

"Well, you're a big fucker, that's for sure. Now, when you get done mingling with the fellas, I'll be in the office. One of these two can show you around," Axton said as he turned toward the shop.

"Got a question, boss," Jack said under his breath.

Axton turned around and crossed his arms over his chest. As he stood and studied Jack, he flexed his biceps. A small show of testosterone, and one of Axton's signature poses, it was obvious Axton needed Jack to know regardless of his size, just who it was that was the bigger man.

"What might that be?" Axton asked flatly.

"Who put the money on my books?" Jack asked.

"The club," Axton responded without any emotion.

As Axton turned around, Jack cleared his throat.

"*Who* put the money on my books?" Jack asked again, placing emphasis on the word *who*.

Axton turned around and shook his head.

"Semantics," Axton sighed, "His name's Biscuit. Big barrel-chested fucker with brown hair and a beard. He'll be the one telling some bullshit story in the shop. Just listen for the loudest voice, and look for the crowd. Why?"

"Appreciate what the club's done for me, boss, I really do. And I appreciate the money on my books, much fucking more than the Fury did for me, that's for Goddamned sure. But someone had to take the time to *send* it. You know, take the risk of being on the Fed's radar for sending money to me. Just wanted to thank him, that's all," Jack explained.

"Introduce him to Biscuit," Axton said as he turned around.

"Otis, we met in the courtroom," I said as I extended my hand.

"Heard plenty about you from Syd and Toad here. They say you're good people. If you're good with them, you're good with me," he responded as he shook my hand.

"Likewise," I nodded.

"Follow me? I'll introduce you to Biscuit," I said.

Jack nodded his head.

I turned around and slowly walked inside, making certain to choose my path wisely, and trying to avoid all of the large groups of men who were gathered talking. As we walked into the shop, most of the men stopped what they were doing or talking about, and took a second glance at Jack. There wasn't much that would typically intimidate a Sinner, but if there was, Jack just might be it. As the men gawked at his sheer size and obvious attitude, I walked up to Biscuit. As Axton hinted, he was in the corner of the shop with five of the fellas who stood eagerly listening to a story he was telling.

"Biscuit," I said as we walked up to the group.

"What' shakin' O?" Biscuit said as he stopped talking and turned away from the group.

I raised my chin slightly and tilted my head toward Jack, "Man wanted to talk to ya."

Biscuit studied Jack for a second, and stepped to the side of the group. Biscuit was as full of shit as a Christmas turkey, but intimidating him would take an army of men, not one.

"What can I help ya with?" Biscuit asked as he looked up and down Jack's frame.

"Heard you were the one who put the money on my books," Jack said.

Biscuit shook his head and glanced down at Jack's boots, "Money came from the club."

"Heard you were the one who *sent* me the money. The money the club raised for me. *You* were the one who put it on my books," Jack said flatly.

Biscuit shifted his gaze to mine, then toward Toad, and quickly shifted his eyes to meet Jack's, "You got the right fella. Is there a problem?"

"Just wanted to personally thank ya for sending it. I appreciate ya. If you ever need anything, just let me know. Name's Jack. *Big Jack*," Jack said as he extended his hand.

Biscuit grinned and shook his hand, "Biscuit. Stick around and have a beer."

Jack crossed his arms in front of his chest and nodded his head once, "I'll be back. Just got to see the boss about my cut."

"I'll be right here," Biscuit said as he leaned forward and immediately began talking.

"He good people?" Jack asked as we turned to walk away.

"One of the few I'll run with," I responded, "Biscuit, Slice - the President, and Toad here, that's about it."

Jack nodded his head in acknowledgement as the three of us walked toward the office. As we stepped through the door, Axton held a cut up in the air and studied it.

"This is an extra-large, try it," he said as he handed the cut to Jack.

"Everything's American made as far as the leather goes, and I sew it all myself. Sometimes the patches look shaky, but I embroider the name's myself," Axton explained as Jack tried on the cut.

"Fits perfect," Jack said.

Axton nodded his head in agreement, "Looks good."

'Sew 'em up yourself, huh?" Jack asked as he removed the cut.

Axton nodded his head as he reached for the cut, "Can't think of doing it any other way."

"Says a lot about your pride in being the boss of the club, that's for damned sure. Can't ever go wrong with American made, either," Jack said.

"We'll agree on that, and I appreciate it. I take a lot of pride in this club, my brothers, and the quality of members. No worries about some ATF wannabe fucking with you in here," Axton bragged.

"We'll see about that," Jack growled, "Far as I'm concerned, I'll stick close to the three of you and that Biscuit fella. I'm not here to swap stories, make friends, or learn how to be a bad-ass. Nobody'd believe my stories, I'll never have many friends, and I ain't met a man yet who's big or mean enough to whip me," he paused and glanced toward me.

"Except maybe this big fucker here," he said as he slapped his hand against my back.

Axton crossed his arms in front of his chest and grinned as he alternated glances between us, "Some fellas are lovers and some are fighters. Toad? He's a little of both. Otis? He doesn't know a damned thing about loving, but fighting? He could probably write a best-selling book on the subject."

"Good to know," Jack said.

"Have the cut ready tomorrow night," Axton said.

Jack shifted his gaze to meet mine and tilted his head toward the door, "Appreciate it, feel naked without one. We'll leave you to your business."

After we walked through the door and into the shop, Jack turned to face me, "Any chance you two and that Biscuit fella want to get a little riding in? It's been a bit since I spent any time on a bike, and I'm itching to get out on the road."

"I'm game," I shrugged as I glanced at Toad.

"Same," Toad responded, "Head to town and get a beer?"

"As long as we're headed to Avery's old joint, I'm sure Biscuit'll agree," I said with a laugh.

"Why's that?" Toad asked.

"New girl in there. Tall, thin, and kind of a dirty blonde named Kat. Cute little bitch. She's Biscuit's new bitch," I said.

Toad shook his head as we walked toward the group of men gathered around Biscuit.

"When you gonna find you an Ol' Lady?" Toad asked over his shoulder.

I shrugged my shoulders, "You heard the man. I'll leave the loving up to you and Slice. I'm not a lover, I'm a fighter."

And, as much as I wanted to embrace the statement, and had truly come to believe it was where I'd remain, I had my reservations as to whether or not it was where I belonged.

OTIS

The forty minute ride in the hot summer air made each of us more than ready for a cold drink by the time we rolled into the bar. The atmosphere wasn't much different than the night Biscuit and I met Kat; with the exception of us, four patrons, a waitress, and a bartender were all that occupied the establishment. Kat not working was a minor setback as far as Biscuit was concerned, but in my eyes it allowed us to get to know Jack without any distractions.

"Otis tells me you been fucking some college girl who works here. What the hell's wrong with you, Biscuit?" Toad asked as we sat down in the booth.

Biscuit ran his hand through his hair as he shook his head, "Shit brother, ain't a damned thing wrong with me, wait 'till you see her. I think you'll agree Biscuit's doin' pretty damned good with this one, college girl or not. We've been fuckin' like a couple of Catholic rabbits. That girl's got the sexual drive of a three peckered billy goat."

"She is cute as fuck," I agreed.

"Right now, I think I'd fuck anyone who agreed to hold still long enough for me to poke 'em," Jack chuckled, "And that'd be about ten seconds worth, it's been quite a stretch for me."

Biscuit leaned into the table and rubbed his beard with his hand as he turned toward Jack, "I bet you're hornier than a fourteen year old boy who just found daddy's Playboy collection."

"Pretty damned close," Jack chuckled.

"Kitchen closes in twenty minutes if you want food. If not, the bar's open till two. Want to see a menu?" the waitress asked.

"What? Just get some beers?" Biscuit shrugged.

"Budweiser. I don't want Toad trying to order beers. We'll end up with some pale ale orange apple cider bullshit," I said jokingly.

The thirty-something year old waitress was attractive, but looked like she probably had a houseful of kids and a husband at home. The diamond ring on her finger could have been a gimmick, but the depression that had developed in the skin on her finger came from wearing it for many years if it was.

"Four Bud's?" she asked.

"Make it twelve. We'll go through the first four in about a *minute*," Biscuit responded.

She titled her head to the side playfully and turned toward Biscuit, "I'll bring eight and as soon as you set your empties at the side of the table, I'll bring four more. You don't want to drink hot beers, do you?"

"Smart girl right there," Biscuit said as he tossed his head her direction, "Make it eight."

"Be right back," she said as she turned away.

Biscuit glanced around the group and eventually shifted his gaze upward as he rubbed his beard. It appeared he was thinking of which story he wanted to grace us with. As he searched through his memory for something to reveal to the group, Jack broke the silence.

"So you fellas take any long rides? Go to Sturgis?" Jack asked.

I shook my head, "Don't go to Sturgis, but we make some pretty good runs. Austin for the ROT Rally, and down to Phoenix for the

Arizona Bike Week. Some of the fellas go down to Daytona, but it's a long ride and still winter here when that fucker pops off."

"No Sturgis, huh?" Jack chuckled.

"Sturgis has become a trailer-fest. Every swinging dick in the country drags his bike there on a trailer and then rides the fucker around town for a few days. Some of the fellas head up there alone, but we don't make a club run," Toad responded.

Jack nodded his head and grinned as the waitress dropped off the beers. After he nervously grabbed the first beer, we all reached for a bottle.

"Never cared for that Rally myself; bunch of amateurs," Jack said as he held his beer elevated over the center of the table.

Each of us grabbed a beer, opened it, and raised them for the obvious toast Jack intended. As our bottles clanked together, Jack spoke.

"Here's to being free, riding hard, and sleeping on a soft bed," Jack said.

After drinking half his bottle of beer in one gulp, he raised his bottle again. We immediately followed and waited for his next bit of wisdom.

"And here's to Slice's Ol' Lady Avery. Without her, I'd still be eating Star Crunch and drinking cold instant coffee in my cell," he said as he tilted his bottle into ours.

"Damned fine woman right there," Biscuit said as he lowered his bottle to the table.

I gazed toward the bathroom entrance blankly as *Citizen Cope's Sideways* began to play over the sound system. As I mentally faded away for a moment and became engrossed in the words of the music, I realized I was seated in a position which made me slightly uncomfortable. Naturally, I always tried to position myself facing the entrance of any bar I was seated in. If not, I generally stood by the door, and felt as if I was guarding the fellas from any potential harm or threat who might choose to enter. Having my back to the door made me nervous. Toad's PTSD made him far more skittish than I was, and he always demanded he *never* be seated with his back facing the door. Tonight, Jack and Toad sat facing the door with Biscuit and I facing the restrooms in the rear of the bar. Although I felt a little uneasy, I realized having Jack's back to the door probably wasn't an option considering his just having been released from prison. As I tried to comprehend what Jack had been through for the many years he was locked up in prison, Biscuit's elevated tone brought me back to a conscious state of mind.

"So, we were supposed to leave to go to the ROT Rally in about a week. There was this cute little Asian bitch working at this Thai place, and at the time, I hadn't fucked me an Asian yet. So I'd been goin' in there and bein' sweet on this little bitch," Biscuit paused and took a drink of his beer.

He rested his forearms on the table, leaned almost to the center, and widened his eyes, "So she's a little fucker 'bout four foot nothin' and has these little titties that look big because she's so damned tiny. Had an ass about the size of a Jonathan apple, but on them skinny little legs and against that eighteen inch waist it looked like Kim fucking Kardashian's ass. So anyway, we're a week out, and I head in there to get me some Asian pussy before the run."

"So I get in there, and she ain't my waitress, this other cute little chick is. But that ain't what this is about. So I order my food and get that spicy peanut chicken shit they sell. You guys eat Thai food?" he asked with wide eyes.

"Had some," Toad nodded.

I shook my head.

Jack shook his head and laughed, "Don't fuck with the stuff."

"Well, lemme tell ya, it ain't spicy, it's fucking *hot*. So anyway, I order this shit, and after a bit, a big plate of it shows up. Now I'm about half pissed this little Vietnamese princess ain't working, so I gobble this shit down. Now I'm waitin' on my check, and my gut starts making them noises. You know them noises when you *know* something's gonna happen and it ain't gonna be good?"

Jack nodded his head and lifted his beer, "Like after eatin' a burrito out of the toilet."

"What?" Biscuit snapped back, "A *toilet* burrito?"

Jack nodded his head and laughed, "Contraband. If you get caught with them, you go to the hole, so you can't leave 'em out in the cell, and you need to keep 'em cold anyway. So the Mexican's would steal the food from the kitchen and smuggle it to the cells and make up burritos. They'd sell 'em for stamps and store. They'd come wrapped in a piece of plastic, like from a garbage bag. The end was tied and it'd be air tight, and we kept 'em in the toilet to keep 'em cold until we wanted to eat 'em. Toilet's kind of like a 'fridge in the joint. Got sick on a few of those fuckers, that's for sure. Sorry for interrupting, go ahead."

Biscuit leaned away from the table and widened his eyes, "You ate shit out of a toilet?"

Jack nodded his head, "Didn't have a choice. Food, drinks, everything. You tie a string to it, shove it in the toilet, and pull it out when you want it. If the cops come, you flush it. After they leave, if they don't find the end of your string, you pull it back out of the sewer and either eat it or drink it."

"God damn," Biscuit said as he shook his head from side-to-side.

I felt the same way, but didn't dare embarrass Jack by saying so. Life in prison was without a doubt different than life on the outside. To imagine living every day confined, under the watchful eye of the guards, and having a few thousand people who wanted to try and test your ability to fight on a daily basis was more than I wanted to try and imagine.

"Go ahead," Jack said, "I apologize for interrupting."

Biscuit narrowed his gaze as he stared down at the table and shook his head, "Okay, so I'm waitin' on my check, and my gut's a rumblin' and makin' noise, and I know it's time to go. I reach into my wallet, pull out a twenty, and drop it on the table. I run out to my bike and ride that fucker home like I'd stole it. Whole way, it's a coin toss as to whether I'm gonna shit my pants or make it on time. I pull that fucker in the drive, hop off, and run into the house, dropping my pants as I'm runnin'."

"So I get into the shitter, and just explode. A miracle I even made it, I'm tellin' ya. So for about four hours, I got the shits. Now for situations like this, I keep them pills, the anti-diarrhea stuff, *Imodium AD*. I take about ten of those fuckers and finally it stops," he paused and reached for another bottle of beer.

He held his finger in the air as he took a drink to make sure we all knew the story wasn't over. As he lowered his bottle to the table, he continued.

"So that ain't even the story, the story's *this*. I took so many of those damned pills that I didn't shit for a week, and we got the rally comin' up in two days. Finally, it came. When it did, it was a week's worth, and about the size of a ten year old boy's arm. Fucker ripped my ass to shreds. Now, although I finally took a shit, I'm in pretty sad shape and I got a hemorrhoid the size of a Johnsonville Bratwurst hanging out of my ass," he hesitated, turned his palms up, and widened his eyes.

"God damn," Jack sighed, "That's a bitch. And the run's a few days out?"

I'd heard the story ten times over the years from half a dozen different people. The first time it made me about half sick, but every time after the first, I couldn't help but laugh. I was curious to hear Jack's response to Biscuit's problem solving skills, and sat anxiously waiting for Biscuit to continue his tale.

"Precisely. Two days until we're gonna spend ten hours on the road, and I've got a little friend hangin' outta my ass like I just gave birth. So I know I can't make it with this hot dog hanging out of my ass. Hell, I can't even sit down. Sleepin' on my belly and shit, and I fuckin' *hate* sleepin' on my belly, I'm a back sleeper. So I get me a rubber glove and I poke this fucker back up in there. Hell, after a few minutes, I feel pretty good and forget it's even there. I stand up and take a few steps," he paused for effect and took another drink.

He shoved his beer to the side and leaned into the center of the table. After making eye contact with each of us individually, he continued his story.

"And *bloop* - out the fucker comes. Another rubber glove, poke him back in there, and everything's fine. Take a few steps and *bloop* - out he comes again. Now I *know* I can't ride to Austin with my finger in my ass, so I start to thinkin'. And all of a sudden it comes to me, so I have Tater come get me in his truck and take to me that dildo shop out east. After a look around a bit, I find one of them butt plugs. Did you know they come in about ten different sizes?"

Toad, who I was quite certain had heard the story no fewer times than me, shrugged. Jack, obviously slightly uncomfortable, sat back in his seat, wrinkled his nose, and crossed his arms.

"Had no idea," Jack responded under his breath.

"Well they do. Picked me out a little red number on the small side of things. And it had this little ring in the end made it look like a pacifier. So Tater takes me home, and I glove up, shove the hotdog inside, and poke the little pacifier in my ass. After I wiggle around a bit, it feels pretty good. Now as far as I'm concerned, problem's solved. I'm a day out and ready to ride. Just for shits and grins, later on that night, I reach back there to check on things, you know, make sure everything's where it should be. And I'll be damned if that little ring, you know the part you hold on to? It's fucking gone!"

"Huh?" Jack shrugged.

Biscuit nodded his head, "Yep. Fucker sucked right up there in my ass. So, now I got to go fishin' for this little fucker. I glove up *again*, stick my finger up there, and fish around and find it. I pull her out, wash her up, and grease it with Vaseline and poke it back inside. Couple a minutes, and *bloop*. You guessed it, it disappears."

"So I just say fuck it. At this point in time, I feel pretty good, other'n knowing I got a butt plug in my ass. I hop on the bike and ride out to the snow ski and mountain climbin' store out on Central. Buy me one of those spring loaded carabiner D-rings. After I rode home, I gloved up one last time, found the little fucker, pulled it out, and hooked that D-Ring to it. Then I shoved her back in, and let the hook just hang out of my ass," he paused and nodded his head proudly as if he'd just cured cancer.

"Rode to Austin with a rappelling D-ring hanging out of your ass?" Jack winced.

"Sure did, left it there for a fucking *week*. Don't know if it was a conscious thing, or just because I had that little rubber plug in there or what, but I didn't shit for a week. When we got home, I reached back, grabbed the D-ring and gave it a tug. Damned thing popped out, and my little friend the hotdog was gone. Problem solved," he shrugged.

Biscuit sat back in his seat, crossed his arms, and nodded his head. As Toad shook his head in what was probably a combination of disbelief and disgust, Jack leaned forward and grabbed his second beer from the table. After he took a long drink, he shook his head and laughed.

"You're funnier than a motherfucker," Jack chuckled.

"Club joker, that's me," Biscuit responded proudly.

Jack shook his head and took another drink. He inhaled a shallow breath and appeared to be preparing to speak when his eyes widened and his jaw dropped open. Toad's eyes widened slightly immediately following, and his head tilted to the side.

"Holy. Fucking. Shit. Now, *that's* a woman," Jack said as he craned his neck to see.

Toad tilted his head to the side as his eyes appeared to bulge out of his head. I turned my head and glanced over my shoulder toward the door.

Holy fucking shit was right.

A lump began to immediately rise in my throat. I blindly fumbled for my beer as I continued to study the tall blonde woman as she slowly walked toward the bar. After taking a drink of my beer and washing the lump down my throat, she was directly in front of me, facing sideways. My eyes fixed on her, I fumbled to find the table, and released the bottle of beer. As my heart began to pound from my chest, I stood from my seat and turned to face her.

It had been fifteen years, but I was pretty damned sure. Not based so much on what she looked like, but how she made me feel when she walked into the room. I swallowed heavily and rubbed my sweaty hands against the thighs of my jeans.

"Sam," I breathed.

Nothing.

"Sam!" I said with a tone of authority.

Slowly, she turned around.

Her eyes immediately widened, and she raised her hands to her mouth as if in shock.

"Steve?" she whimpered.

As our eyes met, it felt as if my heart completely stopped beating. Somehow, in spite of it, I found a way to take the few steps across the floor of the bar and open my arms. As soon as she wrapped her arms around me and rested her face on my chest, my heart began to beat again.

After a long hug, she released me and pulled away slightly. As she stood in front of me, I glanced up and down her long frame. She looked no differently than she did fifteen years prior. What little she had aged did nothing but add to her beauty. Eventually, I fixed my eyes fixed on her left hand.

No ring.

And my heart stopped beating again.

SAM

I sat in the kitchen wondering if one day an answer would come. I knew - or at least I suspected - my mother's death would come long before mine; but knowing did little to prepare me for her departure from my life. As I was sure all children did, I wished I had spent more time with her, called her more frequently, and came home on a more regular basis. Changing it now would be impossible, and all I hoped for was to ease what little pain remained.

I lifted my coffee cup halfway to my mouth and gazed down into the cup. Realizing it was one of the cups I used to drink out as a young girl brought back memories, and as they filtered through my mind, a smile came to my face. Although I was a girl, blonde, and somewhat of a ding-dong, I wasn't so idiotic or mentally impaired that I wasn't able to accept her death as being just what it was.

The completion of her cycle of life.

No newcomer to losing someone I loved, I grinned and lifted the cup to my mouth with my mind filled with fond memories of my childhood. As my mind slowly searched for even more tender recollections from my youth, her not so dead cat walked into the kitchen and meowed.

Fucking cat.

I hated cats. Now, along with everything else in the home, I had inherited a fucking cat. The grey tabby looked like a small version of her larger vermin cousins, and was possessed by none other than the devil himself. In the several days I had spent inventorying the contents of the house and searching for small pieces of my mother's life, the cat followed me everywhere I went. When I stopped, it stopped. As I worked, it sat and stared at me with golden snake-like eyes that seemed to burn holes through my skin and into my flesh. The one thing that prevented me from stepping on it or placing it out with the many bags of trash was the fact it was my mother's only true friend, and my single living tie to my mother's former life.

"Go away!" I hissed as I swatted my hand in the direction of the filthy feline.

"Meow!" it responded.

"No," I screeched.

"*This*," I swatted my hand in her direction again, "Means *go away*."

She meowed again, obviously confused regarding my demand, and began walking toward me. As I watched in sheer horror, she walked alongside the table, turned at the last moment, and before I could lift my leg, slithered to the side and rubbed her body against my shin. The many hours I spent at the gym combined with my quick reflexes paid off in the form of a swift leg extension which sent her sliding across the kitchen floor.

"Stay over there before I put your sickening ass in the freezer," I snapped as I stood from my seat.

I stared down at my leg as if I expected to see my calf withering away from some form of staph infection. After brushing her residue from my skin, I finished my coffee and walked to the sink. Gazing into the back yard provided a rush of memories from my high school years, and the time I had spent with my then lover, Steve.

If anyone ever was, we were meant for each other. The type of couple that made everyone else sick when we showed up at a party, we were the two people who always finished each other's sentences, poked food into each other's mouths, and tasted each other's drinks we concocted at parties or fast-food restaurants.

My life had never felt as *in order* as it was then. In Steve's presence I was able to exhale, and had no worries whatsoever. He was a huge guy, standing more than six feet five, wasn't overweight, and actually was quite the opposite. In high school, he played football and basketball, and always stayed in great physical condition. After school was over, he continued to stay in great shape by constantly lifting weights and running. His physical presence combined with his protective nature made me feel comfortable that no matter what, no harm would ever come to me.

Other than spending time with me, his only other true love was riding his Harley. He found freedom in riding it, and often spent countless hours on the road - often with me on the back – riding to a place that we rarely *planned* on going. I was young at the time, but there was no mistaking that our love was not only genuine, but it was the type of love most women would never find in a lifetime.

To try and describe the love we shared would be impossible. Words like *perfect* and phrases like *once in a lifetime* came to mind when thinking about it, but there were no words in my vocabulary that would accurately describe our relationship with any level of justice. When we were twenty-one years old, I decided I needed to act as if I was an adult, and the selfish side of me desired children.

Steve wanted nothing more than to live his life free, and love me until the end. In time I'm quite sure children would have been possible with him, but at the time I asked, I gave very little, if any, room for negotiation. His response was not what I wanted but what I should have expected.

And we parted ways.

Incapable of living in the same city as Steve lived without having him in my life, I left the city with tear-filled eyes, a broken heart, and no plan for my future. I moved as far away as geography and common sense would allow, and came to rest in New York City. Within a year I was married to a workaholic who could care less about anything but how many commas were in his paycheck.

After a year of marriage, a terrorist flew a commercial airliner into the building he worked in, and he never came home from work. No body, no clothes, no jewelry, and no closure to a loss I was ill prepared for.

I recovered quickly, as I always did, with the understanding living life was a mystery; and solving it, no different than watching a movie, didn't come until the bitter end. With the exception of losing Steve, I had accepted everything life had thrown my direction, and never once complained.

Losing him, however, remained the one thing for the last fourteen years I never accepted. I knew I couldn't change it and would never be granted an opportunity to fix it, but accepting it as being a good decision haunted me on a daily basis.

After the death of my husband, I left New York and moved to St. Louis - the second worst decision I ever made in my life. There I remained, single, uninterested, and gainfully employed as a hairstylist at an upscale salon I dreamed of one day owning. The untimely death of my mother brought me back to Wichita, a city I had very little intention of ever returning to full time, and in fact I dreaded even the short visits to my mother prior to her death. My underlying fear of encountering Steve, and finding him living a happy life with someone other than me made me feel ill.

Immediately following our breakup, I had snooped on Myspace hoping to find a glimpse of him or a morsel from his life without me. As the years passed, I had spent countless unsuccessful hours attempting to find him on Facebook, Twitter, Tumblr, and even scoured the popular dating forums. It came as no surprise that I never found anything; Steve was always a person who enjoyed living out of the view and away from the scrutiny of others. A few years into this century, and I'd given up any hope of ever learning *anything* about him. In time, I began to live my life as the single *arrogant bitch* most of my clients described me as.

Arrogant? *No.*

Dissatisfied with the loss of the one man I loved, and the other who I had simply settled for? *Yes.*

I gazed at the concrete bench situated underneath the pergola, recalling the time Steve and I had spent there. As my focus shifted to the entire yard, I appreciated the small changes my mother had made since I'd seen it last. The sides of the brick walkway leading to the fountain in the rear of the yard once adorned with large leaf periwinkle and various hostas was now beautifully landscaped with lavender, daisies, and an occasional black-eyed Susan. The back yard had always been my mother's place of escape, and in many respects, it was mine as well. She used the yard for therapeutic reasons after the death of my father, and I sometimes felt guilty for my less relaxing use of the beautiful space she had created. The smell of the flowers combined with the seclusion created by the depth of landscape made it a perfect area for sex. Steve and I had spent countless hours in the yard fucking on various large stones, the concrete bench, and even in the fountain. I loved fucking him in my mother's back yard, and generally speaking, I preferred it to my bedroom. Steve's bad-boy attitude, his take charge personality and my willingness to please the man I truly loved caused me to agree to some pretty risqué sexual situations in the five years we were in a relationship.

My eyes once again shifted to the bench and became fixed. I grinned, wondering just how many times I had pressed my chest against the cold concrete while arching my back, forcing my ass high enough in the air for Steve to satisfy my sexual desires. Many times I had bit my lower lip so hard while he fucked me that impressions of my teeth remained in my lip for an hour after we returned into the house. Although my mother never questioned me, I always felt she knew I loved the yard just as much as her, but for different reasons.

There were times when I would lay on the bench with my eyes closed as he knelt beside it. As I lay in wait, he would take his hands and…

His hands.

Oh dear God, his *hands*. He was a master with his hands; where to place them, and just how delicately or deliberately to use them. And there was always the issue with the use of his lips. He spent more time kissing my body than he did my mouth. He seemed to enjoy dragging his lips, teeth, and tongue along my body; teasing me until I was a frantic mess. Only when I was no longer mentally, physically, or sexually able to allow him to continue would he agree to stop. To describe Steve as sexually torturous would be an accurate understatement.

I rinsed the cup, placed it in the dishwasher, and turned off the kitchen lights. After quickly checking the house for other lights I had left on through the course of the day, I walked to the front door, reached for the door handle, and hesitated. I turned and gazed into the house which was illuminated solely by the glow of the lamp in the living room. I stood and grinned at the memories the home brought, sad I wasn't able to bring myself to stay overnight. As I gazed down the hallway toward the door of my childhood bedroom, I felt something press against my ankle.

Somewhat confused, I glanced down at my feet.

"Meow…"

Fucking cat.

Reluctantly, I reached down and patted the cat on the head. As I turned for the door, I wiped my hand against my thigh, freeing it of the matter the cretin was certain to have left. I opened the door, stepped onto the porch and glanced inside; making certain the cat hadn't followed me. Sitting in the entrance, the cat stared back at me with golden eyes now filled with huge black pupils, undoubtedly allowing it to sneak through the house in the dark and wreak havoc on the organized piles I had created.

I glared at her and shook my head.

"Good night Taylor. I'm going to the hotel. I'll see your nasty little ass tomorrow."

I closed the door, locked it, and turned toward the driveway. I glanced down at my watch as I walked to the car. As it was still quite early and not quite dark yet, I decided to stop for a much needed drink before I retired for the night. A drink would allow me to relax and get a good night's sleep, something I felt I desperately needed.

Stopping at the shitty little bar beside the hotel would be easy, and no doubt would allow me to enjoy a drink without seeing anyone I knew. I didn't need any sympathetic apologies for the loss of my mother.

I needed to relax alone and try to rid my mind of memories of the only man I ever loved and how my selfish wishes tore us apart.

SAM

I pulled into the parking lot of the bar and parked the car. The bar's lot, as I had suspected, was all but empty. Having passed by it for more than a week in my evening drives back to the hotel, it seemed to *always* be empty during the weekdays. There were times when I *wanted* a drink, and times when I felt I *needed* them, and tonight was a *need* night. Having made contact with the disease ridden feline no less than a dozen times throughout the course of the day- combined with my walk down memory lane - left liquid sedation as my only hope for a good night's sleep.

My stroll to the door produced four motorcycles parked along the sidewalk leading to the entrance. Carefully parked in a perfect line side by side, they reminded me of Steve and his friends, and how they used to make sure their motorcycles were always parked neatly and in an almost picturesque manner.

Great, another reminder of him.

Frustrated and suffering from more than a decade of sexual deprivation, I considered kicking the first motorcycle in the line and causing them to spill over like dominoes. After a moment's worth of hesitation, I admired the motorcycles, turned to the door, pushed it open.

As I stepped through the door, *Lenny Kravitz' Can't Get You Off My Mind* played. A great choice of music, and one of my all-time favorite songs, but it was about as ironic of a song as anyone could have chosen. After rolling my eyes and shaking my head lightly, I stepped into the empty bar.

A muscular tattooed biker in a ribbed tank top and another seated beside him with olive colored skin and a gorgeous smile sat in a booth facing me. Two other bikers outfitted with their motorcycle gang attire had their backs facing me. As I turned to the bar, the muscular one in the tank top craned his neck to catch another glimpse.

Stare all you want, gym rat, I'm not available.

Memories of Steve again began to float around in my head as I walked toward the empty bar. I glanced along the barstools, grateful the bar was empty. I should be able to toss down a quick triple vodka before any of the bikers developed enough courage to approach me and escape without incident.

"Sam," a voice from behind me hollered.

My muscles tensed as I stopped right where I was standing. Half scared to turn around, I stood, petrified of encountering an old friend from the past who would assuredly provide me with stories of how my high school sweetheart, Steve, had eventually married and now lived happily with his wife, children, and two pet cats. The endless silence that followed filled me with hope that whoever had shouted was talking to someone other than me.

"Sam!" the voice bellowed in more of a commanding tone.

It seemed…

I slowly turned around.

Oh dear God.

Every emotion imaginable filled me at once. I raised my shaking hands to my face and pressed them against my cheeks, attempting to hide the tears that were sure to come next.

He was gorgeous. Much bigger and in what appeared to be the best physical condition I'd ever seen him in, he stood and stared. It had been fourteen years since I'd seen him, but he hadn't aged one bit. It seemed he had simply been transformed from a boy into the man who stood before me. As I stood still and fought back tears, he slowly approached me with his arms outstretched.

I wanted to turn and run away.

I glanced at the palms of his hands as he excitedly made his way to where I stood. Before I could see if he was wearing a ring, he had me wrapped up in his muscular arms.

I can't do this.

As he released me, I couldn't help but admire him as I fumbled for a way to explain my desire to leave. I considered pulling my phone from my purse and claim to have received a text message emergency. To have him even begin to explain of his wife, children and what the past fourteen years had graced him with would crush me.

He crossed his arms in front of his chest as he seemed to study me, and as he did, the fingers of his left hand rested on the outer portion of his right bicep.

No ring.

Not one hundred percent certain if my eyes were seeing what was truly in front of me, or what they *desired* to see, I blinked my eyes and gazed at his hand.

No ring.

I blinked again.

Oh fuck it, I've never been known being subtle.

"So, are you divorced?" I shrugged as I nodded my head toward his hand.

He uncrossed his arms and glanced down at his left hand as his mouth formed into a grin.

"Never married," he said as he shook his head from side-to-side.

Oh dear God.

Please make him single, available, and interested.

I stood like a loon, exchanging glances between the muscles in his arms and his gorgeous face. He appeared to have gotten a dozen or more tattoos since the last time I had seen him, which did nothing more but add to his already striking outward appearance. I found a man with tattoos to be far more attractive than a man without, and his recent additions weren't helping the situation. Struggling to devise a way to save myself from seeming over eager or desperate, I stood with my mouth agape as he began to speak.

"You look great, Sam," he said as he folded his arms in front of his chest again.

I blinked my eyes.

"Where's your husband?" he asked as he tossed his head playfully toward the door.

I widened my eyes and shrugged my shoulders.

Jesus, Samantha, speak.

He raised his hands to his head and rubbed his temples. It was something he had done since he was a kid when either confused or angry. Now quite certain my silent shrug regarding my husband caught him by surprise, I swallowed heavily and searched my mind for the right words.

"Dead," I blurted before I had a chance to filter my thoughts.

"Sorry to hear that. And I'm sorry about your mother, Sam. I really am," he said as he reached for my arm.

Thoughts of a life with Steve in it began to fill my head. No longer was I concerned with my mother's house, inventorying the boxes of trinkets, or keeping the cat alive. Riding on the back of Steve's motorcycle, having him fuck me breathless in the back yard, and feeling his magical hands against my skin became the only thoughts available within the confines of my biased mind.

"Join me for a drink?" I somehow muttered.

"Sure. Let me introduce you to the fellas first," he grinned as his hand lightly gripped my upper arm.

I allowed him to guide me to his side. His arm wrapped around me as soon as he turned toward the booth where the other men were seated, and in a few short steps, he was introducing me to his biker brethren.

"Fellas, this is Sam. Sam, this is Toad, Biscuit, and Big Jack," he said as we approached the table, pointing to each man as he said their name.

Immediately, the three men stood. As soon as the man he pointed out as Big Jack stepped from the booth, the one he identified as Toad slid from between the table and bench and stood in front of us.

As he extended his arm to shake my hand, he widened his eyes and tilted his head to the side, motioning toward me. As I shook his hand, I glanced at Steve, who nodded his head and grinned in return.

"Pleasure to finally meet you. I've heard a lot about you, Sam," Toad said as he shook my hand.

I grinned and nodded my head, not quite knowing what to say. As the bigger barrel-chested man stepped in front of us, he reached up and ran his hand through his thick brown hair, as if attempting to make himself more presentable. His full beard and sheer size made him rather intimidating, but as he spoke, he seemed to have a very calm and pleasant demeanor.

"Sorry about your mother, Sam. Name's Biscuit. Nice to finally put a face with the name," he said as he reached for my hand.

I glanced at Steve.

You told them about me?

And about my mother?

I swallowed a lump of sentiment which began to rise in my throat. The thought of him telling his friends about me caused me to once again become the emotional little girl I'd spent almost fifteen years trying to abandon. As I gazed at the profile of his face, hoping for him to say *something*, the man in the ribbed tank cleared his throat.

"Pleasure to meet you, ma'am. Otis is a damned fine man," he nodded as he reached for my hand.

I turned toward Steve as I shook the man's hand, "Otis? You're going by Otis? The name your grandfather gave you?"

He shrugged his shoulders and grinned as he pointed to an embroidered patch on his leather vest.

Otis.

Steve's grandfather called him Otis since he was a small child. Although his parents never really adopted the practice, I never heard his grandfather call him anything other than Otis. The thought of Steve using it as his biker name filled me with warmth.

"How's he doing?" I asked.

"He passed about ten years ago," he sighed.

"I'm sorry," I said under my breath.

"Nice to meet all of you guys," I grinned somewhat nervously.

"We're going to go have a drink at the bar, fellas," Steve said as he motioned to toward the bar.

"Let's sit here," I said as I pointed toward the oversized booth where they were seated, "Unless this is private?"

"Nothin' private about this little meetin'. Hell, sit down," Biscuit grumbled as he found his seat.

"Want to sit here?" Steve shrugged.

I glanced toward Steve and grinned, "I'd love to."

And, to be brutally honest, I didn't want to sit in the booth with his friends. I didn't want to be *anywhere* with his friends. I longed to be alone with Steve, catching up on lost time. If it were up to me, he'd follow me back to my mother's house.

And bend me over the bench.

OTIS

Being in Sam's presence caused me to realize not only how much I had missed seeing her, but just how easy it was for the right person - the person we reserve our *true* love for - to completely right everything that may be wrong in our life by simply gracing us with their existence.

I knew if I allowed her to escape my grasp again, my life would return right back to where I had been living prior to her return. Sitting in her hotel room talking made it immediately apparent that where I *had* been living my life was miles away from where I *should have* been living it. As she sat across the couch from me and playfully brushed her hair from her face, it became more difficult to accept her inevitable departure.

"So, you're going back to St. Louis?" I said as I stood.

She stood from the couch, scrunched her nose slightly, and narrowed her eyes as she turned to face me.

"Well, yeah. I mean, eventually I'll have to. I live there," she muttered.

I shook my head as I studied her. Although I was grateful to have seen her, I was frustrated that in a matter of days, things would return back to the way they were. Immediately, my mind began to reel with thoughts of ways to repair what damage I had done to our fifteen year old relationship.

"No chance of you staying? You know, making this your home again?" I shrugged.

"I didn't say *that*. It's just. I'd have to have a good reason. I mean, I wouldn't choose this place over any other place. Well, maybe I'd choose it over St. Louis, but *right now*, St. Louis is home. It's been home for almost fifteen years," she paused and reached for her purse.

"Gum?" she asked as she pulled a pack of gum from her purse.

I shook my head and grinned.

She stills chews gum.

"A good reason?" I shrugged.

"Uh huh," she nodded as she tossed the pack of gum into her purse.

I glanced around the hotel suite and eventually fixed my eyes on hers. "It's really none of my business, but did your mother own her home?"

She nodded her head, "Yes, she did."

I raised my shoulders slightly and widened my eyes, "I'm going to guess you inherited it?"

"I did, like I said earlier. That's what I'm doing, going through stuff now. Why are we standing?" she asked.

"I'm thinking," I responded under my breath, "So, you're going to tell me that you'd rather live in St. Louis, and abandon or sell the home you grew up in? There's a lot of good memories there."

She inhaled a shallow breath and after short a moment, exhaled and fixed her eyes on mine, "That's the problem; the memories. It's the reason I'm staying here. I just can't, Steve. It's really tough, but I just can't stay there."

"Why?" I shrugged, somewhat saddened by the fact she couldn't bring herself to stay in the home we had spent so much time in together.

The thought of her getting rid of the home was almost unthinkable. We had spent the majority of our relationship in her mother's home, and a good part of it was spent outside, fucking in the flower garden her mother had made. As a young man, the sensation of having sex in the *backyard* was almost equal to the initial excitement of having sex itself. Together, it provided a sense of enjoyment well beyond having sex in a bed. Soon, we were not only fucking in the yard, but anywhere and everywhere we could; and the more adventurous it was, the better. We soon learned we both had an inner sexual demon we needed to release, but it was her mother's backyard that made us realize it.

"My mind fills with too many memories when I'm there," she responded through her teeth.

Thank God. I hope you're thinking of me.

I turned my palms up and widened my eyes, "And that's a bad thing?"

She glanced up and nodded her head, "Yeah. It sure is."

Her eyes were glassy and it appeared she was on the verge of crying. Even though it had been a little more than a week, I considered the possibility of her not being quite over the loss of her mother. Sam was always a strong woman, and one thing I always admired was her ability to roll with the punches so to speak. Growing up, it seemed regardless of what life tossed at her, she was able to accept it as being, and simply move on. Her mother's death may have been more difficult for her, and I began to feel insensitive for pushing her about the home.

She glanced upward and fixed her eyes on the ceiling. After a moment, she fixed her eyes on mine and sat down on the couch.

"Sit," she said in a half demanding tone as she patted the cushion beside her.

I sat down, feeling selfish for acting the way I had acted. As I attempted to mentally form an apology worth offering, she began to speak.

"You know, it's tougher than I thought. Much tougher. I was in the kitchen tonight looking out in the back yard. It's changed a lot, but just seeing it is tough," she sighed.

I nodded my head, "I'm sorry Sam, I imagine it is."

I considered how I might feel if I lost my mother; and how seeing the things she loved and cherished - after she had passed away - would affect me. As she bit her lower lip and glanced around the room, I contemplated losing both my parents and how having no one might cause me to react. As my sorrow for Sam's loss began to peak, I once again felt like a selfish idiot.

"Sam, I'm..."

She raised her hand between us to silence me as she inhaled an audible breath. I crossed my arms and leaned into the back of the couch, prepared for her ridicule.

"You know the guy I married? Michael? I really didn't even know him. Not *really*. I met him at the gym. He was really tall, muscular, and he had a tattoo on his bicep I'm sure he must have got as a result of some stupid college bet. But he was as close as I could get. He reminded me of you, Steve. When I looked at him, I saw *you*. But when he spoke or acted, he *wasn't* you. It wasn't long and I realized no one could be. After a while, I realized the kids, having a family…all of that…it wasn't important. What I wanted wasn't a family, kids, or him for that matter, what I wanted was a sense of security in having *you*," she threw her hands in the air as if making the determination was a huge revelation.

Okay, that wasn't what I expected.

"When he died, I hate to say this, but it's true. You're the first person I've said anything to about this…" she paused as her voice began to fill with emotion.

"When they announced what happened, after the terrorists flew the planes into the buildings, and they were collapsing," she hesitated and swallowed heavily.

After a moment of staring at the ceiling and attempting to steady her breathing, she continued.

"I hoped…I wanted…" she shook her head as she bit into her lower lip.

After a long silence, she stared down at the floor and continued, "When I got the word that he was dead, I was *relieved*. I know it sounds morbid and selfish or whatever, especially to everyone else who lost someone in the tragedy, but for me? I was relieved."

In some respects, the world we live in had just shrunk into a very personal sized ball. To think she had lost someone in what I assumed to be the terrorist act of 9/11 made the terrorist act much more real. Even though, I sat and stared, shocked by the statement she had made.

"I was relieved he was gone, because it would allow me to move on and live my life with the memories of you without feeling guilty for doing so. I've never got over losing you, Steve, and I'm pretty damn sure I never will," she said as she turned toward me.

What?

As somber as the mood had become, I felt there were many things I should have said in an effort to comfort her for the loss of her husband. My excitement after hearing her more recent statement made regarding never getting over losing me prevented me from saying what I should have, and caused me to say what I was actually thinking.

"You've never got over losing me?" I snapped back as I sat up in my seat.

She shook her head from side to side as she wiped her eyes with the tips of her fingers.

"No, and I'm afraid I never will. It's really hard seeing you again," she blubbered.

Fuck it, we're both adults.

I'm thinking you're feeling the same way I am.

"Sam," I said as I slowly stood.

She wiped her tear filled eyes. After what seemed like an eternity, she shifted her gaze upward.

"Yeah," she breathed.

Here we go.

"I love you, Sam," I said as I opened my arms.

She sat for a split-second and stared with wide eyes.

Bad idea.

You should have kept your mouth shut, Otis.

She stood, screeched like she'd just seen a snake, and jumped into my arms.

"Oh God, I love you, too. I never stopped loving you. I tried...I tried to change the way I felt, but...I couldn't..." she breathed into the side of my neck.

How quickly a person's life can change...

One simple statement or event can flip your life into a completely different direction. No differently than Jack being released from prison, or the bikers in Waco who were thrown in jail for being in a bar at the wrong time, holding Sam in my arms made an immediate and unscheduled change in my life. A change for what I assumed would be the better, but a change nonetheless. As I held her in my arms, a rush of memories filled my mind, and I quickly came to realize one thing for absolute certain.

I wasn't ever going to let her escape my grasp again.

SAM

My entire life away from Steve, I had one desire and one desire only.

To be with him again.

Under the assumption I had lost him for good, and certain a man as attractive as him would have easily had women tossing themselves in his direction, I preserved what little remaining dignity I had by not exposing myself to him in the years which had passed since we were apart. Now, finding out we shared the same feelings over the years caused me to feel as if we had never been apart.

"No, as soon as I'd meet a woman, I would compare her to you. They never measured up so I couldn't see wasting my time - or theirs for that matter," he said.

Shocked, but quite relieved, I suddenly began to itch all over.

"And you've pretty much been single? Since we broke up?" I shrugged.

"Yep," he said as he nodded his head, "You know how I am about trusting people. I feel like I can't really trust just *anyone* now. That was another excuse I used."

Steve was a very tall man. I had always perceived myself as being tall for a woman, and stood 5'-7", but standing beside him made me feel small. The fact he towered almost twelve inches over me not only made me feel secure in his presence, but for some weird reason it excited me to no end. As I stood and absorbed just how large of a man he had become, I admired his handsome looks.

And I couldn't help myself.

"So, you've loved me since then? Since I left?" I asked as I shifted my eyes toward the crotch of his jeans.

Still rocking that big bulge, aren't you?

"I never stopped, Sam. I've always loved you. Felt kind of stupid for ever being so selfish that I let you go," he sighed.

You felt selfish?

I felt selfish.

But I'll let you keep on feeling like it was your fault.

"So it's kind of like we've never been apart," I said as I shrugged my shoulders.

He nodded his head and grinned, "Yep."

"I want to fuck," I said flatly.

His eyes widened considerably. He raised his hands to his face and began to rub his temples, a strong sign he was either considering my request, or for some reason the thought of fucking me had become repulsive. I didn't have to wait long to find out which one he was thinking.

"Right now?" he sighed as he lowered his hands.

"Now? No not *here*," I responded as if I clearly had other plans.

"Follow me," I said as I turned toward the door.

I stepped past him and opened the door. As he stood and gawked at me, I glanced down the empty hallway, reached for his hand, and began walking toward the elevator. As he followed behind me, he chuckled.

"Where are we going, Sam?" he asked as we walked down the hallway.

I silently walked to the elevator and pressed the button. As we stepped inside, he glanced in my direction and simply shook his head.

"It's a surprise," I responded as I inhaled a whiff of his scent.

Still wearing Acqua Di Gio.

Good.

1996, the year we graduated high school, Acqua Di Gio was introduced. I loved the smell, and purchased a bottle for him at the mall for his birthday. While we were together, he never wore any other cologne to the best of my knowledge. It had become his signature scent, and every time I smelled it since, I thought of him. Now, smelling a faint hint of it excited me.

Within a few seconds my pussy began to tingle.

The elevator door opened at the first floor. After glancing down the hallway in each direction, I eagerly began walking toward the indoor swimming area. The indoor pool was separated from the adjoining workout room by a glass wall which was mirrored on the side of the gym. From the pool, a person could see inside the gym, but from the gym, a person attempting to look out at the pool saw nothing but their reflection. The remaining three walls in the pool room were constructed of brick, making it virtually soundproof. Although the lights weren't on, the glow from the hallway entry and the door leading outside illuminated the area more than enough to provide a sexy luminescent lighting perfect for a late night fuck.

I pulled my room keycard from the pocket of my shorts and pressed it into the card reader. Eagerly, I opened the door which led to the pool, pleasantly surprised to find no one inside. The room was hot, humid, and thick with the smell of chlorine. My joy multiplied tenfold when I glanced toward the gym and noticed a couple getting in their late-night workout.

"What are we doing, Sam?" he asked as he glanced around the room.

"I don't have my swimming trunks," he chuckled.

"You're going to fuck me, *Otis,*" I grinned as I cleared the towels from the top of the glass table positioned between the edge of the pool and the glass wall.

Through the one-way glass, I could clearly see the two people inside the gym on elliptical machines, working away while listening to their iPods. The thought of Otis *not* knowing they couldn't see us excited me almost as much as me imagining they *could.*

"Right here? There's people in the gym, Sam," he responded.

I shrugged as I unbuttoned my shorts, "Lose your sense of adventure?"

As he glanced toward the gym the side of his mouth curled slightly.

"No, sure didn't," he responded as he reached for his zipper.

Although he had always been in great physical shape, his arms were not only now covered in tattoos to his wrists, but they were solid muscle from his forearm to his shoulder. His unbuttoned leather vest exposed his massive chest covered only by a sheer white tee shirt he wore underneath his vest. As he pulled against his zipper, I watched intently as the muscles in his bicep flared.

I glanced down and gazed at his zipper as I waited for him to pull his cock out. I'd seen it a million times, but I stood in wait, wanting to catch a glimpse of it, hoping nothing had changed. Not having been with a man for over a decade, and never having had sex with anyone as old as myself, I wondered if at 36 years of age, something might have changed. Thoughts of a wrinkled half shriveled up *old man penis* came to mind. As he unbuckled his belt and pulled his zipper down simultaneously, his thick dick flopped free of the denim which had restrained it.

Oh dear God.

A wrinkle-free cock with the girth of my wrist sprung from his jeans. My hand, which was resting between the upper band of my panties and my hip, quickly moved between my legs as if it had a mind of its own.

Soaked.

"See this," I said as I raised my glistening finger into the air.

His eyes shifted upward as I spoke.

"That's fourteen years of wait," I said as I fixed my eyes on my pussy-soaked finger.

"Fifteen, actually damned near sixteen, but who's counting," he said.

I shrugged my shoulders. I had no intention of arguing over a few months time, I was ready to fuck.

I glanced in his direction as he cleared his throat with a cough.

"See *this*?" he asked.

I shifted my eyes to his cock filled hand and nodded my head.

"This isn't fifteen years of wait, but it's damned sure about ten inches of ready," he said with a smile as he stroked his hand along the rigid shaft.

Feeling an almost giddy degree of excitement I hadn't felt since I'd seen him last, I pressed the waist of my shorts along my thighs and released them as they slid past my knees. As the fabric nestled around my ankles, I leaned over, pressed my forearms onto the top of the glass table and glanced over my shoulder.

He stood ten feet behind me with his cock in hand, his jeans bunched around his thighs, and his eyes fixed on my ass.

"That ass of yours is still incredible," he sighed as he continued to stroke his cock.

"Try this pussy out and see what you think of it," I said with a laugh as I pressed my chest onto the table.

"Smart ass," he breathed.

I exhaled as he rested his hands on my shoulders. As I felt the tip of his cock pressing against my wet pussy, I realized regardless of my overeager state of mind, I hadn't been fucked in almost a decade and a half. As he pushed past my parted lips and began to fill my vaginal walls, I opened my mouth, widened my eyes drastically, and did the only thing I could think of which might provide a little relief.

"Ohhhhhh," I groaned like a woman possessed by demons.

"That's fucking painful…but it feels so good," I moaned.

"Jesus, Sam. Your pussy wasn't this tight when you were sixteen," he said under his breath.

"When I was sixteen," I sighed.

"You were…"

"Fucking me…"

"Three times…"

"A day…" I grunted as he continued to try and force himself inside of me.

I bit my lower lip and laid my head to the side as he pulled against my shoulders and slowly pushed himself deeper and deeper into my not so receptive pussy. As he slowly pressed his cock further and further into me, I gripped the sides of the table tightly and bit down harder on my lip.

As long as I had waited for this day to come, and as excited as I was to be fucking him again, I realized there was no way I was going to last. As much as I wanted it, and even though it felt amazing in an oddly awkward way, having his arm-sized cock inside of me was painful as hell. As I prepared to try and explain my need to throw in the towel and

120

offer him one hell of a blowjob, he pulled up on my shoulders, lifted my chest from the table, and sank his teeth into my neck.

After thirty seconds or so of dragging his teeth along my neck and biting my shoulder, ear, and neck as he did so, his mouth came to rest against my ear. As he exhaled warm breath against my ear, a chill ran down my spine.

"That tight little pussy of yours is pissing me off, Sam," he breathed into my ear.

Goosebumps rose along my arm and my upper body began to tingle.

"I'm about to pull out, shove you down on your knees, and jack off on your pretty little face," he moaned.

The mere mention of having him jack off on my face opened a totally new chapter in my book of memories. The thought of it sent a tingling sensation through my lower region, and suddenly I felt my pussy open up like a blooming rosebud. Within a few seconds, the pain was gone, and Otis was sliding in and out of me not with ease, but definitely without much frustration.

"Oh fuck yes," I moaned as I glanced toward the glass wall.

The two people were in the gym were running on their elliptical machines, staring at the mirror in front of them. In my mind, they were watching Otis fuck me and enjoying what they were seeing. As I felt each individual inch of his stiff shaft slide inside of me, I sighed and grinned, knowing it wouldn't be long before I erupted into an earth shattering orgasm.

"I'm going to pull out and cover your face in cum, you sexy little bitch," he moaned into my ear as he rhythmically worked his manhood in and out of my dripping pussy.

Oh dear God.

"Do it…but make sure they're…watching…when you do," I muttered as he continued to fuck me senseless.

The feeling of his hands pulling on my shoulders, his mouth against my ear, and his cock deep inside of me not only brought back old memories, but was quickly creating a new one as I watched the people on the other side of the glass. While he continued to pound every inch of his swollen rod inside of my sexually out-of-shape pussy, I felt like he was taking my virginity *again*.

When I was sixteen, I was a virgin. I gave my virginity willingly to Otis, because at the time, I knew not only that I was in love with him, but that I wanted to spend my entire life with him as my *other*. He was slightly smaller at the time, and stood roughly six feet tall, but his cock was every bit as large then as it was now. As he pounded away, his hips slapped against my ass, filling the *room* with the sound of sex, and my *mind* with thoughts of whether or not losing my virginity the first time or this time was more pleasurable.

"They're watching you…fuck…me. You know that…right?" I said between choppy breaths.

"They better be," he breathed into my ear as he released my shoulders and slid his hands down to my breasts.

His huge hands massaged my boobs as he continued to slide his cock in and out of my wetness. Each *in* stroke hit a spot deep within me that sent a sensation throughout every inch of my lady bits. As my swollen pussy tingled from the inside out, he began to pinch my nipples between his thumbs and forefingers.

Oh dear God.

Hell yes.

Squeeze my titties while you fuck me.

With his hips pounding against my ass and my back arched, his cock was beating a tune against my g-spot. As his three available fingers continued to squeeze my boobs, his thumb and forefinger maintained pressure on my nipples. The sensation of it all became too much and my body began to shudder.

And that was it.

The beginning of the ever so miraculous orgasm that filled my body, mind, and spirit with hope, desire, dreams, and love shook me to my inner being. As it continued, I groaned into the room.

"Ohhhh God yes," I moaned as he continued to pinch my nipples and pummel my g-spot.

As I continued to float out into orgasmic heaven, I didn't realize he had released my nipples from his grasp. Only when his hand came down against the side of my ass did I realize through my shock, stinging ass cheek, and heightened sense of sexual sensation that he had freed his hands from my boobs.

Slap!

The sound of the skin-on-skin contact echoed throughout the room. I glanced at the glass wall, for some reason expecting the people in the gym to have heard it and now be eagerly watching him continue to fuck me like his little sexual play toy I was eager to become.

"This tight little pussy of yours…" he grunted as he continued to pound his cock into my wetness.

"Is almost…too much," he groaned as he gripped my ass with both hands.

My legs were rubber, my pussy was on fire, and my body felt like I was floating in a cloud of sheer bliss. As much as I wanted to continue to fuck, my poor pussy was incapable of even one more moment of punishment.

I was done.

"Cum on my face," I grunted as he spread my ass cheeks apart with his hands.

I thought the offer alone would excite him enough to get him to stop fucking me for a moment and consider it. During his down time, I figured I could come up with something that might encourage him to pull out of my pussy and finish elsewhere.

"Titty fuck me," I sighed.

"You horny little bitch," he breathed as he slowly pulled his cock from my wet pussy.

"Come here," he growled as he grabbed a fistful of my hair.

I had obviously aroused the alpha male side of him I so desperately desired. As he tugged against my hair, I stood from my position at the table, kicked my shorts and panties to the side, and followed him as he shuffled toward the glass wall, restrained from taking large steps by the jeans still wrapped around his ankles.

As he came to a stop at the glass window, I looked upward and through the glass. The man and woman had stopped their workout, and stood talking beside the machines as they stared into the glass.

"Knees," he demanded as he released my hair.

I eagerly dropped to my knees.

"Open," he breathed.

I opened my mouth and raised my hands to my chest. As I massaged my boobs in my hands, he guided his cock past my waiting lips. He methodically began to work his manhood in and out of my mouth, allowing me to fantasize about the people on the other side of the wall actually witnessing me suck his dick. As I closed my eyes and drifted into la-la land, he slowly pulled his cock from deep inside my throat.

"Watch me," he demanded.

I opened my eyes and anxiously watched as he stroked his cock vigorously. His swollen forearm and bicep were as much of a turn-on as him stroking his cock in my face. After roughly thirty seconds, he arched his back, began to moan, and pressed his free hand against my forehead, tilting my head slightly rearward. As I moaned in anticipation and continued to squeeze my boobs, he released my head and pounded his fist against the glass.

Kneeling in front of him squeezing my boobs like the sexually deprived woman I undoubtedly was, my eyes remained locked on his throbbing cock as his clenched fist worked to milk it of the special gift he reserved for me. I moaned in a combination of excitement and relief as I watched cum spurt from the tip and onto my face, lips, and into my mouth. As he groaned in pleasure, he continued to beat against the glass and grin like a mad man.

When he finally stopped plastering me with his warm wet sentiment, he shuffled to the side and grabbed a folded towel from the table behind him.

"Holy shit Otis, that was a lot of cum," I sighed as I drug my fingers along my face like little squeegees.

"Here, wipe off," he said as he handed me the towel.

As I cleaned my face I noticed he glanced up at the glass and smiled.

Knowing the people in the gym had no earthly idea of what we were *really* doing, I wanted to play along, hoping to prolong Otis' wonder of their voyeuristic nature.

"What?" I asked as I glanced up at him.

He shrugged his shoulders as he reached down to pull up his jeans,

"They left after the show was over, but they got to see me jack it on your pretty little mug."

"Well, at least they stuck around until the grand finale," I said as I tossed the wadded up towel onto the top of the glass table.

After I found my shorts and panties, I got dressed. Otis was good for me in a really, really bad way. Saying *no* to him was impossible, and I liked that about him. He fully realized he was my Kryptonite, rendering me powerless in his presence, but although he might press right up against a few boundaries, he never took advantage of me. Knowing when to stop was a strength he seemed to naturally possess.

As we walked out of the room and into the hallway, he turned toward the gym and grinned.

"They got a hell of a show at the end," he said with a nod.

I stopped and shook my head, laughing inside at the fact the glass was a one-way mirror.

"It's one-way glass," I chuckled.

He shook his head, "Not when the lights are off in the pool room and dimmed in the gym. It reduces the reflective nature of the glass. They saw us, believe me."

I considered what he said, realizing my eyes were closed at the end while he pounded against the glass. After a short consideration, I decided he was simply toying with me. I'd worked out in the gym on several nights of my week long stay, and all I had ever seen was my reflection.

"You're full of shit," I sighed.

He reached toward the door handle and pulled the door open.

"Go inside and look at the glass, smart ass," he said as he tossed his head toward the door.

"Fine," I huffed as I stepped through the open door and into the gym.

Although the lights were on, they were dimmed to a very low level of light, no different than they were when the couple was working out. I glanced around the room, and after a few seconds of my eyes adjusting to the lighting, I glanced at the mirrored wall.

The mirrored wall was no longer a mirror, but only a darkened sheet of glass. I gazed into the adjoining room and focused on the cum-covered towel I had wadded up on the glass table. As my mind filled with shock, my body and spirit filled with an eerie sense of sexual satisfaction knowing the couple had watched him fuck me and jack off on my face.

As I reached for the door handle I realized my life was going to be turned upside down in a very short period of time. Having Otis as a lover was something I knew very few women on this earth could handle, and I was one of the select few who were able.

Hell, I was probably the *only* one.

I opened the door, turned toward him and grinned, "What are we going to do when we get back to the room?"

"Could you see through the glass? See the pool?" he asked over his shoulder as he turned away.

"Yes," I sighed.

He nodded his head.

"So what are we going to do when we get back to the room? Sleep?" I asked again.

"Back to the room? We aren't going to the room," he said as he turned down the hallway which led to the parking lot.

"Where are we going, back to the bar?" I asked.

"Nope, going out to the bike," he said, "I want to lick your pussy while you're sitting on my bike."

Somewhat shocked by his statement, but excited at the thought, I spun in his direction.

"In the parking lot?" I asked excitedly.

"Yep," he responded as he opened the door.

I glanced out into the parking lot at his motorcycle. As I gazed at the silhouette in the glow of the parking lot lights, I began to itch all over. Within a second or so, my pussy began to tingle. I glanced up at him and grinned as I stepped through the door.

"Sounds good to me," I said as I shrugged my shoulders and walked past him.

Having Otis in my life again was not only going to be a challenge, but would require some significant adjustments.

Adjustments I was more than willing to make.

OTIS

When I was eight years old, I wanted a B.B. gun for Christmas. After what seemed to be a lifetime of wait, Christmas morning came. I realized the elongated box Santa Claus had left by the tree could have contained anything, but as I tore the wrapping paper from the box, I hoped it was what I desperately felt I needed to move forward into manhood. Living in the Mid-west, a boy's receipt of a B.B. gun was not only confirmation he was becoming a man, but proof he was a responsible young man worthy of the power the weapon possessed.

Much to my surprise and complete satisfaction, the box was clearly marked *Daisy*, the manufacturer of the undisputed king of B.B. guns. With my heart racing, I cautiously opened the box, being careful not to rip the precious cardboard.

As I hefted the gun from the box my heart swelled with pride. Fighting back tears of joy, I stood in my pajamas with the gun in my arms.

"He knew, Pop. He knew I was ready," I exclaimed.

My father nodded his head, "Did he get you the right one?"

"Pop, it's a Daisy," I grinned, "The Red Ryder."

He narrowed his gaze as he shifted his eyes toward the weapon, "Is that a good one?"

I grinned and nodded my head, "The best, Pop. It's the best one on the entire planet."

He grinned as he turned toward my mother, "Well, sounds like Santa Claus has got his shit together."

And so began my love and respect for guns. I cherished the weapon, and at least initially I took it with me everywhere I went. It sickened me to go to school without it, certain I just might need it for *something* Axton and I encountered in our walk to school or on our way home. The excitement didn't soon fade, and on a typical morning I'd immediately check the wooden rack on the wall of my bedroom as soon as I woke to make sure it remained where I had left it the night before.

At the time, the thought of separating myself from my cherished gift left me feeling empty and exposed. Although I didn't necessarily *need* it, being without it caused me to feel as if I didn't appreciate it for everything it provided me.

With it in my presence, I felt a sense of self-worth and purpose I didn't feel in its absence.

Separating myself from things I cherished for even a moment's time had always been a difficult thing for me to do. The MC was a prime example of my inability to spend time away from something I truly held dear to my heart.

I glanced at my gun safe and grinned, knowing it still contained the B.B gun I had received twenty-eight years prior. Being at home while Sam continued to inventory her mother's house was driving me insane. Similar to going to school without my B.B. gun while I knew it was at my disposal, being at home without Sam at my side left me feeling empty and alone.

I glanced at my two motorcycles and shifted my gaze to the car. Covered with a custom cover to preserve the perfectly restored condition, the car beneath the cover was an absolute pleasure to drive and a high-horsepower beast. I had purchased the car as a basket case when I was sixteen years old. In shambles, incomplete, and without a motor, transmission, or rear axle, my father had trailered the car home in piles and boxes. Together, over an almost two year long time frame, we pieced the car together, and he loaned me the money for a driveline.

One of my father's police force friends painted cars and did bodywork on the side for spare cash. After some negotiation and a little persuasive nature, my father convinced him to repair the car and paint it with a show quality paint job for my return of yard work. Halfway through my senior year in school, we completed the car.

Just in time for my senior prom and graduation.

Now, no differently than most other bikers, the thought of riding in a cage was repulsive to me. I reserved trips in the car for special occasions, often driving it once a month on a Sunday evening or taking it to local car shows. From time to time I'd remove the cover, drive it to Wichita, and street race some unsuspecting Corvette or a local teen with a Subaru WRX turbo he'd tricked out.

My special occasion 1969 Camaro Z-28.

I glanced at my Harley bagger. I shifted my eyes to my Heritage Softail. After a few moments of staring blankly at the bikes, I sighed, took a sip from my cup of coffee, and stared at the Camaro. I raised the coffee cup to my lips, finished the coffee, and placed the cup on the shelf beside the door.

I slowly walked toward the car, carefully removed the cover, and opened the door.

Fuck it.

If this isn't a special occasion, I don't know what is.

SAM

Squatted in the corner of the back bedroom, I began to dig through a box I had found in the closet marked *Samantha School.* As I pulled each item from the box carefully, I realized just how much my participation in school activities meant to my mother. Report cards, photographs of me, and various newspaper articles announcing my successes in track, basketball, and debate were amongst the items I was surprised to find.

As much as I enjoyed the memories the newfound items brought to the surface, I realized I could spend nothing short of forever digging through the boxes in my mother's home. Although she was a very neat woman, it was apparent she was somewhat of a pack rat, boxing up everything her life produced, keeping it for future reference or simply for the joy it brought her.

I glanced around the room as I dropped my 4th grade report card into the box. My mind a whirlwind of thoughts and emotion, I tried to comprehend not only the work which was in front of me at my mother's house, but the fact Otis was now back in my life.

Living in St. Louis wasn't an option now, and although I knew after receiving my inheritance I didn't *need* to work any longer, I felt I should to keep my sanity. Moving back to Wichita was going to take a little time, and thoughts of where I'd live and when I'd be able to move began to swirl in circles in my head.

I stood, stretched my aching legs, and gazed at the doorway.

"Meow…"

You disgusting furball.

Realizing my only way out of the room was blocked by the fuzzy varmint, I stomped my foot on the floor in an effort to scare her away. Although it appeared to initially startle her, she immediately settled into her sphinx-like posture again and stared at me with her golden glassy orbs.

As she stared at me, she blinked her eyes slowly a few times.

You nasty cretin.

I glanced around the room for something soft I could throw in her direction, and eventually decided it didn't necessarily *need* to be soft. After some thought, I reached into the box, removed one of my brass medals from playing basketball, and slid it across the wooden floor, past her, and into the hallway.

Being the utter idiot she was, she quickly turned and ran toward the medallion, assuming it was alive.

While she attempted to bat the medal across the floor with her disgusting paw, I escaped the room, stepped past her, and down the hallway toward the living room. Feeling as if I needed to try and assemble a plan for my near future, what I was going to do about moving, and where I intended to live, my mind instead began to think of Otis and what little precious time we had spent together. As I sat on the loveseat recalled my best version of our pool room sex, a loud rumbling sound from outside caused the hair on the back of my neck to stand up.

It sounded like the world was coming to an end.

Curious as to what the noise might be, I stood and walked across the room. As I got closer to the window, the level of the sound increased and seemed to become closer and closer to the house. As the noise reached an all-time high, I pulled the curtains to the side and peered outside.

Immediately, my stomach filled with butterflies.

Is this even possible?

You still have it?

I ran to the front door and yanked it open. In the driveway, grinning from ear to ear, Otis was seated in what appeared to be a very nice likeness of the 1969 Camaro he drove throughout the latter years of our relationship. There was no doubt he had the ability to excite me sexually, but his car absolutely drove me into an entirely different type of sexual frenzy.

His car made me wet.

"Looks just like your old car," I shouted over the sound of the exhaust.

He turned off the car and stepped into the driveway. Standing beside the car in a tee shirt, jeans, and his sneakers, he looked just like he did when we were in high school. As I stood on the porch admiring him and the car it seemed as if we had never been apart.

"It *is* my old car," he grinned.

"You still have it? *Seriously*, is it?" I screeched.

He nodded his head proudly.

I jumped from the porch, ran to the passenger side of the car, and carefully opened the door. A quick glance of the glove box provided all the confirmation I needed to see. The *Sublime* sticker I had affixed to the center of the glove box door remained right where I had stuck it in 1996.

The lead singer of the band had died of a heroin overdose the day before we graduated high school. Paying tribute to him and my love of the band, I had stuck the sticker on Otis' glove box while I waited in the car as he and Axton discussed our after graduation plans.

I glanced over the top of the car.

"It's still there," I said.

"Right where you left it," he grinned, "I wanted to kill you for sticking that fucker on there, but I could never bring myself to remove it."

"The memories this thing brings back," I sighed as I glanced up and down the side of the car.

"Good ones," he said as he walked around the front of the car.

"Take me for a ride," I said as I reached for the door handle.

He turned around and walked back to the side of the car.

"Get in," he said as he opened the door.

As the engine started, it startled me. The sound of the rumbling exhaust, thoughts of all the times I had sucked his cock while we'd driven to the movies, and the sheer excitement of seeing the car again caused me to begin to shake. I held my arm to the side and flattened my hand as he backed out of the driveway.

"Look," I said as he shifted the car into gear.

"What?"

"I'm shaking," I said as I nodded my head toward my hand.

"Why?" he shrugged as he released the clutch.

I shook my head, "This car, you. Memories. Jesus, Otis. This is just crazy. I can't believe…"

"Well, believe it. I'm not letting you get away this time," he said over his shoulder as the car inched along the street.

"Promise?" I asked.

He released the gear shift, held his right hand at his side, and extended his pinkie finger from his otherwise clenched fist.

"Pinkie promise," he said.

A chill ran down my spine. *He remembered.* We had made dozens of pinkie promises as kids, but he would never pinkie promise we would be together forever because he said he couldn't *guarantee* it. According to Otis, and to his father, breaking a pinkie promise was punishable by cutting off the pinkie of the one who broke the promise.

I pointed my extended pinkie finger at him, "If you break a pinkie promise…"

"I'll let you cut the fucker off with my dad's pocket knife," he said before I finished speaking.

"You sure you want to do this," I asked.

With lightning-like speed, he reached for the gearshift, shifted gears, and thrust his hand into the air, locking my pinkie with his. Now with our hands in the center of the car with our pinkies intertwined, everything I had sat in the room and worried about no longer mattered. Now, I had Otis right where I wanted him.

In my life forever.

"There, now you're stuck," he grinned.

I stared down at our locked pinkies.

"Couldn't be happier," I sighed.

He released my finger and shifted gears again. I gazed at him admiringly, and realized he wasn't wearing his motorcycle vest. Maybe, I decided, it was because he wasn't riding his motorcycle. To let him know I noticed, I opted to mention it.

"Not wearing your biker vest today?" I asked.

He shook his head as he turned the corner onto Central Avenue, "Not allowed to wear them in cars. The vest is called a *cut*. And we call cars or any kind of vehicle a *cage*. And there's no cuts allowed in cages."

I nodded my head as I glanced down at my pinkie.

"I see."

Considering Otis was now in an *actual* motorcycle gang made me a little nervous. Although he and a few friends - Axton included - had ridden motorcycles since they were kids, he was never in a gang in the past. My experience with motorcycle gangs was limited to what I saw on the news, and although I hadn't seen much, I couldn't help but see the nationwide coverage the biker gunfight in Texas was given.

"So, this gang you're in, do you..."

"It's a *club*, not a gang," he interrupted.

"Okay," I shrugged, "Your *club*, what is it that you guys do?"

With his eyes fixed on the road ahead, he responded without emotion.

"We ride bikes and drink beer."

"That's it?" I asked, somewhat relieved and slightly shocked.

"Can't really say, Sam. It's like this," he said over his shoulder and he changed lanes, "We're a private club. Club business is *club* business, and no one else's. We don't discuss it with anyone. It's nothing against you, and even though you're the only woman I truly trust, for sake of the club and everyone in it, I'm sworn to secrecy so to speak."

I turned to the side and faced him directly, "Secrecy? So we're going to keep secrets?"

"Sam..." he sighed.

"You aren't like those guys down in Texas, are you? The ones that got in a gunfight?" I asked.

I stared at him as he gripped the steering wheel in his hands. Obviously he was slightly offended by my question - the muscles on his biceps flared as he clenched the wheel. After swallowing and giving his response some thought, he glanced in my direction.

"There's motorcycle clubs, and there's 1%er motorcycle clubs. The 1% club is a name that dates back to World War one, and is indicative of the belief that only one percent of people who ride motorcycles are outlaws. A 1%er club is called an outlaw club. They were an outlaw club," he explained.

"Are you...or is your club an *outlaw club*," I asked.

He nodded his head, "Yes we are."

"So how long until you guys decide to shoot up a bar and go to prison, *Otis*?" I asked sarcastically.

"We don't shoot up bars, Sam. We're not like that," he said over his shoulder.

I glanced up as he turned the car into the parking lot of a Starbucks coffee shop. Although I'd been to the intersection, the last time I had been there, there wasn't a coffee shop, but a gas station.

"When did they put this here?" I asked.

"Ten, maybe twelve years ago," he shrugged.

As I glanced at the building over my shoulder, I realized in my time away a lot of things had changed. I turned toward Otis and crossed my arms.

"Well, I don't like the secret thing," I huffed.

He raised his hands to his head and rubbed his temples for a long moment. As he lowered his hands, he sighed.

"Look at it this way, Sam. I just made a pinkie promise with you. Do you think I'll break it?" he asked.

"No, I sure don't. I know how you're weird about promises. I like that about you," I responded.

"Okay, look at it this way. I took an oath with the club. I made a promise, under oath, to never discuss the intricacies of the club or club business with an outsider, all in an effort to protect the club and the men in it. For me to break that promise would be no different than breaking my pinkie promise with you. I gave my word. It's all I've got, Sam."

As much as I didn't like it, everything now made perfect sense. Otis was a prideful man, and he had always been a man with tremendous moral values. I'm sure he took great pride in being able to offer the club his absolute silence when questioned of their activities.

"Okay, I'll respect that," I said with a nod, "What are we doing here?"

"Well, now that we're done arguing about that, I'm going to get a cup of coffee. I thought we'd relax out here in the sun before it gets too hot, maybe get lunch, go to a movie, and then we'll see," he shrugged.

"You going to let me suck that big cock of yours in the movie?" I asked.

He reached for the door, opened it, and turned to face me.

"Does a shark shit in the sea?" he responded.

"Sure does," I nodded.

"Answer's yes," he grinned.

As thoughts of sucking Otis' cock in a half filled afternoon movie filled my mind, concerns and worries about his involvement in an outlaw motorcycle club slowly vanished. One thing about being in a relationship with Otis was that all the time I had spent with him was filled with love, sex, and passion, leaving very little time for anything else.

And, as love, sex, and passion were on the top of my relationship priority list, I didn't complain one bit.

"Well, let's choke down a cup of coffee and get to the movie," I said over my shoulder as I reached for the door handle, "I haven't been to the movie in years."

"Been a bit for me, too," Otis said as he opened his door.

I paused and glanced at him over the top of the car, "Last movie you saw?"

"Fight Club," he said with a nod.

"Fight Club? Like *Fight Club* with Brad Pitt and Edward Norton?" I shrugged.

Fight Club was the last movie I had seen with Otis, in the fall of 1999, immediately before we split up. Immediately after that, I moved away. It was late October of 1999, right before my favorite holiday, Halloween.

Otis shrugged his shoulders and tilted his head to the side, "First rule of Fight Club is…"

"First rule of Fight Club is, you do not talk about fight club," I said as I walked around the edge of the car.

"Second rule of Fight Club is…" he said as he stepped toward me and reached for my hand.

"Second rule of Fight Club is, you do not talk about fight club," I said flatly.

He stopped walking and turned to face me, "Third rule of Fight Club is…"

I gazed at him and grinned. For me, this was easy. I'd seen the movie on Netflix and owned the DVD. Watching the movie reminded me of him, and I had watched it no less than fifty times.

"Third rule of Fight Club is, if someone yells stop, goes limp, or taps out, the fight is over," I responded.

"I love you, Sam," he said as he leaned forward and began to kiss me.

As we stood in the middle of the parking lot kissing, I couldn't help but admit that I loved him too. It was almost as if when we split in 1999, progress for both of us had stopped completely. Our lives continued, and the world's clock ticked at the same pace, but neither of us made any progress toward building a new life or moving on. Now, fourteen years later, we were both ready to make up for what we had missed out on for so many years.

As our lips parted, I stood and stared at him admiringly. Although he had gone through changes in his life, he was still very much the same person I fell in love with as a young girl and continued to love until this day. A little older, more than likely a lot wiser, and now in an outlaw motorcycle gang, he was still the same playful, loving, protective person he had always been.

And in considering all of the good he offered me, I decided to cast what little bad he had embraced aside. For me to be critical of him for something he so wholeheartedly believed in would be selfish.

And I had no intention of being selfish.

Not again.

It was time for me to become grateful.

As we walked toward the coffee shop, hand-in-hand, I glanced back toward the Camaro. After all these years he still had it. He had kept it for whatever reason, but ultimately, he had kept it. To me that was all that mattered.

And for that, I was grateful.

OTIS

There was never a doubt in my mind that I had the ability to love. I loved the MC. I loved the passion the men shared, my MC Brothers, and the concept of the club entirely. I loved the brothers I held close to my heart - Axton, Toad, and Biscuit - and without a doubt I loved Avery and Sydney.

The love I felt for my parents was indescribable.

Loving a woman - truly loving a woman who I believed to be my other half - was different.

Much different.

Sam wasn't *in* my world, she *was* my world. I would do anything for her, everything to protect her, and whatever I was required to do to preserve what we had together. As soon as I had her in my arms again, I realized the depth of my love for her.

Although I knew all along that I loved her, I don't think I realized exactly what loving someone completely meant. I was no longer a selfish boy, I had developed into a selfless man, and loving Sam was proving to be something I was not only capable of, but obsessed with. Sam provided me with an entirely new list of reasons to want to live life to the best of my ability.

Loving her didn't keep me from pushing her to her limits. In fact, pushing her was always something she loved about me, and I hoped it would never change.

"You sure as fuck better," I growled.

"Seriously, Otis. There's like," she turned her head and glanced around the theater.

"Like twenty people in here," she sighed as she turned around.

"Look at me, Sam. *Look at me*," I said sternly.

"Okay Otis, I'm looking at you," she whispered.

"Do I look like I give a fuck?" I shrugged.

After a few seconds of studying me, she shrugged her shoulders, "No."

"Okay. Now, do me a favor. *For me*. Stick your finger inside your shorts and feel that little pussy of yours. Tell me if it's wet, Sam," I said flatly.

After glancing around the theater nervously, she lowered her hand between her legs. I gazed toward her lap and watched as she slid her finger beneath the fabric of her shorts. After a few seconds, she sighed, raised her finger in the air, and wiped it on the seat beside her.

"Soaked," she sighed.

"Now, let's agree on something," I whispered.

"Let's hear it," she sighed.

"Well, without a doubt, there are times when a guy wants to fuck, and his cock isn't very cooperative. He might want to go at it, but his junk is limp. And, there are times when a woman spends half an hour kissing a guy, thinks he's pretty hot, and decides she wants to fuck him. The problem is that her pussy isn't wet yet. Now can we agree these types of things happen, and these situations actually exist?" I asked as I glanced down the rows of seats.

"Yeah, I agree," she breathed.

I turned my head to the side and focused on her beautiful face as I continued, "Okay. Good. Now, *conversely*, if a man's cock is rigid as a piece of steel, or a woman's pussy is dripping down her leg, would you not agree that she or he is ready not only from a mental state of being, but physically as well?"

"I suppose so," she sighed.

"Damn, we agreed on something. Good. Okay, now, let me ask you one more thing. Do you love me," I asked as I reached for my belt buckle.

Even though the theater was quite dark and the movie hadn't started yet, it wasn't difficult to see her wrinkled brow or detect her huge attitude.

"You know I do," she hissed in a half-whisper.

"Okay. Well, if you love me, and your pussy is currently a wet little dripping mess, why would you deprive not only me - but your willing and wanting self - of a little cock?" I asked as I unbuttoned my jeans.

She glanced downward, studying my hand as I unbuttoned my jeans. As I pulled my cock free of my pants, she nodded her head toward it and glanced upward.

"*That's* why. In your hand. Look at it, Otis. I'm not depriving myself of a *little cock*. Your cock needs a fucking zip code. It's huge. Now, let me ask *you* something," she said as she alternated glances between my cock and my face.

"Okay?" I shrugged as I began to stroke my cock.

"You've taken a shit before, right," she asked.

I rolled my eyes and glanced up at the ceiling before answering.

"Yes," I sighed.

"Okay. Now you're a pretty big dude, so I'm going to guess you take a pretty big shit. Let's just agree on that, okay?" she said as she nodded her head.

"Alright," I sighed, feeling somewhat frustrated with her line of thinking.

"Okay. Now if you've taken pretty big shits over the years, I'm going to guess your asshole is about as receptive to having something stuffed in it as my pussy is. Probably a pretty good match. Your ass and my twat. Now ask yourself *this*. Do you think I could shove that fucker in you and have you not squeal so loud you'd wake the dead? *Do you?*" she asked.

I shook my head and chuckled. I had no idea where she was headed with the shit-talk, but she made a good point. Sam never had a problem challenging me if she disagreed, and I respected her for it. My *job*, in my opinion, was to make sure she felt the way she *believed* she felt.

I continued to stroke my cock as I stared at her.

"Guess not," I said flatly.

"Huh. Point made," she said as she turned to face the screen.

As the lights began to dim, and the sound system began to emit Dolby THX bouncing ball bullshit around the room, I stroked my cock and tilted my head her direction.

"One more question," I said as I leaned her direction.

"Shoot," she whispered.

I leaned my head onto her shoulder and glanced up into her eyes.

"When you're watching a movie, do you ever turn around and watch the people *behind* you?" I asked.

She shook her head, "No, I watch the movie."

"Who's behind us?" I asked.

"Nobody, Otis. We're in the back row," she whispered.

"So the only people who can see us are in front, right?"

"Yeah," she responded.

"And we just agreed they're not going to turn around, right?" I asked as I lifted my head from her shoulder.

"Forget it, Otis," she sighed.

I released my cock from my grip and reached for her hair. After lifting the blonde strands over her left ear and carefully draping them behind it, I admired her beautiful face. After a few seconds of admiration, I leaned toward her and bit the bottom of her ear between my teeth. With her earlobe in my teeth, I growled into her ear.

"You sexy little bitch," I breathed against her ear.

I reached over with my left hand and grabbed her boob. As I began to squeeze it in my hand, she started to moan quietly. While she wiggled in her seat and groaned, I inhaled an audible breath through my clenched teeth and exhaled slowly into her ear.

"Reach over here and grab my fucking cock, Sam," I breathed.

Without speaking, her hand fumbled in my lap until she found my rigid cock. As she began to slowly stroke it, I bit into her earlobe with slightly more force and exhaled into her ear again. Immediately, her shoulder jerked and she tilted her head to the side, pressing against the side of my face.

"You're driving me crazy," she breathed.

"And you're pissing me off. Since when do you not listen to me? This time I'm not asking, I'm *telling*. Get your sexy little cock sucking mouth down there in front of me and suck my cock, Sam," I breathed as I released her ear and pointed to the floor.

Without releasing my cock from her grasp, she lowered herself to the floor and leaned forward. Wedged between the front of my seat and the seat in front of me, she glanced up and grinned.

"I'm so wet," she sighed as she began to stroke my swollen shaft.

I grinned and glanced around the theater. In front of us, three rows down, were two people on one side, and two people on the far other side. In the lower portion of the theater, and entire row was filled with a group of fifteen or so people, and another couple sat to our immediate left, two rows down. All told, roughly twenty people were in attendance. As the movie began to play, I felt her mouth encompass my cock.

I glanced down and sighed at the sight of her head moving up and down in my lap. Although I'm sure not *all* women enjoy having a cock stuffed into their throat forcefully, Sam was no stranger to the tip of my dick pummeling her mouth like a woodpecker pounding away at a tree trunk. After a quick inventory of the theater again, I lowered my hands onto the back of her head and slowly raised my ass from the seat. As the cowboy on the screen pulled an old man from a burning car, I began to fuck Sam's face like I was trying to put out a fire deep within her throat.

The sound of her sloppy slobbering and gagging was pretty evident where we were seated, but the sound effects and dialogue from the movie masked the sounds of our sexual adventure from everyone else's ears – especially those seated in the in the front of the theater. I knew it would take no more than a minute of my cock in her mouth to drive her insane, and after holding her head tightly in my lap for a few eye-watering seconds, I released her head and leaned forward.

As she pulled her head from my lap she gasped for breath.

"Holy shit, Otis," she sighed as she wiped her mouth with the back of her hand.

"Take off your shorts and turn around," I said flatly.

She glanced over each of her shoulders as she raised herself into a crouched position. After a few seconds of struggling to get them off, she sighed and stood. Now standing beside me, she mumbled a few unintelligible expletives and yanked against the waist of her shorts, pulling them and her panties down to her thighs. A few expletives and a little more struggling later, and she was naked from the waist down.

I glanced around the theater.

Everyone remained focused on the movie as the cowboy walked to the door with a bouquet of flowers.

"Turn around and ride my cock, Sam," I whispered.

"No shit, Sherlock," she said though her teeth, "I thought I'd just stand here."

She turned around, reached back and grabbed her ass with each hand, and as she attempted to spread her glistening pussy as wide as she could, lowered herself onto the tip of my cock. As I guided the tip into her pussy with one hand, I pressed my other into the small of her back. Although fucking in the hotel pool room was torturous, this time I slid with exceptional ease into her wet warm fold.

"Jesus," she sighed as my cock bottomed out.

I reached forward with my right hand and covered her mouth. As I pulled the back of her head toward my chest, I sat up in my seat slightly, forcing her to arch her back. Now incapable of speaking, her back arched, and her hands still gripping her ass, she began to rock back and forth along the length of my swollen shaft.

Her soaking wet but still ever-so-tight pussy worked magic along my stiff dick. Each time she raised her ass or lowered herself onto my lap, I felt as if the tip of my cock was going to explode. Swollen to an all-time high girth and as hard as a diamond, it seemed the skin was hypersensitive to the perfect rhythm of her reverse cowgirl ride. As she bit into my hand, her speed increased and she seemed to become a little more daring. With muffled groans bellowing into my hand, she bounced up and down on my cock as she continued to stretch her ass cheeks apart with her fingers.

Watching her fuck me with such force was beyond any level of *exciting* I could recall from our past. Maybe I wanted it more. Quite possibly I wanted *her* more. Perhaps it was nothing more than being in love as a man instead of being in lust as a boy.

The inside of theater wasn't bright by any means, but the movie provided enough illumination for me to watch my cock disappearing into her pussy. As I glanced up and made note of the cowboy and a blonde girl having a lakeside picnic, Sam groaned into the palm of my hand. To spice things up a little, and to force Sam to exercise a little self-control, I moved my hand from her mouth and twisted her hair in my hand.

I pulled her hair tightly, forcing her head to the side of mine. With her back now against my chest and her ear beside my lips, I turned my head to the side and pressed my mouth against her ear.

"Slow down, little girl. You're going to get us thrown out of here," I whispered.

She continued to bounce up and down on my cock like we were filming a porno movie and this was going to be the climactic ending. Her very audible breathing was animal-like and increasing in volume with each stroke.

"Lose…"

"Your sense…"

"Of adventure…" she breathed

I pressed my mouth firm against her ear and exhaled, "You little smart ass."

I pulled her hair rearward and raised my butt from the seat. In perfect timing against the predictable rhythm of the movement of her ass, I forced myself into her as deep as I was able. Almost standing in my seat, I pressed the front of her thighs into the back of the seat in front of us, grabbed my belt, and pushed the waist of my jeans to mid-thigh.

Now fucking her as if to prove a point, she was grunting each time my cock bottomed out inside of her. As she released the cheeks of her ass and gripped the backs of the two seats directly in front of us in her hands, I pounded myself into her like I was in some kind of grudge fucking contest.

"You smart mouthed little bitch," I breathed.

"You need to remember who's fucking boss," I sighed as I pulled upward on her hair.

The sound of my hips slapping up against her bare ass echoed over the sound of the quiet conversation the couple was having on the screen. A person in front of us turned around and immediately turned back toward the screen after seeing what was going on. Within a few seconds, several people turned around. The thought of them seeing us, even for a split-second, fueled me to continue to fuck her without mercy.

I felt my cock begin to swell and realized my breathing was not only labored, but quite loud. The theatre was filled with the sound of sex. My hips against Sam's ass, her groaning from me pulling her hair, and her grunts with each in stroke were enough to make even the more focused moviegoers understand fully what we were doing in the rear of the theater. As I felt my scrotum begin to tingle, I realized I was on the verge of climax.

I released Sam's hair and gripped her neck in my hand. As I squeezed her neck with my fingertips and pulled her body backward against mine, her pussy began to contract around the shaft of my throbbing cock. In perfect timing, I exploded into her wet pussy as she groaned in pleasure into the not so vacant theater.

I arched my back and bit my lip as I continued to enjoy what seemed to be a never ending orgasm.

"Oh dear God…" she moaned as her knees buckled.

I exhaled, opened my eyes, and gazed down into the theater. More than half of the people in the theater were focused on Sam and I.

After a few seconds of standing motionless and regaining my senses, I released her neck, slid my hand up to her cheek, and turned her head to the side. A very long passionate kiss and a solid heartfelt hug later, and I collapsed into the seat, exhausted from the excitement of our sexual escapade.

"Take off your boot and give me your sock," Sam whispered over her shoulder.

I turned to the side and scrunched my brow, "What?"

"I've got about a quart of your cum trying to fall out of my pussy, Superman. I need something. Give me a sock to mop this up with," she sighed.

I reached down, pulled up my jeans, and unlaced my shoes. After removing them both, I handed her my socks. The thought of having on only one didn't seem to appealing.

She stared down into her hand and chuckled.

"You wear no-shows?" she said with a laugh.

"Huh?" I responded.

"No-shows. Little bootie socks. You *wear* these?" she asked.

"When I'm wearing shoes, yeah," I nodded.

"I fucking love you," she sighed as she reached between her legs.

"Love you too, Sam," I grinned as I reached down and pulled on my shoes.

After what seemed to be a matter of minutes, the movie ended. Fully understanding it had been much longer than the few minutes it seemed to be, I realized I had watched the remaining portion of the movie in a daze, daydreaming about my future with Sam. She, on the other hand, sat quietly and enjoyed the romantic movie. As the credits rolled across the screen, I held my hand in front of her chest, and cautioned her from immediately standing.

"Let's wait a minute," I chuckled.

"Right," she grinned.

After several minutes, the theater emptied, short of the long row of people still seated in the front. Realizing for some reason they had no intention of leaving the theatre, I stood from my seat, held Sam's hand, and began to walk toward the steps. As we walked down the steps, a few of the people turned around. As the theater was well-lighted now that the movie was over, I could clearly see the group was a combination of college aged couples, without a doubt out of school for the summer. As we passed the group and turned toward the aisle leading to the exit, the sound of a person clapping caused me to pause and turn around.

After a few claps, another joined. Within a few seconds, the entire group stood, faced us, and continued clapping. Half embarrassed, and half proud, I stood and stared blankly at the group and smiled.

Sam released my hand, situated one arm in front of her and the other behind, and performed a very well executed bow. After standing, she reached for my hand and glanced up at me.

"Neither one of us have a tremendous amount of sense, you know that, right?' she chuckled.

"Well aware," I said as I turned toward the door.

And almost more than anything else, that was what I had always loved about Sam. Now, more than ever, I was able to be myself around her, which was something I hadn't really done since she left. As we quietly walked toward the door hand-in-hand, I realized the person I was becoming was the person I had always been, but that I had no one to share being myself with.

Sam caused me to act without inhibition or concern. Anxious to see just who it was that resided beneath my exterior shell, I released her hand, turned to face her, and pressed her against the wall.

I kissed her passionately, as my hands fumbled along her body, exploring every inch of her as we continued to kiss. Eventually, I raised my hands and cleared her hair away from her face and our lips parted. As I stared into her beautiful brown eyes, incapable of speaking exactly what I was thinking, one of the couples of college kids walked past.

"Get a room," he laughed over his shoulder as he walked through the door.

"We don't fuck in rooms!" Sam shouted back.

I shook my head and grinned, "Do you think there's something wrong with us?"

"No," she snapped back, "It's everyone else who's losing out. Fucking prudes."

As we walked toward the door, Sam reaching into her purse, pulled out my wadded socks, and tossed them into the trash can.

"I want to see Axton," she said as we walked down the hallway.

I nodded my head, "I was thinking the same thing. And there's a few others I want you to meet. A few of the girls. Axton's Ol' Lady and

Toad's Ol' Lady."

"Am I your Ol' Lady, Otis? Is that what I am?" she grinned.

"You God damned sure are," I responded.

As strange as it seemed to say, and as much as she may not understand the sincerity and seriousness of the label, Sam was none other than Otis' Ol' Lady.

And now it was time I made her part of my family.

SAM

Accepting a woman as a friend was something I never did without tremendous resistance. Their competitive nature, catty attitudes, and unstable emotions made me reluctant to invite one into my life as a true friend. Over the years I had developed several friendships with women, but oddly enough, I never really considered them to be *true* friends. Opening up and being *me* around them never happened, and it seemed the person I often chose to be in their presence was a small portion of who I really was.

An abbreviated version.

Something seemed different about the two girls in front of me.

Much different.

"No, I work at an attorney's office as a para. *Her* brother's Jack, you met him at the bar the other day, he's the one who's all buff and covered in prison tats. I'm the one who wrote the appeal and got him a new trial. I'm Axton's Ol' Lady, she's Toad's, you got us mixed up," the girl with the darker hair said in one breathless sentence.

She talked a hundred miles an hour, and was difficult to follow, but she had a great outgoing personality.

"Sydney? Syd?" I said as I pointed toward the more reserved blonde.

She raised her hand in the air and nodded her head, "That's me. I'm Jack's sister."

157

"And I'm Avery. She's Syd, and I'm Avery. Just remember, Sydney, *shitty haircut*. Avery, *awesome bitch*. It's easy that way," Avery chuckled.

Sydney glanced in Avery's direction and rolled her eyes.

"Shitty hair's right, but you're far from an awesome, bitch," she laughed.

Avery shrugged her shoulders as she puckered her lips and kissed the air.

I nodded my head and grinned, "Hair, awesome. Got it."

"And you're engaged? To Toad? The cute Italian guy?" I asked as I turned toward Sydney.

"Yep. That's me?" she smiled as she reached for her glass of tea.

"Okay, well. Let's get to know each other. Where'd you guys meet?" I asked.

"You'll love this," Avery blurted.

"You really want to know?" Sydney asked.

"Sure," I responded, "Why not?"

She shook her head and pushed her glass of tea to the center of the table.

"Well," she inhaled a deep breath, held it for a moment, and exhaled.

"It was at a bank robbery. I guess it's kind of common knowledge now, so I'll tell you the real story. I was homeless at the time, and I had used this guy the night before for a shower, and no I didn't fuck him," she paused as she raised her eyebrows comically.

"You were *homeless*?" I asked, shocked at the statement.

She nodded her head, "Homeless, jobless, penniless, yep. All of the above."

"Oh. Wow," I responded as I reached for my drink.

The thought of such a gorgeous woman who also seemed to be so well put together being homeless was almost unbelievable to me. As I attempted to wrap my mind around the complications of being homeless, she continued to tell her story.

"Okay, so I went into the bank with this guy while he was taking me back to my car, thinking he's going to deposit money or make a withdrawal or whatever, and the fucker pulls out a gun and starts robbing the bank. No shit. I'm standing there confused, scared, and wondering how long of a prison sentence I'm going to get when they catch *us,* and this guy who I'd watched walk into the bank in front of us leans over and says *stand by the door, I don't want you to get hurt,*" she paused and raised her eyebrows.

Okay, this is exciting stuff.

"Toad?" I asked.

She nodded her head, "And he asks me if I want a way out of this deal. Of course I say yes. So anyway, the numbskull I'm with walks up to Cambio - that's his real name by the way - and he asks him for his deposit bag. Toad shrugs his shoulder and acts like he's scared, and the guy points the gun right at his face."

She paused and pointed her finger at my face.

"Holy crap," I sighed as I drained my drink.

"Not really. Cambio pulled some Marine judo shit and snatches the gun from the guy's hand, kicks him in the chest, and knocks him on the floor in like one half a second. The dumb fucker's on his back on the floor now, and Cambio's got the gun in *his* face," she shook her head and grinned.

"Wow. That's kind of sexy. So what did the cops say when they got there?" I asked.

She shrugged her shoulders, "I don't know really, I left right after that."

I shook my head and stared blankly, causing her to explain further.

"While he had the gun on the robber, he turned to me and said *go tell the big fucker outside that the devil looks after his own and tell him to take you to Biscuit's house.* Hell, I was scared to death and I took off running. I had no idea who these guys were, but it just seemed right at the time. Being around bikers my entire life, I figured they were good solid dudes, so I ran into the parking lot like I was leaving a burning building, and ran up to Otis and said *devil looks after his own,*" she shrugged as she reached for her tea.

I widened my eyes and swallowed heavily, "Oh dear God. The guy in the lot was Otis? *My* Otis?"

"The one and only, yes ma'am. He didn't ask any questions, just grinned and fired up his bike. The only thing I remember is him saying *you better hold on* right before he gunned it and shot out of the lot," she said as she lowered her glass to the table again.

"Devil looks after his own?" I said as I shook my head, "huh…"

I turned toward Avery and gazed past her as I tried to think of being a part of a bank robbery in the first place.

Avery nodded and tilted her head to the side playfully, "Club motto."

"I see," I sighed.

"So, the cops showed up, the news interviewed Cambio, and the rest is history," she shrugged.

"Wow," I said as I lifted my glass and stared into it.

Empty.

Avery turned toward the bar, raised her hand, and waved at the waitress.

"Went a lot better than the next time a guy pulled a gun on Toad, that's for sure. Now *that* was scary," Avery said as she turned around.

I widened my eyes and glanced at Sydney, "There was another time?"

"Guy in Texas," she nodded as she took a drink of tea.

"Shot him in the chest. Collapsed lung, coma, damned near died," she said flatly.

What the fuck have I got myself into?

"Let's hear it," I sighed as I picked up my glass again.

"Get her another, make it a double," Avery chuckled as the waitress walked to her side.

"It *was* a double," I laughed.

Avery raised her eyebrows, "Triple?"

"Hell, why not," I sighed as I turned toward Sydney.

She tossed her hair over her shoulder and began talking as if it was just another day.

"Okay, they all rode down to Texas, Biscuit, Cambio, Slice, and Otis. They had a meeting down there. When the meeting ended, a guy walked out of the building who Cambio recognized as one of his former Marine friends he hadn't seen for years. He'd actually lived his entire life, post war, thinking this guy was dead. After a little reunion in the parking lot of sorts, a car pulled up alongside the group, and the driver pulled out a gun, threatening Cambio's Marine friend. And, Cambio being Cambio, he jumped in front of the barrel just before the guy pulled the trigger, saving the life of his friend. He took the bullet in the chest. It collapsed his lung and broke his collarbone, but he's fine now. Well, pretty much anyway."

"Oh dear God. When did all this happen?" I asked as the waitress handed me my drink.

161

"Uhhm. Let's see. The bank robbery was about four months or so ago. Give or take. The Texas deal, maybe two months ago," she shrugged.

"All of that, in the last four months?" I gasped as I raised my glass to my lips and drank half the drink in one gulp.

She nodded her head, "Yep."

I glanced at Avery.

She grinned and shrugged her shoulders.

I turned toward Sydney and stared for a long moment.

"So the homeless thing, what happened there?" I asked.

"Oh, right after the robbery Cambio gave me a house to live in. It was one of his rental houses. And he gave me a job at his barbeque restaurant as a waitress, which I love by the way. Then, we got engaged, I moved in to his house, and now we live together," she responded.

"Wow," I said as I drank my remaining vodka cranberry.

I turned toward Avery and sighed.

"And you and Axton? How'd that come about if you don't mind me asking?" I asked.

"Don't mind at all. We met at the bar I was working at. I was still in school, a senior. I hit on him, and hit on him, trying to get him to like me, but it didn't work. We were just hanging out every now and again, but no sex or anything. You know, just me riding on his bike and stuff. One night a few months later, we were at a party at the clubhouse, and some doofus started hitting on me. Axton just lost it. He beat the guy half to death, tossed him in the street, and told me to get on his bike. I got on, and the rest is history," she blurted.

I glanced at Sydney, stared blankly for a moment, and turned to face Avery.

"Beat the guy half to death?" I asked.

"Yeah, it was pretty bad," she sighed.

"Couple of shootings and a beating in the course of a few months?" I asked as I reached for my glass.

The two girls turned to face each other and started laughing. As they each turned to face me, they nodded their heads at the same time.

"Yeah, that's about it," Sydney laughed, "I wouldn't trade or change Cambio for the world."

"Me neither," Avery shrugged, "Axton's as good as gold."

As I stared at my glass, wishing it was a quintuple, the waitress passed. As she noticed me gazing into the empty glass, she pointed at me and raised her eyebrows. I nodded my head as I raised my glass in the air. She raised her hand and extended two fingers. I shook my head. She raised three. I nodded. She turned toward the bar and walked away.

"That's a good waitress," I said as I turned toward the girls.

"Kat?" Avery said, "She's the best."

"You know her?" I asked.

She nodded her head, "She went to school with me and played volleyball. She's a year younger than me. She graduates this year."

I nodded my head.

"She's fucking Biscuit," she chuckled.

"Big guy with the beard?" I nodded.

"That's Biscuit," she sighed.

As the waitress placed the drink on the table, Avery stared down at it and laughed.

"You're going to be a mess here pretty quick, Sam. That's what, eight shots in half an hour?" she asked.

She was right for the most part, but I was already a little more than half drunk. Generally speaking, my limit was one drink, knowing if I had two, I'd be drunk. Having had a double, and a triple, and now having another triple, it would stand to reason with a matter of minutes I'd need someone to take me home in a shopping cart. I felt an almost necessity to tell some kind of a story to compete with what they had shared, but I had very little to offer. I glanced down at the drink, shifted my gaze to meet Avery's, and shrugged my shoulders as my mouth curled into a smile.

"Hell, I walked here. I've only got to stumble about two hundred feet to get *home*. It's been a long day. Otis and I went to a movie and he fucked me half senseless in the theatre, which was fabulous by the way. Now I'm just unwinding and trying desperately to be social. I normally hate girls because they're so competitive and catty, but you two are fun," I said as I reached for my drink.

"You had sex in the theater? Which one, that ratty one on east Kellogg?" Avery laughed.

I shook my head, "No, the Warren Theater. The really nice one right up the street here."

"You fucked in the Warren?" she gasped.

"Sure did," I said as I took a sip of my drink.

"Holy shit," Avery gasped.

"Like fucked? *Fucked around*, or fucked?" she asked as she leaned into the table.

I took another short sip of my drink and grinned, "Well, I got down on my knees in front of him while the movie was starting and sucked his cock first. Then I got up and rode him reverse cowgirl until I came all over his cock. It was awesome. Oh, and we got a standing ovation on the way out. No joke, the entire front row stood up and clapped as we left."

Avery raised her hand in the air and turned her palm to face me. I raised my hand in the air and slapped it against hers. As she shook her head from side-to-side, Sydney raised her hand. I slapped mine against hers and nodded my head.

"To the Sinners," Sydney said as she raised her glass of tea, "Never a dull moment."

"To the Sinners," Avery said as she raised her glass.

I glanced down at my glass. With blurred vision and an unsteady hand, I picked it up and somehow raised it to the toast. As our glasses clanked together, I burped, sloshed half my drink onto the table, and said my own toast.

"To the Sinners, and to being stuffed full of so much dick that it hurts to sit down," I giggled, "and to getting standing ovations, and cleaning up the quart of cum with Otis' no-shows."

"Otis wears no-shows," Avery laughed.

"He sure does, and gather 'round, ladies. I've got a few stories to tell you about Otis," I said as I raised my glass to my lips.

Yeah, I think we're going to get along just fine, ladies.

I clanked my glass onto the table, sat back in my seat, and began to tell the story of the night Otis duct taped me naked to a tree while wearing a kilt.

Not because I felt a need to be competitive, but because I wanted to make sure they knew I was one of them.

An equal.

The Ol' Lady of a Sinner.

OTIS

If the life of a Sinner had taught me nothing else, it taught me to always keep my guard up, regardless of the company I was keeping or the events surrounding me. When life seemed too good to be true, it was always time to glance over my shoulders and make sure of who or what was behind me. It wasn't that I believed life wouldn't offer me what was good, it was more my belief that the laws of average would always make sure to keep me in check by tossing me a shit sandwich from time to time.

The thing about a shit sandwich is this.

As soon as you bite into it, you know one thing for absolute certain.

You just bit into a shit sandwich.

"So both of you want to go in there with me?" Jack asked nervously.

"If you really think we need to," Toad shrugged.

"Same as going to talk to the cops in the joint far as I'm concerned. You never go alone to talk to the man. Always go in pairs, that way nobody can start the *he said she said* shit. I just want witnesses," Jack said as he peered into the shop.

"Sure, we'll go," I said as I stepped past him, "Come on."

We walked to the office door together, and after making sure they were at my side, I knocked on it sharply.

Axton, obviously recognizing my knock, responded through the closed door, "Otis? Come on in."

I pulled the door open slightly and peeked inside, "It's the three of us, Slice. Toad and Jack are with me, got a minute?"

"Always, as far as you three fuckers are concerned. Come on in," he responded as he closed the book in front of him.

"Come on," I said as I waved my arm toward the two men.

I pulled a chair from the table and sat down, and Toad did the same. Jack began to nervously pace back and forth across the floor, staring down at his boots as he walked.

"You alright, Big Jack?" Axton asked as his eyes followed Jack's steps.

"Be fine boss. Just thinking," he said as he glanced up.

After walking back and forth a few more times, he stopped, pulled out a chair at the corner of the table, and sat down.

"Permission to speak candidly," Jack sighed.

Axton glanced at me, shifted his eyes toward Toad, and eventually fixed his eyes on Jack.

"What the fuck's going on?" Axton asked as he stood from his seat and crossed his arms.

Immediately, Jack stood from his seat.

"Sit down," Axton snapped, "What the fuck's going on here?"

Jack sat down, glanced down at his boots for a moment, and sighed.

"Sure, whatever. Speak freely," Axton huffed.

"Think we've got a cop in the club, boss?" Jack said as he glanced up.

What the fuck?

"What the *fuck* are you talking about?" Axton bellowed.

Toad immediately stood and turned toward Jack.

"Sit the fuck down, Toad," Axton demanded as he uncrossed his arms.

"There ain't a cop patched in in *this* MC, I can guarantee you that much. Now what brought you in here? What happened?" Axton barked.

Jack stood from his seat, "Sorry, boss. I got to stand. Hear me out, okay?"

Axton nodded his head, "Fuck it, I guess you can walk. And I'm listening."

As Jack paced the floor, he began to speak, "Well, when I was in the joint, we had cops that took us to the hole in the elevator when we got a write up. They had this special key, it looks like one of them round keys for a soda machine, but it's about half inch longer. Elevator repairmen have 'em too, but that's about it. It lets you stick the key in the elevator, turn on an override, and make it go to the roof or the basement or whatever. Now when I was in court the first time, and the second time for that matter, I saw the same thing. The US Marshall and the ATF fellas that took me to court in the beginning, and again the other day, they both had 'em. They had to put 'em in the elevator to get down to the basement to their cars."

Axton crossed his arms in front of his chest and inhaled a long slow breath as he waited for Jack to continue.

"There's only a couple of elevator manufacturers, *Dover* and *Otis.* Most of the keys say one of those two names on 'em. Kind of looks like a Harley key too, now that I think of it," he said.

"God damn it, Big Jack, get to the point," Axton growled.

Jack stopped pacing, turned to face Axton, and crossed his arms, "That fella they call Gunner, boss. He's got one of them keys on his key ring. It says Dover on it for sure, I looked at it. And unless he's repairing elevators on the side, he's probably a fed or a prison guard."

"I fucking knew it. Phony ass piece of lying shit. Motherfucker says he was in the shit, I never trusted his phony ass," Toad blurted as he stood from his seat.

"God damn son of a motherfucking bitch," Axton said as he turned toward the cabinets on the wall.

"Hell, he's been here for years, he can't be a cop. Who vouched him in the club?" Axton asked as he reached for the *Members* book.

"Don't need the book, Slice. I can tell you who vouched him in," I sighed.

"Who?" Axton asked as he turned around.

Simultaneously, Toad and I responded, "Hollywood."

"Fuck!" Axton shouted as he kicked the table with the toe of his boot, almost knocking it over entirely.

He glared at Toad for a long moment, and then fixed his eyes on me. I sat silently, and attempted to think of why Gunner would need an elevator key. As I drew an absolute blank, Axton kicked the table again.

"Fuck! Fuck! Fuck!" he screamed as he turned toward the door.

"Who's that cock sucker run with?" he asked.

I shrugged my shoulders. Axton turned to face Toad.

"Ran with 'Wood. Well, till 'Wood committed suicide," Toad sighed.

"Fuck!" Axton yelled as he kicked the table again.

"You God damned one fucking hundred percent sure he's got an elevator override key? One fucking hundred, not ninety-nine. You sure?" Axton asked as he turned toward Jack.

"Wouldn't be here if I wasn't boss. Hundred percent," Jack nodded.

"Fuck!" Axton shouted.

In an attempt to settle Axton down, I stood from my seat.

"Let's talk about this, what are we going to do?" I asked.

"Torture his ass, get him to admit it, and kill the fucker. Pretty simple shit," Axton shrugged.

"I'll do it," Toad said as he stood.

Axton shook his head, "I'll fucking do it."

"Hold up, boss," Jack said as he raised his hand in the air.

"You kill this fucker now or you even kill him later, fed's will be on this club like shit on a shoe. Whoever sent him knows he's *here*. He comes up missing or turns up dead, we're fucked," Jack explained.

Axton turned toward Jack and shook his head from side-to-side and sighed.

"Well, what the fuck do you suggest?" he growled.

The thought of a cop being in the group was unthinkable to me. Gunner being the cop was much more believable than anyone else, he seemed to always be around, but in the same respect, he wasn't around when he needed to be. As I sat and thought about it, he did seem to ask a hell of a lot of questions. He damned sure didn't look like a *typical* cop, but after seeing what the ATF agent looked like in court, he damned sure could be an ATF agent.

Doing life in prison under the RICO act didn't appeal to me *at all*.

"I say we kill the prick," I said as I looked up.

Jack shook his head, "It'll bring the heat in here so God damned quick, it'll make your heads spin."

"What's the answer?" Axton asked.

"Well, he's gonna be wearing a wire, you can bet on that. So we need to get him where we can talk to him and the wire ain't any good. Won't be easy, him being a cop and all, but we'll have to do it. Anybody got a swimming pool?" Jack asked.

"A what? A fucking swimming pool?" Axton huffed.

Jack nodded his head, "Yeah a pool. Make his ass get in the pool. Water will ruin the wire. Only way I know for sure, other than stripping him down, and then you still don't know. Fucking things can be in their hair, ears, hell some of the fellas in the joint said they even had 'em sewn into their clothes. So if you make him strip, and he tosses his clothes in a pile beside him, he can still be listening," Jack said as he raised his hand to his ear.

"Biscuit's got a pool," I said.

"Sure does," Axton agreed.

"Fuck. Alright. I'll get with Biscuit. We'll need to get him over there without making him nervous. How in the absolute fuck are we going to do that?" Axton shrugged.

"Have Biscuit tell him we've got some pussy over there?" Jack shrugged, "But don't tell him there's a pool, fed's hate being around pools. He'll know what's up for sure and he'll call in the troops."

"And we won't say anything out loud. I know that much," Axton said as he pulled his note pad out and shook it.

"I'll write everything down and make him do the same. Son of a fucking bitch, I hope you're wrong," Axton said as he tossed his pad on the table.

"You fellas go out in the shop and act like nothing happened. Is the fucker out there now?" Axton asked.

I nodded my head.

Axton swung his leg up and kicked the table hard enough to lift it from the floor three feet.

"Fuck!" he yelled.

"Biscuit?" he asked.

"Nope, think he's fucking the girl from the bar," I responded.

"Alright, I'll call him. Stay out in the shop, and just follow my lead. I'll be out in a minute," Axton said.

As we walked to the door, Axton cleared his throat, "Big Jack?"

"Yeah boss," Jack said as he turned to face Axton.

"Cut looks good. And about this…" Axton sighed and shook his head as he gazed down at the floor.

As Axton glanced up, he continued, "Good lookin' out, Jack. Good lookin' out."

Jack nodded his head, "Just doin' my job, boss."

An ounce of devotion is more powerful than a lifetime of knowledge or a heart filled with faith. Devotion has the ability to make even the weakest men develop strength, and the fear-filled become brave.

Jack was devoted to the club, there was no doubt in my mind.

I was devoted to the club, and to the woman I loved, Sam. If Jack was correct, and Gunner was a cop, he threatened to take the two things from me I was devoted to and truly loved.

And in no way was I going to let that happen.

Not without one hell of a fight.

SAM

I sat on the porch with my head in my hands and cried. I had never really cried much as a child or an adult, but I seemed to be making up for it now. The loss of my father as pre-teen was difficult, but I somehow accepted it. The loss of my mother, although untimely and by a very odd series of circumstances, had also been accepted. The loss of her beloved cat, however, was the straw that broke the camel's back.

In my excitement to see Otis' car, I had left in a hurry, leaving the front door open. After the movie and my trip to the bar, I stumbled to my hotel room in a drunken stupor. Returning to my mother's house the next day revealed the door had been left open, but my thoughts didn't immediately include the cat. Only after an entire day of working without interruption did I realize the cat was gone.

I wiped my eyes and glanced to my side. A dish of food, another of water, and three small stuffed toys sat beside me. I gazed out into the dark yard and attempted to regain my composure. After a moment of sniveling and wiping my tired eyes, I raised my cupped hand to my mouth.

"Taaaaaylor. Kitty, kitty…Taaaaaylor…come here kitty," I blubbered.

I scanned the yard for any movement.

Nothing.

As I lowered my face into my hands, my phone beeped. I picked it up and swiped my finger across the screen. A message from Avery revealed her best advice regarding the loss of my mother's cat.

I stared down at the screen.

Avery: Shake a bag of cat food and make it rattle. It works every time.

After typing a quick *thank you* response, I set my phone aside and picked up the sack of cat food. It seemed ridiculous, but I stood up and began to shake the sack violently. After what seemed like no more than a few seconds of shaking it, I heard a rustling sound in the shrubbery beside the house, and Taylor jumped onto the porch.

"Meow…"

I dropped the sack of food onto the porch and reached down with both hands and picked her up. Immediately, she began to purr. I held her close to my chest, walked into the house, and closed the door. I'd never actually held a cat before and therefore had no experience doing so, but she seemed to like the way I was holding her. I walked to the loveseat, sat down and placed her beside where I was sitting.

She immediately jumped in my lap, walked in a few circles, and flopped down on her side. As she lay in my lap continuing to purr, she gazed up at me with her golden eyes and blinked a few times very slowly. Within a few minutes, she was asleep. I sat on the couch for some time, thinking of my mother, and what satisfaction she must have received from having the cat as her only house mate. There was no doubt in my mind my mother had loved the cat, and out of respect, I decided I needed to do the same, even if it proved difficult.

Carefully, I lifted the cat from my lap and set her aside on the loveseat. After cleaning the porch of her food, water, and toys, I walked back to the loveseat and sat down. Still asleep in a ball, Taylor appeared to be unaware or uncaring of the grief she had caused me. I shook my head, grinned, and sent Avery a text message letting her know I had found the cat.

Tired, relieved, and slightly bored, I opened the browser of my phone and typed a few words into the *Google* search window.

What does it mean when a cat blinks slowly

A screen full of answers popped up, and I clicked on the first one and read the article.

Slow blinking by a cat (sort of an eyes-almost-closed look, almost trance-like) is a good sign — one that says, "You're my buddy, and I feel comfortable hanging out with you."

I finished the article, tossed the phone to my side, and shifted my eyes toward the sleeping cat.

After a few seconds of watching her sleep, I reached down and ran my hand along her body. Her fur was soft, similar to the faux fur coats for sale in the mall at wintertime. I ran my hand along her fur again, amazed by the softness of it. She turned her head and opened her eyes. As the slits in the center increased into large black dots, I smiled at her and blinked my eyes a few times.

Slowly.

OTIS

Axton sat in a chair on Biscuit's patio staring down at the table in front of him. On the table - a Sig Sauer pistol, Axton's pistol, a keychain, and Axton's note pad. The clothes that Gunner had been wearing were in Biscuit's garage. Although we didn't find a wire, and Gunner swore he wasn't wearing one, we had found enough evidence to believe Jack was correct in his assumption.

The pistol we found in the saddle bag on Gunner's bike had magazines in it marked "Law Enforcement Only" and his keychain included an elevator override key.

After several minutes of awkward silence, Axton picked up Gunner's pistol and walked along the edge of the pool.

"Do not say a fucking word until I ask you to," Axton said as he reached the area of the pool where Gunner was treading water.

"Don't think for one motherfucking minute that I won't kill you and make it look like a suicide, you piece of shit," Axton said as he knelt beside the pool.

"I'm going to ask you a few questions, and based on your responses, I'll make a few decisions on what's in the clubs best interest," Axton said as he raised the pistol in the air.

"This is yours, by the way. Just to clear things up," Axton said flatly.

"I realize contrary to popular belief you're not bound by law to answer this question truthfully, but I'll ask you anyway. Are you law enforcement?" Axton asked without so much as an ounce of emotion.

As Gunner continued to tread water, he closed his eyes momentarily, opened them, and sighed, "Yes."

Axton closed his eyes and shook his head, "Fed?"

"ATF," Gunner responded almost breathlessly.

He had been treading water for at least thirty minutes, and was breathing pretty heavily.

"Outfuckingstanding. Now, if you're a fed why are you telling me this?" Axton asked as he opened his eyes.

"Far as I know…there's only one way…out of this…and it includes me walking away…from here. Anything else happens and they'll… come down on you…and the Sinners…like the wrath of God. Let me out of the pool…and we'll discuss it," he responded in a broken sentence.

"Fuck you, motherfucker. Shoot this prick, Slice," Biscuit hollered as he reached out with the long rod and pulled the pool cleaning net over Gunners head again.

As Biscuit pushed Gunner under the water for the umpteenth time, Axton shook his head and stood.

"God damn it, Biscuit, I don't like it any more than you do, but our options are limited. Let him up," Axton growled as he pushed the pistol into the waist of his pants.

"Hear what he's got to say, boss," Jack said.

Axton glanced toward Biscuit and sighed, "Let him up, Biscuit. He can swim his fucking ass over to the shallow end and stand there."

He shifted his eyes toward Gunner and his face changed to one of disgust.

"Go down there and stand, I'm not letting you get out of the fucking pool," Axton said as he pointed to the shallow end of the pool.

After Biscuit lifted the net from Gunner's head, he struggled to swim to the other end of the pool. Clearly exhausted, scared, and uncertain of what his future held, I hoped whatever he planned on telling Axton was enough to convince all of us of what he hoped to convince us of. Right now, the majority of the men in attendance preferred him dead. As he waded through the shallow water, Axton barked out his order.

"Stop right there, whatever your fucking name is," Axton said as he reached the thigh deep water.

After Axton walked to the shallow end of the pool and crouched down, Toad, Jack, Biscuit and I followed. Upon our reaching the other end and standing behind Axton, Gunner began to speak.

"You've been my field assignment for two and almost one half years. There's no one else on this investigation. I swear to you. I had a meeting a few weeks ago with the director, and he's pissed because I claimed I wasn't ready to testify before a Federal Grand Jury..."

Axton interrupted him as he stood from his kneeling position. In his signature *I'm not very fucking happy pose*, he crossed his arms and flexed his biceps.

"What in the fuck does this have to do with anything? Let's get one thing straight. I don't like cops. You're a cop. If I took a vote right now, at least four of these fellas would agree to kill you. My math skills aren't too damned shabby, and that's eighty fucking percent, excluding you. Damned sure a majority," Axton said.

"Look," Gunner said as he raised his hands in the air.

"I started investigating you on guns. In the last two years, you really haven't done anything contrary to law. Might be a stretch, but possibly selling guns to a prohibited person is all I can come up with. To indict you, I need to testify and turn in my reports. Reports come first. If I don't, there's no case. Period. End of story. I'll agree to not testify, how's that?" Gunner asked.

"You've got to be fuckin' shittin' me," Biscuit said as he swung the ten foot long pole from the net into Gunner's head.

Whack!

The pole glanced down across his brow and cut his nose. As Biscuit raised the steel rod over his head, obviously preparing to smack him again, Toad, Jack, and I all stood chuckling at Biscuit's behavior. Axton, however, wasn't amused.

"You no good son-of-a-fuckin'-cop-bitch," Biscuit howled as he raised the pole, "I'll just beat you to death if they won't let me shoot you."

"God fucking damn it, Biscuit. Put the pole down," Axton hollered as he raised his hands in the air.

"Ain't happenin', Slice. These fuckin' cops, you can't trust 'em. Probably got a Smith and Wesson .44 Magnum shoved up his ass as a backup piece. I'm keepin' the pole," Biscuit said as he held the pole in his hands like a Lacrosse stick.

Axton shook his head as he looked down at Gunner, and eventually he began to laugh.

"Well, don't hit him with the fucker again unless I tell you to," he chuckled.

"I don't trust you any further than I can throw your fat ass. Don't think I can agree to that," Axton sighed as he knelt down at the edge of the pool.

"You've got two options," Gunner sighed, "Kill me, or let me go. That's it."

"Fuck this motherfucker, Slice. He's tryin' that cop psycho-babble mind game shit on us," Biscuit said as he raised the pole over his head.

Axton raised his hand in the air, "Put it down, God damn it, Biscuit."

"Man's got a point, boss," Jack sighed, "We've got two options. Kill him, or let him go."

Axton, clearly well beyond frustrated, tossed his hands in the air as if giving up, "Well, what the fuck do you four fuckers want to do?"

"Kill him," Biscuit said.

"Same. I say we kill him," Toad nodded.

"Want to kill him boss, but it isn't too practical. Soon as he doesn't report in, they'll come to the clubhouse," Jack shrugged.

My thoughts mirrored Jack's. My knee jerk reaction was to kill him, but for some reason I questioned my natural thoughts and considered what might be more sensible, something I had not always done in the past. In matters regarding the club, I almost immediately went with my gut feeling and dealt with the consequences later. I stood quietly thinking, sensing all of the men's eyes were fixed on me; waiting on my response. I glanced up at Axton, fully realizing it was Sam and my love for her that caused my reservation to murder him, but knew not to reveal my thoughts.

What it is we love immediately becomes sacred, and we'll do whatever we must to preserve it.

"Hand me the gun," I said flatly as I extended my arm.

"We need to talk about this, my fucking head's spinning," Axton shrugged as he shook his head.

I rolled my shoulders rearward, flexed my chest and changed my tone to a very demanding one, "Hand me…"

"The fucking gun," I said as I took a step toward Axton.

Axton's eyes widened as he took a step rearward.

I turned toward the deep end of the pool and stomped toward the table where Axton had been sitting. After grabbing his personal pistol from the table, I slid the slide rearward and checked to ensure there was a round in the chamber. As I took the few steps back toward the shallow end of the pool, all five men began to speak at once.

"Shut the fuck up. Every fucking one of you. Just shut the fuck up, especially *you*," I said as I pointed the pistol at Gunner.

Gunner stood approximately five feet from the end of the pool in thigh deep water. As long as my legs were, reaching him in one surprising step wouldn't be difficult at all. Without a hint of revelation of my thoughts, I leaped into the pool and before he was able to react, grabbed a handful of his hair in my left hand. As I pulled his head rearward, I pressed the barrel of the pistol into his eye socket.

"God damn it, Otis," Axton screamed.

"Shoot the motherfucker!" Biscuit hollered.

"Otis!" Axton yelled again.

"Shut the fuck up!" I screamed over my shoulder.

I turned my head to face Gunner, and fixed my eyes on his one available eye. As I spoke, I twisted the barrel of the pistol into his eye socket, making the situation as uncomfortable for him as I could.

"Listen to me, motherfucker, and listen *good*. I'm not like these other four fuckers. I'm the quiet one you need to worry about. You've been here two and a half years, so you know I'm the protector of this fucking MC, regardless of who wears the SAA patch," I growled.

"You've got one opportunity to answer each question I ask. *One*. If you don't, I'll pull this fucking trigger," I said as I pulled the hammer of the pistol rearward until it clicked into place.

Axton's pistol was a double action H&K, and didn't require that I pull the hammer rearward to fire it. Pulling the trigger without pulling the hammer rearward required a more lengthy pull of the trigger, and more force. Pulling the trigger with the hammer *cocked* required minimal effort. Some called the trigger effort required in this position a *hair trigger*, because all you had to do to fire the weapon was move the trigger a hair, and with his ATF training, Gunner would know this if anyone did.

"Otis!" Axton screamed as I cocked the hammer.

"What's your God given name?" I demanded.

"Allen. Allen Pintler," Gunner coughed.

"Current place of residence," I grunted.

After no more than a long second of silence, I pushed the pistol into his eye and closed my eyes.

"Wichita. Right here in Wichita," he cried.

"Got a wife and kids?" I asked.

"Uhhm. I uhhm, yeah. I have a family," he blubbered.

Good, then this should be easy.

"You've got one option and one option only, and I'm going to explain it to you. You're going to get out of this pool, dry off, get dressed in some of Biscuit's clothes, and you and I are going to go to your house in Biscuit's truck. You're going to prove to me that it's your house by showing me your fucking mail, pictures of you with your fucking wife, and pictures of you with your kids. Your kids old enough to have laptops?" I asked.

"What? Laptops?" he muttered.

"Easy question, motherfucker. Do your fucking kids have laptops?" I growled.

"Yeah, they both do," he snapped back.

"Alright, again, listen carefully," I said as I changed my voice to a more calm tone.

"You're going to allow us access to their laptops, and we're going to put a *LoJack* on them, just to make sure you don't try and run anywhere. We'll track your kid's whereabouts, and we're going to put one on your bike and your personal car as well. And we'll track you. You either refuse to testify to the Grand Jury, or I'm going to kill your wife and kids. It's that simple. This isn't a threat, it's a solemn promise. If I'm going to spend life in prison, it isn't going to be on your terms, it's going to be on mine," I paused and raised my eyebrows, giving him a moment to consider what I had said.

"You agree to these conditions?" I asked as I pressed the pistol against his eye.

"Oh fuck. Uhhm, yeah, I agree. Don't hurt my kids, just don't hurt my kids," he began to blubber.

"It's all up to you, Special Agent Allen Pintler. It's all up to you," I said as I pulled the pistol away from his face, lowered the hammer, and extended my right arm rearward.

As I continued to hold his hair in my left fist, someone took the pistol from my grasp. I released his hair and walked to the corner of the pool. After walking up the steps and onto the deck, all eyes were fixed on me.

"Sorry, Slice. It was the only thing I could think of," I shrugged.

Axton shook his head and grinned, "LoJack's? Where the fuck did you come up with that?"

"Got one on *my* car and *my* laptop," I shrugged, "They work good, you can track them in real time on the internet."

186

"Get out of the pool," Axton growled as he handed Toad the agent's gun.

"Toad's going with you. Toad, if he tries anything, and I mean *anything*, do whatever a war torn Marine thinks is best," Axton said.

"Got it, Slice," Toad responded.

Agent Pintler surely loved his children, and he was doing what he must to preserve that love, and keep it sacred.

And in many respects, I was simply doing the same.

SAM

Yet another week and a half had passed, and as much as I knew at some point in time I would need to go back to St. Louis, doing so was a different story. To leave Wichita, even for a few days, was unthinkable to me. Leaving my mother's home, leaving the only girlfriends I felt I ever had, and leaving Otis was more than I was able to agree to do.

Although I believed they would all be waiting for me upon my return, the thought of walking away from the ones I loved wasn't something I was comfortable doing. The longer I thought about it, the clearer it became - my *fear* was the potential loss of one or all of them.

I had lost everyone I cared for in my life; my father, Otis, and then my mother. Now, feeling as if I had reconnected with Otis, leaving him, even for a short period of time, was to risk losing him.

And losing him was not an option.

I pushed the box to the side, stood, and glanced around the room. As my head began to spin from the thought of it all, my stomach began to heave. What my mother had warned me of since my childhood was actually happening – I had clearly worried myself sick.

I ran down the hallway and reached the toilet just in time to vomit. As I knelt on the floor, hugging the cold porcelain in my arms, I decided if I was going to leave, right now wasn't the time to think about it. Maybe I just needed to see if I could convince Otis to go with me and help me pack.

After the patch in party was over, I could see if he would go. At that time he'd have no real reason to stay, at least there was nothing scheduled with the club as far as I knew. When I finally felt like I was done vomiting up what little breakfast I had eaten, I stood, washed my face, brushed my teeth, and wandered into the back bedroom.

Having a family is somewhat of an assurance that there will always be people you can confide in, trust, and will be there when you need them to be; all because of the binding love of family. Family will always provide unconditional love because they are, well, family. It is not a conscious decision or a choice, it just is.

Choosing to love a person is different. At any point in time, the person you have chosen can change their mind, fall in love with someone else, or be scared away by some ridiculous statement, exposed belief, or expressed desire. Losing Otis the first time was proof of a long love filled relationship's ability to crumble over an expressed desire. My longing to have children was more than likely a result of me feeling a need to secure my place with Otis, but the expression of my thoughts provide results which were the exact opposite.

In hindsight, I should have known. Otis had always been a person who needed to feel as if he was free from what bound most everyone else on this earth. Conforming to society's beliefs, systems, and procedures was something he was never comfortable with. Even as young boys, Axton and Otis thumbed their noses at authority, society, rules, and regulations. A little internet research confirmed my suspicions of his motorcycle club standing for nothing more than the expression of freedom, therefore nothing had changed.

For me to attempt to take his freedom from him then, or attempt to take it now would result in nothing short of disaster. Our pinkie promise was all I needed to spend a lifetime with Otis, and I could do so happily knowing I needed nothing else from him to feel secure.

As I gazed blankly into the room I considered my position on matters may not be clear to Otis. I walked to where I had been sitting before, picked up my phone, and drafted a text message to clear things up.

I want you to know the fact you're in a motorcycle club doesn't bother me, and in fact, I'm happy you are. I'll be here for you always, Sam

I stared down at the message. After reading it several times, I backspaced through it and erased it. A few taps with my very capable fingers, and I stared once again at the screen.

You and Axton seem right at home with the motorcycle club, and I like it that you appear to be at peace now

Jesus, Sam. That looks ridiculous.

I backspaced until the message was gone.

I fumbled with the phone for a moment and gazed down at the screen.

I want you to know something

I love you and will always support you

I grinned and pressed *send*.

I glanced around the room at the various boxes scattered on the floor. I would have a lifetime to inventory my mother's house, and doing so now wasn't necessary. It provided me with a sense of self-worth, and allowed me to feel I was paying a tribute of sorts to my mother by doing so, but it wasn't *necessary*.

"Meow."

I turned toward the door.

Taylor sat in the opening, staring in my direction. After a few second stare-off, she blinked her eyes slowly.

I returned the gesture.

"I think I'm done for the day, Taylor. Let's go lay on the couch and listen to music. Maybe I'll see if the girls want to come over and hang out later," I said as I walked her direction.

As I passed her, I glanced over my shoulder. By the time I was halfway down the hallway, she turned and began walking in my direction. Maintaining her pace, but following ten feet behind me, she followed me to the loveseat. I no more than sat down and placed my phone at my side, and she jumped into my lap, walked in a few circles, and flopped down. A few blinks of her eyes later, and she was asleep.

As I sat and stared at her, watching her body expand and contract from her breathing, it dawned on me why my mother had the cat as a pet.

The cat offered her the same thing it offered me. No differently than family, the cat didn't question her - or me for that matter. Without thought and without prejudice, the cat offered her love.

Unconditional love.

As I stroked the cat's fur, my phone beeped. Being cautious not to wake the cat, I leaned to the side and picked up my phone.

Otis: Love you, Sam. And I'll always support you.

Hey Moms cooking dinner. Eat around 4. You want to come?

Using my thumb, I pressed the keys for my one word response and pressed *send.*

Yes

I hadn't seen Otis' parents for fourteen years. When we were together, I perceived his parents no differently than I perceived mine. To me, they were an extension of my family, and losing them, in many respects, was as difficult as losing Otis. Having them in my life would provide me with a sense of family I would never be able to feel again in their absence. Eager to see them, and excited for the dinner, I lifted Taylor from my lap, stood, and walked into the kitchen with her.

Although it was only 8:30 in the morning, it wasn't too early to try and make something to take to the dinner. Holding Taylor in my arm, I opened the refrigerator door and gazed inside.

Empty.

After realizing I wasn't in *my* home, I closed the refrigerator door, frustrated there wasn't anything in it to prepare a dessert. I dropped the cat on the floor, pulled my phone from my pocket, and sent Sydney a quick message.

Help? Good dessert to take to dinner at Otis' parents?

Almost immediately, the phone beeped. I glanced at the screen.

Sydney: Bee's apple pie. Best in the entire world. Too long to text. Want me to come over?

I grinned as I read the message and promptly responded.

IDK if you want

My phone beeped instantly.

Sydney: Text me your address. Be there in 20. Toad and Jack are doing yardwork.

I typed my address into the phone, and sent it to Sydney, beyond grateful to have her help with the dessert. I didn't cook much, but I *was* a woman, and knew how to. Having a family recipe would make taking the dessert much more enjoyable than getting something from the internet.

I slipped my phone into the pocket of my shorts and glanced around the room. Although the house was empty short of Taylor and me, I felt as if I was blessed with having a family of sorts. Albeit unconventional, it seemed like it was a family nonetheless.

And my sister I never had while growing up was coming over to help me make a pie.

OTIS

"Well, it just seems like a weird choice to serve to a guest, Marge. Not everyone likes shit like this," my father sighed as he glanced down at his plate.

"Ken, it's not *shit*. And if Sam doesn't like it, she doesn't have to eat it," my mother responded.

Sam reached down and turned her plate a quarter of a turn and glanced toward my mother, "I love stuffed peppers, Mrs. Milner. It smells wonderful."

"What's this pile of stuff, Marge?" my father asked as he poked his fork into the potatoes.

My mother looked up from her plate and shook her head, "It's a casserole. Potatoes, cheese, sour cream, butter, and cream of chicken soup. Taste it, you'll like it."

"Get the recipe off Facebook?" My father asked as he scooped up a forkful of the potatoes.

"No, not Facebook. I got it from Pinterest. Same as the stuffed pepper recipe. Just eat it, Ken," my mother snapped.

I glanced at Sam. Her head swiveled from side-to-side as she followed my parent's conversation, watching each of them intently as they spoke. As our eyes met, I pointed the end of my fork at the countertop where her apple pie was sitting.

"Sam didn't get her apple pie recipe from Pinterest, so maybe you'll like it," I chuckled.

"Family recipe?" my mother asked without looking up from her plate.

"Sydney gave it to me. It's her friend's mother's recipe. We made it together this afternoon," Sam grinned.

"Sydney is the Marine's fiancée from the barbeque joint, ma. And the big black kid that works for him doing the yard work around town, it's his mother's recipe," I said as I cut into my stuffed pepper.

My mother looked up from her plate and turned toward Sam, "Shirley. She won an award down at the festival with that pie."

Sam nodded her head, "That's what Sydney said."

My father thrust his hands in the air and shook his head, "Sam brings award winners, and you're cooking shit some eight year old Pakistani kid is posting on the internet."

"Eat, Ken," my mother snapped.

"Good peppers ma," I said as I swallowed a bite of the stuffed pepper.

"Thank you," she responded.

With her fork still stuck into her potatoes, and without taking a single bite of her food, my mother turned to face Sam. I often wondered if my mother ate small meals throughout the day to stay alive, because at the dinner table she often picked at her food while my father and I ate, never actually eating what was on her plate. As Sam turned her direction and smiled, my mother spoke.

"Now Samantha. Steve tells us you're going to be coming back here to live. Is that right?" my mother asked.

"Let her eat, ma," I sighed.

My mother slowly turned my direction and widened her eyes. "I was talking to Samantha. Eat your dinner, Steve."

I glanced at my father, who was finishing the mound of potatoes from his plate. As he shoveled another forkful into his mouth, he looked up and grinned, "She said no pie 'till we're done with this shit. Better eat up."

Sam shifted her gaze back and forth between my mother and me as she spoke, "I'm going to go back to St. Louis one of these days, and get my stuff. I'll just bring everything back here and probably live in my mother's house."

"The house in Lakepoint? On the east side?" my mother asked.

"Yes, the same house I grew up in," Sam nodded.

My mother tilted her head my direction, "Steve, you need to go with her and help her. She doesn't need to go by herself and get her things. She needs a man to help her, so you go with her."

I glanced up from my plate and shook my head, "I'll probably go, ma."

"No *probably*. You need to go," my mother sighed.

"Get you some tie down straps from work so nothing blows out," my father muttered as he shoved a forkful of pepper into his mouth.

"Let Sam eat, ma," I sighed.

"Speaking of work, Clyde had sex with the cock-eyed girl at the south register," my father said as he glanced up from his plate.

"Ken!" my mother gasped.

"Well, he did. Sam - Sam from work, not this Sam - he caught 'em back in the store room. Had that cock-eyed gal bent over a row of boxes," he paused and swallowed the bite of food he was chewing.

"Ken, stop!" my mother sighed as she tossed her head toward Sam.

"Does sex talk bother you, Samantha?" my father asked.

Sam glanced at my mother, shifted her eyes toward my father, and shrugged.

"She's a lady, Ken. It's rude," my mother hissed.

"Well, I wasn't going to go into graphic detail, Marge. I'm just making conversation. So anyway, this cock-eyed gal that works the south register has the body of a porn star, but when she looks at you, her eyes are all cock-eyed," he paused, glanced at me, and made his eyes go crossed.

As he looked around the table with crossed eyes, my mother covered her eyes, and Sam laughed so hard she almost spit her food out.

"Ken, that's *rude*," my mother said.

"What's rude is to see her body, and then have her turn around and look at you. That's rude. So anyway, she gets a divorce maybe a month ago. And then she'd been complaining to the other gals at work that no one would take her out on a date," he paused, sliced off a chunk of his stuffed pepper, and poked it with his fork.

As he poked the food in his mouth, he continued before he even started chewing, "So I told Clyde, I said *Clyde, if she wasn't cock-eyed, guys would be lined up to the bank*, you know the one way up on the overpass, *they'd be lined up to the bank to get a piece of that*. And Clyde looks at me and smiles. He says *Ken, as long as she's facing the other way, what's it matter*. Hell, I thought he was joking, so I just shrugged my shoulders and said *I guess it don't, Clyde*. I guess it don't, that's what I told him."

As my mother stared down at her plate, more than likely praying, Sam's eyes were fixed on my father's. Although she hadn't heard his dinnertime stories for years, she was no newbie to his tall tales. Even back when we were in high school, my father told stories at dinner no differently than he did now. As he swallowed his food, Sam spooned a fork full of potatoes up and waited.

"So it hadn't been a couple days, and Sam goes to the store room to get one of them mini air compressors for this guy, and that gal was bent over with her pants around her ankles, and her top off, and that damned Clyde was just a poking away. Sam said she spun around and hell he couldn't even tell where she was looking. I told him she was looking at *everything*. She may be gaggle eyed, but I bet that gal's got the peripheral vision of a God damned Owl. Anyway, Sam says her boobs are fake. She had her top off when the whole deal went down," he nodded his head once toward Sam, turned toward me, and poked the last bite of pepper with his fork.

"Ken, that's not dinner table talk," my mother said as she looked up.

"Well, I want Samantha to feel like she's at home, Marge. Damn. If I sat here and ate without speaking you'd wonder about me wouldn't you, Samantha?" my father asked as he glanced toward Sam.

"I suppose so," she said with a laugh.

"Never would have guessed her boobs were fake. Hell, they jiggle when she walks," My father said under his breath as he pushed himself from the table.

"I'm going to get some of this pie sliced and ready. Marge, you haven't touched your food, are you going to eat pie?" my father asked as he stood from his seat.

My mother glanced up from her plate and nodded her head, "I'd planned on it, yes."

"I'm done and Sam's close, pop. Bring us a slice," I said as my father walked into the kitchen.

I pushed myself away from the table slightly and leaned back in my chair as I studied Sam. She looked exceptionally beautiful. Her hair was generally straight, but she had taken time to curl it and spruce it up. Now, it seemed she had ten times as much hair as she normally did. Curled, pinned, and placed just perfectly, she looked like she could be in a hair product commercial. The golden skin on her face was clear and smooth, and unlike many other girls, the color of her face matched the color of the skin on her neck, shoulders, and arms.

One of my pet peeves had always been women wearing make-up that caused their face to clearly be a color in contrast with the rest of their body.

In her sleeveless knit top, shorts and sandals, she looked adorable. As I sat and admired her while my father cut the pie, she sat and quietly talked to my mother. Unfocused on their conversation, I continued to sit and stare; grateful she was once again in my life.

"What? What's wrong?" she asked as she shifted her eyes to meet mine.

I shook my head, "Nothing."

She cocked her head to the side, "You were looking at me funny."

I shook my head, "Just admiring you."

"Is something wrong with my hair?" she asked as she reached for her hair.

I shook my head, "It's perfect."

"Your hair looks wonderful, Samantha," my mother breathed.

"I was going to say the same thing. Don't remember seeing you with so much of it. It looks real nice, Samantha. Here," my father said as he slid a piece of pie beside her plate.

"And here's one for you," my father said as he reached across the table.

"Thanks Pop," I said as I grabbed the plate.

My father disappeared momentarily, and then walked back into the room with a plate in his hand. As he sat down, he glanced at my mother and grinned.

"You can have one when you're finished," he said as he sat down.

My mother rolled her eyes as she took a small nibble of the potatoes, "I'll get my own, thank you."

Sam looked up from her plate, "Thank you. It's pretty much the same, I just fixed it."

"Looks big," my father said as he pushed his fork into the corner of his pie.

Sam nodded her head and chuckled, "That's what they call it. Big hair. I've got big hair."

"Well, seems appropriate. *It's big.* I like it. Reminds me of when Marilyn Monroe would fix hers all curly," he said as he poked the pie into his mouth.

As he chewed the pie, he dropped the fork from his grasp and it hit the plate with a clank. Immediately, he raised his right hand and held it to his chest as if having a heart attack.

"Now *that's* an apple pie. What's in it that makes it so damned good?" he asked as he pointed toward the plate with his left hand.

"I'm sworn to secrecy," Sam grinned.

"Well, I guess we'll just have to make sure you're going to be around a little more often, so you can bring the pie if nothing else," my father said as he reached for his fork.

"She'll be around plenty, pop," I said as I cut off a piece of pie.

My mother glanced up from her plate and fixed her eyes on me, "So are you two dating again?"

I shifted my eyes toward Sam, "We're together, yes."

"But you aren't *dating*?" my mother shrugged.

"We're together, ma," I half shouted in response.

She scrunched her nose slightly and stared, "What does that mean?"

"Ma, we're adults. Adults don't date," I said as I lifted the bite of pie to my mouth.

"Since when?" she asked.

"Since I don't know when, ma. But we're adults, and we're together. She's moving back here, and we're going to be together," I said as I poked the bite of pie into my mouth.

The pie was fabulous. As I chewed it, I turned to face Sam, smiled, and pointed to my mouth.

My mother pointed the end of her fork at me and shook it, "Together as in *you're a couple*?"

"Yeah, ma. We're a couple," I shrugged.

I glanced at Sam. She was grinning from ear to ear. I realized as I spoke that although she and I hadn't discussed these things, I simply suspected it went without saying. I had expressed to her that I loved her, and she agreed she had felt the same. As she seemed to enjoy hearing what it was I had to say about us being a couple, I considered expanding on it. Before I had a chance to speak, my mother interrupted my thoughts.

"Well, then you're *dating*. When can I have a grandchild?" she asked flatly as she shifted her eyes back and forth between Sam and me.

I shrugged my shoulders and glanced at Sam. Sam's eyes quickly shifted toward my mother. Almost immediately her face was filled with shock and wonder.

"No kids," Sam said sharply as she shook her head from side-to-side.

Shocked at her response, I sat and stared.

"Oh?" my mother responded with wide eyes.

"I'm past my prime," Sam responded, "I don't even know if I can have kids."

"Well, there's one way to find out," my father laughed as he slapped my shoulder.

"Let's just hope you can, and one day God blesses us all with one," my mother said as she stood from the table.

I sat and studied Sam and wondered what changed. Fifteen years prior, her only reason for leaving was that she wanted kids and I didn't. Now, it seemed she either no longer cared to have children or she wasn't able to. Either way, I decided it didn't matter. What mattered was that we loved each other, and we were devoted to each other. As I sat and watched her cut into the pie, I grinned.

She was beautiful. I glanced around the table. If nothing else, I could offer her a family which included a mother, father, and me.

And in my eyes, despite our individual faults, this family was perfect.

SAM

Spending time with Otis' family was so much more enjoyable than I expected it to be. I went to the dinner excited and a little nervous, not necessarily knowing what to expect. What I received was a heartwarming welcome from his parents, and in many respects, it felt as if I had only been away from them for a short period of time, definitely not the fourteen years I had been gone.

His mother's question regarding children caught me slightly off guard and made me extremely uncomfortable. I expected my quick *no* response comforted Otis, but I felt sorry for his mother and her desire to have a grandchild, knowing her longing for us to have kids would never be met. I hoped as time passed, having me for a daughter-in-law might suffice to fill the void.

As much as the maternal part of me once wanted children, I realized the longing stemmed from my feeling of insecurity regarding my relationship with Otis. Losing him once as a result of my request was one time too many, and losing him again would crush me. Our pinkie promise had no clause in it for children, and I felt comfortable as long as kids *weren't* in the picture Otis and I would be together for a lifetime.

I stood, gazing into the mirror, and tried to recall the last time I had been on an actual date. After moving to St Louis, I had gone on a few dates, but eventually decided dating was senseless, as my heart belonged, and had always belonged to Otis.

Michael died in 2001, and I moved to St. Louis immediately following his death. A year later I stopped dating. Maybe it was two years, but certainly not longer than that. So roughly 2003 would have been my last *date*.

Twelve years.

I lifted the hem of my dress slightly and spun in a circle, watching myself in the mirror as I did so.

Wear a comfortable dress and shoes you're comfortable walking in. I'll be there at seven.

I picked up my phone and glanced at the screen. 6:50. Out of my peripheral I saw Taylor approach the doorway.

"Meow…"

"I know, right?" I sighed as I shifted my eyes in her direction.

"I didn't have one, so I ran to the mall and bought it. Cute, huh?" I asked as I turned toward the mirror again.

"Meow…"

"I feel the same way. Where do you think he's going to take me?" I asked as I turned toward the doorway and took a step in her direction.

Silence.

I walked past her, down the hallway, and toward the living room. As I reached the edge of the loveseat, I glanced over my shoulder.

"I don't know either. Come on, we don't have much time," I said as I patted my hand on the arm of the loveseat.

She ran down the hallway and leaped toward my hand, landing gracefully beside it. After peering down in my lap and studying me for a short moment, she carefully stepped between my thighs and curled into a ball. After a few seconds of petting her, the unmistakable rumble of the Camaro coming down the street broke the silence.

"Well, it sounds like he's here," I shrugged as I picked her up and placed her at my side.

As he rolled into the driveway, I ran in the kitchen, grabbed my purse, and literally sprinted for the door. I pulled the curtains to the side slightly and watched, hoping he'd eventually step out of the car. After what seemed to be an eternity, he opened the door and stepped into the driveway.

Dressed in dark designer jeans, black dress boots, and a well-fitted dark grey V-neck tee, he looked amazingly handsome. I loved the entire biker look thing, but seeing him dressed like this was a very nice change. After admiring his slow confident swagger as he worked his way toward the door, I pulled the curtains to the side and reached for the door.

"Oh, wow. You look nice," I sighed as I stepped onto the porch.

He stopped in his tracks and glanced up at me.

"Damn, Sam. You look incredible. That dress looks fucking *good*," he said as he pushed his thumbs into his front pockets.

His arms looked like they were about to bust right out of the shirt. It wasn't too small, and it actually fit perfectly, but for him to buy a shirt that would allow his massive arms to actually fit the sleeves would be impossible. The upper portion of the shirt clung to his massive chest, and hung slightly loose around his rather trim waist. As I stood admiring his little thumbs in pocket pose, I had to consciously prevent myself from slobbering on my new dress.

"Thank you," I said as I did my best to curtsy, "So, you ready?"

"If you are, I am," he responded as he turned toward the car.

I stepped off the porch and glanced toward the car. He stood at the passenger door, holding it open for me, grinning from ear to ear.

As I held my dress to my thighs and attempted to slide gracefully into the low-sitting car, he bent down and kissed me softly. As soon as our lips parted, I collapsed into the seat feeling rather satisfied I could get used to this type of treatment with ease.

"So where are we going?" I asked as he got in the car.

"Surprise," he responded over his shoulder as he started the car.

I clutched my purse in my hands and grinned. I liked surprises as long as they were well natured. A surprise date seemed more romantic to me than an unplanned one, and made me feel a little more special than if we'd have simply gone to some random restaurant to eat dinner. As he pulled out of the neighborhood and sped into traffic, the sound of the car and the sheer force of the acceleration did to me what it always did to me.

Wet.

"In a hurry?" I asked as I reached over to buckle my lap belt.

He grabbed the gear shifter and slapped the car into another gear without letting his foot off the gas pedal, causing the car to lurch forward even more.

"Kind of," he said as he glanced in my direction for a split-second.

"Okay," I said under my breath.

"Does it end soon? Are we going to miss it?" I asked.

"Nope. Not really," he said as he swept past a car on the right side.

"Is it inside or outside?" I asked.

"Good question," he responded without shifting his eyes from the road, "Outside."

I nodded my head, "Is there a large body of water?"

He shook his head and laughed, "No. There's *some* water, but not much."

"Hmmm," I said as I raised my index finger to my lips.

"Just the two of us, or will there be more people?" I asked.

"There will probably be a *lot* of people," he responded.

His focus on driving and having both hands on the steering wheel caused me to focus more on his flexing biceps that I probably should have. Regardless of how much time I had to admire him, not staring at his bulging muscles was extremely difficult. As I studied the tattoos on his forearms admiringly, he turned a sharp corner, causing me to look out at the road.

"Where are we?" I asked as I looked around the unfamiliar neighborhood.

Several parks and a small river lined the streets on either side of the car.

"Almost there," he said as he down shifted the car into a lower gear.

As he slowed the car to an almost stop and turned into a parking area, I glanced around, trying to determine where we were. Although I had grown up in Wichita, so much had changed since I'd spent any time in the inner city that nothing seemed familiar anymore.

"What is this place?" I asked excitedly.

He pointed out the window to a large wooden sign.

Botanica.

"Botanica? The flower garden?" I said under my breath.

"It's more than a flower garden, Sam. Website said they've got fountains, paths, A Shakespeare garden, a rose and wildflower garden, a Chinese garden, butterfly garden - hell I don't even remember how many they have. Ten acres worth," he said as he shut off the car.

I stared out the window at the entrance. I would have never guessed he would take me to such a place, so it was in fact a huge surprise. As

I sat and admired what I could see through the window of the car, he reached over and touched my shoulder.

"I always loved your mother's back yard, and I know you did too. I thought this would be just like it, only a lot bigger. It'll be more enjoyable if you get out," he chuckled.

"I love you," I sighed as I turned to face him.

"Love you too, Sam," he said as he reached for the door handle.

We walked toward the entrance hand in hand, and as we entered the park, my breath was taken away by the sheer beauty of the landscape. A central fountain surrounded by various flowers, shrubs, and a walkway looked like something out of a fairytale, and it was only the entrance to the garden. As he paid for our tickets, I eagerly scanned the landscape for more to see.

"This is beautiful," I sighed as I gazed at the fountain.

As we walked past the fountain and into the park, I gazed at the beautiful flowers, shrubs and trees in an almost trance-like state. Although there were people everywhere, it didn't seem at all overcrowded. The aroma of the surrounding flowers created an almost sensory overload as I attempted to identify all of the individual flowers creating the beautiful scent.

I closed my eyes and inhaled slowly through my nose.

Roses. Honeysuckle.

Gardenias.

Uhhh, Uhhm.

Garden Phlox.

I opened my eyes to a beautiful display of purple Garden Phlox.

"I love this place," I said as I squeezed his hand in mine.

He shifted his eyes from the garden ahead, "Beautiful, isn't it?"

I nodded my head as we walked under an ornamental concrete structure marking the entrance to another area of the garden.

The sound of running water made the entire area seem more peaceful than it already was. After searching along the landscape, I noticed a stone-filled creek beside the walking path with water flowing through it freely. On the side of the path as we curved to the left, a large pool of water with beautiful coy fish playfully swimming about caught my attention.

I pointed to the pool as we passed, incapable of saying anything to describe the beauty of it all.

Two breathless gardens later, and I stood in the center of a rest area with my eyes closed, once again attempting to identify the aroma of a particular flower which had commanded my attention. As I inhaled another slow shallow breath through my nose, Otis' hands on my cheeks caused me to open my eyes.

"I love you, Sam," he said as he leaned down and kissed me lightly.

"I love this place, and I love you too," I sighed.

"Have you enjoyed it?" he asked.

I wrinkled my brow and narrowed my eyes, "Enjoyed it? That's a stupid question. Yes *Otis*, I've *enjoyed* it."

"Good," he said as he glanced over each shoulder somewhat nervously.

"You know what would make it better?" he asked as he turned to face me.

I shrugged my shoulders, "I dunno."

"I want to fuck the shit out of you. Right here," he said as he pointed to the side of the path.

I glanced to where he pointed and stared. The side of the path was lined with flowers, and behind them a more elevated row of shrubbery, and behind it, another row of various flowers. The entire height of the uppermost obstruction was maybe four feet high. People passing by could undoubtedly see us if they simply peered to the side of the path and over the flowers.

"You're crazy, not *here*," I sighed.

"Why? It's beautiful," he shrugged as he glanced around us.

"It is," I said as I stepped to the side, allowing a person walk past.

I tossed my head toward the woman who had just passed and widened my eyes, "See? There are too many people, and it's not even dark yet."

He glanced to the side of the path, turned around and peered around the corner of the display behind him, and reached down and gripped the top of an ornamental concrete bench at his side. As he grunted and pulled against the bench, slowly it began to rise from the concrete slab below it.

"Mother…fucker…this is heavy…as…fuck," he grunted as he lifted the bench.

What the fuck?

I watched in amazement as he carried what was probably a four hundred pound bench to the side of the flowers behind me, setting it on the grass beyond the four feet high row of flowers lining the path. As he walked around the end of the path to where he was standing before I stood with my mouth agape.

"There," he said as he wiped his hands on the thighs of his jeans.

"Now we got us a little place," he grinned.

"People can see us. Like *see* us. *No*," I huffed.

He glanced over his shoulders, turned around, and sighed. Before I had a chance to do or say much of anything, he slid one arm behind my thighs, the other over my shoulders, picked me up from my feet, and held me in his arms.

"Otis," I said through my teeth as I peered over my shoulder and along the path.

He promptly walked around the entrance, to the bench he had placed on the grass, and plopped me down on the bench.

"Lay down flat, and they won't see you," he said as he pointed toward the shrubbery behind us.

I glanced to the side, and although I was able to see the concrete structure, I couldn't see the pathway hidden by the shrubs and flowers.

"If people walk by, they'll see us," I whispered.

As he shook his head from side-to-side, he reached under my dress and grabbed the waist of my panties. Somewhat reluctantly, I lowered my shoulders to the bench and hoisted my ass from the concrete, allowing him to freely pull the panties off.

"Put your feet up on the bench and spread your knees apart," he said in an almost demanding tone.

"I'm not going to show the entire park my twat, Otis," I snapped back as I clenched my knees together.

He pressed his hands down in between my thighs and spread my legs against what little resistance I was able to provide.

"The park isn't going to see your twat, Sam. They'll see the back of my head buried in your twat. *Now spread your legs*," he growled.

"Oh dear God," I sighed as I eagerly flopped my legs to the side.

There weren't enough people in the entire world to keep me from letting Otis lick my pussy; even if we were in public. It was one of the many things he did *extremely* well. As I closed my eyes and gripped the sides of the concrete bench in my hands, I heard a couple walk past us, talking as they enjoyed the beautiful view of the flowers along the path.

As I felt the sides of his head between my thighs, I inhaled a shallow breath in anticipation of what was certain to come. As his tongue slowly licked from the bottom of my pussy to the top, I exhaled sharply.

His tongue began flicking against my clit, sending me into a frenzy of flinching with each touch of the tip of his tongue against my swollen nub. I sank my teeth into my lower lip, hopefully preventing me from howling out a moan of pleasure into the busy park.

I raised my shoulders from the bench, resting on my elbows as his finger began to slide in and out of my wetness. As he continued to lick my pussy and nibble my clit with his soft lips, I stared down between my legs in shock.

This was only the beginning.

And as long as we didn't get caught, it was certain to be a long and very pleasurable night.

SAM

"The next time you try and squirm away from me, I'm going to slap that ass of yours so hard the entire park comes over here," he said between his teeth in a harsh tone.

He'd been fucking me from behind while I was bent over the park bench with my dress around my neck. My bra and panties were beside the bench in the grass, and the cold concrete against my bare boobs reminded me of when he used to fuck me in my mother's back yard, adding to the sensuality of it all. Allowing Otis to fuck me however he wanted was a specialty of mine, but being quiet and holding still weren't necessarily my forte.

As the sound of his hips pounding against my ass rang throughout the entrance of the Shakespeare Garden, I bit into my lower lip so hard it began to bleed. I gripped the edges of the bench and lifted my chest from the bench, along my nipples to barely graze against the edge of the cold concrete.

The consistent sound of not so distant voices kept my level of excitement elevated and provided an assurance my pussy wasn't going to dry up anytime soon.

My eyes naturally rolled back into my head as my overly sensitive nipples danced along the top of the concrete bench. The sensation was almost too much for me to bear. Although my pussy wasn't ready for his thick cock a few weeks before, the excitement of him fucking me in the park combined with actually seeing people walk past as we did so caused my pussy to become a wet and very willing receptacle for his swollen rod.

As his balls slapped against my clit for the thousandth time, I released my lip and groaned into the late evening air. One more thrust, and I made a feeble attempt to escape as his cock pounded deep into me, pressing my thighs into the end of the bench.

"What the fuck did I tell you?" he growled.

"Still," I heaved.

"Stay…"

"Still…"

He bent over, forcing his chest into my back and pressing me against the cool concrete slab. As he ground his face into the side of mine, he breathed into my ear.

"And fucking quiet," he whispered.

The warm air that escaped from his lips caused me to shudder. As goosebumps rose along my left arm, he lifted his chest from my back and slapped my ass with the palm of his hand. As I felt his cock slide from my ever so wanting pussy, I gasped as I turned around.

"Don't stop, I'm sorry, I'll be good," I begged.

I watched in utter horror as he pulled his jeans up and over his still stiff cock. As he buckled his belt and narrowed his eyes, I stood and sadly pulled down my dress. He pressed his hands into his hips glared at me for a few seconds and eventually crossed his arms and sighed loudly.

"Don't fucking move, Sam. Sit right there, out of fucking sight," he demanded as he turned away.

"But…" I began.

216

He stopped and glanced over his shoulder.

"Don't. Fucking. Move."

In what was no more than a matter of seconds, but seemed to be an eternity, I sat nervously - hidden by the shrubbery - and waited as I heard a hint of his voice as he was talking to someone. Although he wasn't within my range of vision, he didn't sound like he was very far away. Another male voice I didn't recognize appeared to be talking to him. After a few seconds, the voices became closer, clear, and more distinct. As Otis came around the corner of the entrance another much younger man followed. Shocked, I stood from my seat.

"Sit the fuck down," Otis demanded.

"Dude..." the other man said as we made eye contact.

Before he had a chance to continue, Otis interrupted him, "Just shut the fuck up for a minute, before I slap the shit out of you."

The man, who appeared to be a hipster in his early twenties, stood immediately behind Otis, attempting to peer over his shoulder. As Otis stepped to the side, the tall, thin, bearded youngster stood in apparent shock staring at me.

"She's my girlfriend, there's nothing funny going on, other than we're a couple of sexual weirdos. All you're going to do is hold her down," Otis explained.

"Otis!" I hissed in a loud whisper.

He crossed his arms and sighed harshly as he shook his head, "I'm not going to warn you again, Sam."

As I gazed beyond him and focused on the tall thin man, the thought of him holding me down while Otis fucked me caused me to writhe where I stood in anticipated pleasure. If anyone could pull it off, Otis could.

"Dude, I'm not..." the thin hipster began.

Otis turned to face him.

"Name's not Dude, it's Otis. Do I look like a guy you want to argue with?" Otis asked as he flexed his biceps and flared his chest.

The thin man shook his head, "Uhhm, no. No, you sure don't."

"Look at it this way. It'll give you something to tell your buddies about," Otis paused and turned to face me.

"Pull your dress up and bend over, Sam. Just like you were a minute ago," Otis sighed as he reached for his belt.

"But I had my dress up on my..." I began to explain.

He released his belt and glared at me as if I were frustrating him to no end, "Just. Like. You. Were."

I turned around and pulled my dress to my shoulders, exposing my entire naked backside to the stranger. Instantly, my pussy began to tingle. The sensation was an entirely new one, and brought a level of pleasure to my mind that was incapable of compare. For the sole purpose of entertainment, I slid my hand between my legs and rubbed my two middle fingers along the length of my dripping wet pussy.

Half bent over, I turned to the side, exposing my breasts to the stranger. As he gawked in obvious pleasure, I shifted my eyes to his crotch and held my gaze. As the seconds quickly passed, his bulge became more apparent.

"Look babe. My pussy's a mess," I said as I raised my soaked hand, hoping to excite the stranger even more.

"Go over there and hold her shoulders down," Otis demanded as he pointed to the far end of the bench from where he stood.

Still standing a few feet behind Otis, the man began with his best effort to talk his way out of the awkward situation, "I uhhm, I really don't think she needs me to do…"

"Tell you what. What's your name again?" Otis growled.

"Alan," the man answered.

Peering over my shoulder, I was enjoying the show in its entirety. Now standing with a full-fledged hard-on, Alan was obviously uncomfortable. The entire situation to me was nothing short of insanity, but with Otis involved, nothing was out of the realm of possibilities. As my swollen pussy continued to send shock waves up and down my torso, I waited for Otis to respond.

"Tell you what, Alan. You either go grab her by the shoulders and hold her down on that bench or I'm going to just knock your skinny little ass out right now. How's that sound?" Otis said flatly.

"Sounds like I'm going to hold her down," he said as he pressed the heel of his palm against his crotch.

As Alan walked in front of me, I straightened my stance slightly, showing him a full view of my perky boobs. As his eyes locked on my chest, I slowly reached for them, fully suspecting Otis to tell me to stop.

Well, until you say something…

I grasped my boobs in my hands and began to squeeze them and pinch my nipples as Alan stood and stared. As I heard the clanking sound of Otis' belt buckle, I turned and glanced over my shoulder. His pants now around his thighs, it was pretty apparent he was as excited as I was. His stiff cock stood at attention, pointing up at the sky at a forty-five degree angle. As I watched it twitch, I released my right boob, stood more erect, and stuck my first two fingers into my pussy.

"Turn around, you horny little bitch," Otis demanded.

I turned away from Otis, and while still standing half erect, pulled my fingers from my pussy and slid them into my mouth while Alan watched in absolute shock.

"Now, Alan, you do what I tell you to, and nothing more. You understand?" Otis asked from behind me.

"Uhhm yeah. Sure," Alan nodded nervously.

"You'll be fine," I whispered.

"Bend over Sam," Otis sighed.

I bent over the bench and pressed my tits onto the now very cool concrete. It wasn't quite dark outside, but it was getting closer and closer with each passing minute. The sun had already set, and although there wasn't any need for additional lighting to see, it was clearly almost dusk.

As Otis spread my ass cheeks and slid his fat cock into my sopping wet pussy, I gripped the edges of the concrete slab beneath me.

"Grab her shoulders and hold her down," Otis demanded.

Alan placed his hands against my shoulders lightly. The mere touch of his hands against my skin while Otis fucked me was enough to send me over the edge, but I wanted more. The thought of him holding me against my will was even more exciting. To test my theory, I raised my chest from the bench and began to turn my shoulders toward Otis.

"God damn it," Otis bellowed as he released one of his hands from my hips.

"*Hold her down!*" he shouted.

Alan's hands pressed against my shoulders. I resisted considerably, and he pressed harder – forcing my breasts flat against the bench. As Otis continued to pound himself into me, I glanced up at Alan's stiff cock and stared. I didn't want Alan to play a part in what we doing from a *sexual* standpoint, but knowing he was just some stranger - and that he was not only watching Otis fuck me - but participating in it…

My tingling pussy stuffed full of Otis' swollen dick, his hips slapping a rhythmic beat against my ass, the lingering aroma of the flowers, being fucked in public, and Alan's hands against my shoulders were simply too much. My entire body began to tingle, from my ever-so-dripping pussy to my nipples and back, I trembled like I had been left naked in a snow drift.

My pussy began to clench around Otis' cock. I bit into my lip, and after a few seconds, began to release an orgasm from the absolute depth of whatever hell the big one's come from. I released my lip and moaned like a wolf howling at the moon.

"You noisy little bitch. Let her go, Alan," Otis hollered.

"Turn around Sam," Otis demanded.

Oh well, fuck it.

As Alan released my shoulders, I stood from the bench, pulled my dress from my shoulders, and tossed it into the grass beside the bench. As a few distant voices added to the excitement of it all, I waited for my instructions.

"Knees," Otis sighed as he pointed at the ground in front of him.

I lowered myself to the ground and began to squeeze my tits in my hands.

"Grab her head and force her to suck my cock," Otis bellowed.

Fuck yes. I love it.

"I uhhm, I..." Alan stammered.

"Grab her fucking head and shove my cock down her throat," Otis growled as he stood in front of me stroking his shiny stiff cock.

As I felt Alan's hands against the back of my head, I resisted, pushing with all my might against him. This, over and above all, excited me greatly. The thought of a stranger making me suck Otis cock was beyond sensual. A word to describe what I felt in anticipation of what was going to happen hadn't even been invented yet.

As Alan's hands pressed against the back of my head, I glanced upward toward Otis. He gazed down at me, grinned, and interlocked his fingers. I opened my mouth further as he raised his arms and positioned his hands behind his head, arching his back as he did so. Still wanting to resist, but with his twitching cock now forced into my face, I leaned forward slightly. I desperately wanted Otis' cock in my mouth. As he pushed forward, forcing the tip past my lips, I eagerly accepted it into my wet mouth. To make the situation work out to both Otis' and my advantage, I pushed myself, swallowing almost every inch of his length, held it for a few seconds, and pulled my head rearward quickly, falsely gasping for air as I did so.

As soon as my mouth released the tip of his cock, I glanced upward, knowing full well he'd take care of Alan.

"God damn you, Alan. Make her deep throat my cock. You fuck this up, and I'll beat you senseless," Otis barked.

Voices along the path became more and more distinct. As they became close enough to understand what they were saying, Alan's hand grabbed my hair and began forcing me onto Otis cock like a jackhammer.

Truly gagging and coughing slobber from my mouth as Alan shoved my throat full of cock, my eyes began to water. As slobber dripped from my mouth and along the shaft of Otis' dick, I reached up and cupped his soaked balls in my hand.

As I rubbed and played with his slippery balls, I closed my eyes and became lost in the smell, sounds of voices, and Alan's incessant slamming of my head onto Otis' cock. With his cock deep in my throat, I felt as if I was going to either puke or die from lack of oxygen. I released his balls and slapped my hands against his thighs, hoping for a little relief.

As I prepared to pass out, Otis pulled his cock from my mouth. I gasped for air and opened my eyes at the same time Otis barked out his final order.

"Hold her head still," he grunted as he stroked his fat cock.

Within a matter of seconds, much to my complete satisfaction, Otis began to cum all over my face, tits, stomach, and mouth. As the warm cum droplets landed against my face, I reached for my pussy, moaning with pleasure. When he finally stopped ejaculating and stood still, I moaned a moan of newfound pleasure. With my fingers knuckle deep in my pussy, I extended my tongue and licked what cum from my face I was able to reach.

"Thanks for your help," Otis chuckled.

"Sorry about the threats. It just kind of added to the excitement," Otis explained as he pulled his pants up.

I stood and took the few steps to my dress. After picking it up from the grass, I turned the inside of it outward and wiped the cum from my face. As Alan quietly walked away shaking his head, I got dressed and turned toward Otis.

"Enjoy yourself?" he asked, smiling from ear to ear.

"Best fucking date ever," I grinned.

He nodded his head as he buckled his belt, "Feel the same way."

And, as fucked up as most people would see it, and as few would believe it if ever told the story, the sexual adventures of our night were absolutely perfect.

And I couldn't wait to see what Otis dreamed up for our next date.

OTIS

The exposure of Gunner as an ATF agent left me feeling as if the club needed to remain as it was from a membership standpoint, and never add anyone else. Knowing that was not only impossible, but certainly not in the club's interest, I tried to wrap my mind around a better process of accepting prospects into the club.

Cash had prospected for a year, and although I vouched for him to be accepted as a prospect, adding him to the ranks of Sinners seemed risky and potentially threatening. For the last year, I had supported Cash, his foolish behavior, and his childish antics. His constant discussions with outsiders regarding club business - often bragging about what was done and who was involved - had caused several meetings to be held between Axton and me regarding a means of forcing him to adhere to the code of silence.

His patch in party was being held, and for lack of a better place to have a pig roast, the club voted to have the party at Cash's home in the country and not at Tater's farm as usual. The home Cash lived in had several acres of grass behind the home, and no farm animals. Tater's home was an actual farm, and had livestock close to the home, making the smell of livestock – especially his pigs – a part of the party.

Mentally struggling with adding *anyone* to the club, I dismissed my thoughts as nervous inconsistencies based on Gunner's not having refused to testify to the Federal Grand Jury yet. His lack of adhering to his end of the agreement had me on edge and worried about the potential incarceration of not only me, but of every member of the club. As I sat on my bike contemplating what to do regarding Gunner, Sam walked out of the house and onto the porch.

Dressed in jeans, Converse sneakers, and a short sleeved button down Harley-Davidson shirt, she looked adorable as she twisted her hair into a ponytail.

"Ready," she hollered as she released her ponytail.

"Well get on," I sighed sarcastically as I pressed the *start* button.

After she was secure on the back of the bike and had her glasses on, I sped out of the driveway and down the winding road that led from her neighborhood. The ride from Wichita to Winfield typically took forty minutes, and although I had no real recollection of the trip from her mother's house to Cash's, our arrival at 7:00 indicated I had made the trip in a little less than thirty minutes.

Bikes were parked in front of the garage, beside the driveway on both sides, and throughout the entire front yard. Counting them would have been impossible, but an educated guess would have been close to sixty motorcycles and several cages. As I slowly rolled into the driveway, cautious of the bikes parked on either side, I was a little embarrassed of my late arrival and the way I was feeling about adding Cash to the club.

"There's a lot of people here. Wow," Sam said as we came to a stop in the drive.

As I positioned the bike beside one I didn't recognize, I began once again to feel uneasy about the event. Being nervous about *anything* wasn't typical for me, and considering everything about the night was making me feel ill, my soul searching for what was in the club's best interest simply made matters worse.

"Well, let's go back there and mingle," I said as I swung the kickstand into place.

"Are we late?" she asked as she stepped off the back of the bike.

"Kind of," I sighed as I locked the ignition of the bike.

"Should have got here at 6:00 with everyone else, patch in's at 7:00," I said flatly.

"You didn't get to my house until 6:30. That's what time you said to be ready," she shrugged.

"I know, Sam. I *know*. I'm not feeling this," I sighed as we slowly walked up the drive.

"What's wrong?" she asked.

I glanced over my shoulder and studied her as we walked. I loved her dearly, and the thought of losing her again was incomprehensible. My position on life, the club, being in a relationship, and being in love had changed in the last month and I felt I needed to do whatever was within my power to preserve the things I loved and held sacred. Keeping the club from harm was my top priority, and doing so also kept Sam and me safe and in a solid relationship.

I shrugged my shoulders, "Nothing's wrong. There's going to be a hundred or so people back here. It might be a little overwhelming. I'll apologize in advance, but I'm going to be tied up with the fellas until the patch in is over. Just mingle with Syd and Avery for a bit, okay?" I said.

She smiled and nodded her head, "Okay."

As we came around the back side of the house, it was clear the party was well underway. The sheer size of the crowd was staggering. The music blaring the unmistakable beats of the *Black Keys*, kegs of beer in trash cans scattered about, several long tables surrounded by folding chairs - mostly occupied by Ol' Ladies - and more cuts than I could count wandering about added to my level of frustration.

"God damn, the VP made it," Axton hollered over his shoulder from the circle of men surrounding him.

Several of the Ol' Ladies, including Sydney, Avery - and to my surprise - Biscuit's newfound playmate Kat, were gathered at the corner of the garage.

"Sam!" Sydney shouted from behind us.

Sam glanced in my direction and held her gaze as she waited for my instructions on what she should do.

"Just go have fun. I'll be a while with this deal. I'll find you in a bit, okay?" I shrugged.

"Love you," she said with a smile.

"Same, Sam. Love you too," I said as I leaned over and kissed her lightly.

"Oh wow. I didn't know we could kiss at these things," she chuckled.

I rolled my eyes and tossed my head toward the girls, "Go."

I turned around and walked toward Axton, who was surrounded by Biscuit, Toad, and a few other men who were wearing cuts that I didn't immediately recognize. As I approached, Axton stepped back and opened his arms.

"Better late than not at all," he said as he slapped his hand against my back.

"Knock you off a piece of ass in the produce aisle at the grocery store?" Biscuit chuckled as he wrapped his arms around me.

I slapped my hand against his back and shook my head, "No, just running late, brother."

As I hugged Toad, he whispered into my ear, "Everything alright, brother?"

I broke the hug and nodded my head, "I'm good."

But I wasn't.

"Otis, need you to meet a few fellas from the *Fire and Iron MC*. Big fucker here's Doc. Doc, this is our VP, Otis," Axton said as he pointed to a man wearing a cut who stood beside him.

Barely an inch or so shorter than me, and covered in tattoos to one wrist and to his elbow on the other arm, the man had a certain presence to him that supported his *I don't take shit from anyone* posture. As he stood stone-faced and shook my hand, I studied his cut.

President.

"He's the president of the Wichita chapter of the MC we rode down to Texas about. And this fella here could give Biscuit a run for his money on telling stories. Teddy, this is Otis," Axton said as he tilted his head toward a barrel-chested monster of a man with a full beard and black curly hair.

"Pleasure to meet ya," Teddy said as he extended his hand.

His hand engulfed mine as he shook my hand in his. I glanced down, shocked at the size of his hands. As he released my grip, I made note of his sausage-sized fingers and huge hands. My guess, based on the condition of his knuckles, was that he was the club brawler.

"Likewise," I grinned.

"We was just talkin' about that fuckin' A-Train gettin' your Sergeant-At-Arms shot. Gotta keep your eye on that God damned A-Train, he's a hot-head," Teddy chuckled.

"Seemed like a pretty solid fella," I responded.

"Oh he's solid as fourteen motherfuckers, but he's a hot-head. We had to ship his ass down to Texas just to keep him from killin' everybody that pissed him off. I'm just glad ol' Toad here ain't pushin' up daisies," he chuckled as he wrapped his arm around Toad's shoulder.

"Toad's a tough fucker, and a little of a hot-head himself," I chuckled as I slapped Toad's bicep with the back of my hand.

"Fuckin' Marines," Teddy sighed.

"So, are the fellas from Texas going to make it?" I asked.

Doc shook his head from side-to-side, "The entire state was flooded a week ago from all of the rain they got. Hell, Obama declared it a Federal emergency. Our Texas chapter assembled and is doing work for charity. The boxer's donating a bunch of money and all of their time to help clean up the mess, so they won't be here."

I pressed my hands into my hips and sighed, remembering the news segment on the flooding, "Yeah, I heard about that. Fucking highways were under water."

"Well, I hate to break up this little party, but we've got to get this kid patched in. It'll just take fifteen minutes or so, then we'll all get back together and solve the world's problems. Sound good?" Axton asked.

"Nice seein' ya again, Slice," Teddy said.

"Slice," Doc nodded.

Axton shook Doc's hand and turned around to face me.

"You straight," Axton asked.

I nodded my head, "Just worried about the club."

He shrugged his shoulders, "Anything serious?"

I shook my head, "Nothing you aren't aware of."

I knew Axton had very little use for Cash. Although the bylaws required a vote by all members in the club to allow Cash to be patched in, I'd never seen anyone denied their patch after prospecting, and I didn't suspect Cash would be any different in Axton's eyes than any of the other half-assed members we'd allowed into the club in the past, Gunner included.

"Well, let me get this microphone and make an announcement," Axton said.

I raised my hands to my temples and nodded my head as I began to rub my fingers against the sides of my head. Axton walked to where the speakers were positioned behind the house. Between the speakers, an amplifier, stereo equipment, and a microphone sat on top of a table. As I made eye contact with Sam, I tossed my head toward Axton and raised my right index finger to my lips.

She nodded her head in acknowledgement.

"Listen up!" Axton's voice blared over the sound system.

"I need complete silence, people," he said as he raised his free hand in the air.

After a half-minute wait, the sound from the large crowd was down to a dull roar.

"I appreciate everyone coming to celebrate a prospect being patched into our club," Axton said into the microphone.

"Cash had been a hang around with the club for about six months before becoming a prospect, and although it's been a rough twelve months for all of us, his year of prospecting is finally over…"

Miscellaneous whoops, shouts, and amen's came from the crowd as Axton paused.

"So we're here to witness this event, and watch him ride a moped around the fucking yard while he wears a shock collar around his skinny little neck," Axton chuckled as he raised the remote control for the shock collar into the air.

Again, Axton paused, allowing several shouts from the crowd to be heard by everyone.

"So, without further ado, we'll get back to it. Todd Parker, known by the club as Cash, has fulfilled his requirement of prospecting for twelve months. All patched in Selected Sinners in favor of his advancement into the club and acceptance as a fully patched member respond in the form of *aye*," Axton said into the microphone.

The crowd erupted into a universal "Aye."

Axton nodded his head.

"Requires a one hundred percent vote to be a Sinner, any opposed respond in the form of nay," he shouted.

I glanced around the crowd.

Silence.

As Axton lifted the microphone to his mouth, I fixed my eyes on Sam, sighed, and raised my hand.

"Nay," the word barely escaped my mouth.

"Well, it appears…" Axton began, clearly not having heard me.

"Nay!" I shouted.

Axton lowered the microphone and shifted his eyes to meet mine.

"Do I have one opposed?" Axton asked.

I nodded my head, "Yes you do. My vote is *nay*," I said.

Cash, standing twenty or so feet from me with his arms folded in front of his chest, dropped his hands to his sides as his eyes widened.

"Is this a joke?" he hollered.

I shook my head.

"Are you fucking kidding?" he shouted.

I glanced at Sam, shifted my eyes toward Cash, and shook my head again.

As he walked my direction, he began to express his displeasure of my vote.

"I've been living in hell for twelve fucking months for this. I washed bikes. I got cigarettes. I cleaned the shop. I got in fucking fights with people I don't even know for no reason other than a patch told me to. This is fucking bullshit, and I say your vote doesn't count, Otis. I've…"

I shifted my feet to the side slightly and widened my stance. As he continued to approach me, I raised my hands in front of my chest and clenched my fists.

"You see, that's the problem. You have no respect, no tact, and no regard for authority or anyone who's your senior. Keep walking this direction all puffed up like that and I'll knock your little ass out," I growled.

He slowed his walk, but continued to advance in my direction slowly.

"I'm not fucking around, little man," I said through my teeth.

As he continued to walk my direction, Axton dropped the microphone and began to walk in his direction, more than likely to intercept him before he got hurt.

With Toad and Biscuit standing slightly behind me telling me to *take it easy*, Cash continued to nonchalantly walk closer and closer, his chest thrust forward and his shoulders rolled back as if he was prepared to fight.

"You're a cocksucking prick," he said as he stepped almost close enough for me to punch.

"Don't take another step, Cash," I seethed.

"And…" he said as he took the last step separating us.

I swiveled my hips and swung a right uppercut into his jaw. No differently than I would have guessed, the punch lifted him from his feet, and sent him into a pile of motionless flesh a few feet behind where he was standing. As he was now clearly unconscious, and in no need of more, I took a step back and sighed as I rubbed my knuckles.

"Didn't see that coming," Axton said.

"Neither did he," I responded.

"No, the vote in opposition; good looking out," he said through his teeth as he lifted Cash's shoulders from the ground.

Sam, now standing behind Axton as he raised Cash to his feet, stood with wide eyes and a worried face, "Are you okay?"

"I'm fine. Guess the party's over," I shrugged.

Although I felt my vote against Cash's acceptance into the club was in my - and the Sinners - best interest, it didn't make me feel any better. Having Cash disrespect me afterward by calling me a cocksucker wasn't *totally* unexpected, but I didn't anticipate it either. Now feeling like I'd ruined a long awaited party, I stared down at the toes of my boots and wondered what the remainder of the night would bring.

I watched as Axton helped Cash into the back door of the house, followed by Cash's wife. After they disappeared into the house, Axton emerged and walked our direction. As soon as it was clear he was coming to where we stood, I fixed my eyes on Sam and tilted my head to the side.

"Go back over with Syd and Avery for a bit, Sam. I'll come over there here in a few, okay?" I sighed.

Sam was no stranger to seeing me fight. In her presence over the years we were together, she had seen me in no less than a dozen fights, maybe more. Without so much as an ounce of argument, she slowly turned around and walked away.

"God damn, Otis. So was that why you were late? Pondering your decision?" Axton asked as he stepped in front of us.

"No, just wasn't looking forward to saying it, I guess. Hell, I knew all along – or at least for the last few months anyway – that I didn't like his arrogance and attitude, but the deal with Gunner sealed it for me," I shrugged, "We don't need anybody in this club that isn't a hundred percent."

Axton pursed his lips and studied me for a moment. "Agreed," he breathed.

"Otis, help!" a voice screamed from my left.

I spun toward the voice. Cash's wife Karen stood on the back porch waving her arms and blubbering.

"Help, he's…" she shouted as she pointed toward the door.

I began swiftly walking toward the house as Axton, Toad and Biscuit followed. Upon reaching Karen, her blubbering, crying and waving her arms did little to let us know what was going on. After pulling the door open and pointing inside, she covered her face with her hands.

After an audible sigh, she pulled her hands away from her face and exposed her quivering lip.

"In…the…kitchen," she sobbed.

"He's got…a…gun," she muttered.

I glanced at Axton, uncertain of whether or not to proceed. As Axton took a deep breath, Toad shoved me to the side, pushed his way past Axton, and stepped into the house. As he quickly disappeared to my left, I yanked the door to the side and ran inside the house.

"God damn it Toad, no!" I shouted, knowing he wouldn't hesitate to try and take the weapon from Cash.

Toad couldn't stand to be shot again, and although I was sure he knew it, his pride and eagerness to resolve problems wouldn't prevent him from exposing himself to harm. As I followed immediately behind

Toad, Axton and Biscuit were right behind me.

As soon as I stepped into the kitchen, Toad stopped in his tracks and held his hand to his side, instructing me to stop.

Cash stood in the center of the kitchen, holding a pistol in his hand, and pointing it at his temple.

"Ain't got nothing to say to you, Toad. I want to talk to Otis," Cash said in a surprisingly calm voice.

"Put the gun down, Cash," Axton said as he stepped beside me.

Cash chuckled and shook his head, "Sorry *Slice*. Don't want to talk to you, either."

"Why?' he said as he turned my direction.

I shrugged my shoulders, not knowing exactly what to say, considering all things.

"You had to have a reason," he shrugged.

I nodded my head and swallowed the lump that was quickly rising in my throat.

Still holding the pistol to his temple, he widened his eyes, "What was it?"

"You weren't ready. Put the gun down and we'll discuss it," I said under my breath as I raised both my hand into the air, hoping to comfort him that I wasn't trying to be a threat.

He shook his head, "Not ready? The year just wasn't enough for *you*, huh?"

"That's not it. Hell, Cash, this is just proof. Hell, you're in the kitchen threatening suicide. How stable does that make you?" I asked.

"Cash please," his wife wept from behind me.

His eyes widened as he tilted his head slightly to the side and fixed his gaze on me.

"Not very," he sighed.

The repercussion from the weapon firing exploded into the room. The deafening sound, dulled slightly from the bodies surrounding him, pushed painfully into my ears. As the acrid taste of cordite filled the air, Karen screamed, and Cash fell to the floor.

"Oh my God, no! Call an ambulance," she screamed.

I clenched my jaw muscles and turned my head toward the doorway behind me.

No need for an ambulance.

He was dead before he hit the floor.

SAM

Cash's suicide at the party had hit me pretty hard. The local police interviewing Otis, Axton, and the rest of the people who were in the house made me feel extremely uneasy. Although I hadn't second guessed my decision to be in a relationship with Otis, two suicides, a random shooting, and a bank robbery over the course of six months caused me to wonder just what the future might bring.

Otis didn't seem to be too troubled by the suicide. I realized we all deal with death and loss in a different manner, but he seemed to be more concerned with the welfare of Cash's wife than the fact Cash had committed suicide.

He went on to explain how he felt no guilt whatsoever regarding the death, and that Cash shooting himself was further proof that his decision to oppose Cash's acceptance into to club was warranted. Cash's inability to handle the day-to-day pressures of being in the club, Otis made clear, was proven by committing suicide.

I didn't necessarily disagree with anything he had said. It didn't, however, make the entire thing any more acceptable to me as being just another day in the life of a Sinner's Ol' Lady. I stared into the back yard wishing for a normal life and far less drama.

Two cups of coffee into my morning and I felt half sick. I pushed my cup to the center of the table and held my hand a few inches over the top of the table and attempted to steady it. As I watched it shaking no differently than if I was a recovering crack addict, I wondered if something might be wrong with me, or if my nerves were continuing to get the best of me.

My otherwise drama free life of the last fourteen years had been filled with the death of my mother, a suicide, and my knowledge of the other than legitimate activities of an outlaw motorcycle club. On the upside, I guessed, I had reunited with the man I so dearly loved, enjoyed time with his parent's, and made friends with two women who I suspected would be friends for life. Hesitant to naturally accept the events of the last month as being part of *my* preferred way of living life, I found it much easier accepting them as being an extension of Otis' life, and therefore a part of my life with him.

As I sat there feeling significantly more satisfied about it than I had felt earlier in the morning, I stared at the cup of coffee, almost repulsed by the smell of it. After deciding I was on the verge of worrying myself sick again, I decided to dump the remaining coffee in the sink and make something to eat. The aroma of the warm coffee as I dumped it into the sink caused me to gag, and within a moment's time I was running to the bathroom.

I dropped to the knees, vomiting into the toilet and onto the floor as I attempted to position myself over the stool. Feeling as if something was undoubtedly wrong with my digestive system or my nerves, I proceeded to vomit the two cups of morning coffee I had just finished drinking. After being convinced I was done with the spectacle, I stood from the floor and cleaned my face in the sink. As I brushed my teeth, Taylor announced her concerns.

"Meow."

Still brushing my teeth, I turned to face her and shrugged my shoulders.

"Meow."

I rinsed my mouth and turned around.

"I know. I've got to get a handle on these nerves."

"Meow."

I stared blankly at her, still feeling queasy. As I studied her, my mind filled with many thoughts not all of which were on my list of preferred reasons for my recent bouts of sickness. I extended my shaking hand, thought of what day I had arrived in Kansas, and began to count weeks, days, and events on my fingers.

After counting and recounting, I bit my quivering lip and walked to the kitchen. After opening my purse and staring into it for a long moment, my head began to spin again.

This can't be.

I recounted the days on my fingers and stared down at the floor.

"Meow."

"Shhh, I'm thinking."

There's no way.

"Meow."

I clutched my purse in my hand and stumbled blindly toward the door. If my math was correct, I'd need to do something quickly and without anyone knowing about it.

Having Otis in my life was the best thing to ever happen to me.

And I wasn't about to chance losing him.

Not again.

OTIS

Axton looked up from his ledger and closed the cover. I had sat quietly as he finished reciting his account of the patch in party into the book. A creature of habit, and a methodical one at that, Axton kept track of all of the major highlights of his life as a Sinner, and did so in writing for future reference. More than ten years of activities, stories, events, and strange happenings were explained in detail in the many leather bound books, but only in a manner that made sense to Axton. Some might call him paranoid, others would describe him as cautious, and a select few believed he was nothing short of a genius.

Me?

He was just Axton, the president of the club.

"Kind of nice having Sam around again," he said as he slid the book to his side.

"Real nice," I responded.

"So, Avery says she's moving back?" he asked as he stood.

I widened my eyes in acknowledgement as I lifted the bottle of beer to my lips. After a long drink, I stood from my seat and turned to face the door.

"Yeah. Probably go help her get her shit loaded into a truck; might take the Toad and Biscuit with me. They don't know it yet," I said over my shoulder as I opened the office door.

"If you're getting another, be sure and leave that stinking motherfucker in the shop," Axton said as I walked into the hallway.

No shit.

I tossed the empty beer into the trash can and walked to the fridge. After pulled two more bottles from the shelf and opening one, I turned toward the hallway and lifted the bottle to my mouth. As I walked to the office, I took a slow drink of the cold beer and thought of my future with Sam, and just what it might include long term. Although she and I hadn't spoken about it, I suspected as soon as she returned we'd end up living together.

Something I hadn't given a moment's thought to in the last decade and a half, I now felt almost obligated to do so – allowing us to become as close to a conventional couple as I was able. Axton sat at the table reading from the ledger as I walked in, but closed the book and shoved it aside as I sat down.

"Everything in there that needs to be," I asked.

He nodded his head and patted his hand on the top of the book, "Looks like it. Just making sure I had everything. Everything alright?"

"Yep. Golden."

"Well, reason I'm asking is you're two-fisting the beers tonight and it's mid-fucking-week. Just wondering if everything in your world's good," he asked as he leaned forward and rested his elbows on the edge of the table.

"It's not your fault, you know," he sighed.

I rolled my eyes as the corner of my mouth curled into a smirk. "Oh shit, I'm not worried about *that*."

"Tell you what I told Sam. That fucker shooting himself provided support of my thoughts that he wasn't going to be able to *handle* being a Sinner. He was weak," I said as I tilted the neck of my beer bottle toward him.

"Don't disagree," he nodded.

I gazed down at my bottle of beer as I spoke, wondering if what I was going to say would make as much sense coming out of my mouth as it did rattling around in my head, "I think Gunner and the entire ATF thing might have made me a little more cautious about who we let in this club, Ax. It's *our* club you know. It's our fucking responsibility to keep it…well…you know what I mean. This place, this club, it's my family. And it isn't everyone that gets to pick who's in their family. The fact we get to should mean we've got nothing but a good solid bunch of brothers."

He leaned away from the table and crossed his arms.

"Two weeks ago, I would have bet folding money we had the best bunch of hand-picked fellas in existence. Now, I'm pretty sure we've got it whittled down to where it needs to be. And I've got to agree with you on Gunner, I'm still nervous about that."

I picked up my bottle of beer, took a slow drink, and gazed his direction as I let the bottle dangle from my thumb and forefinger.

His eyes widened slightly as he cleared his throat.

"So, something's eating at you. What's going on?" he asked.

"Do you love Avery?" I asked as I gazed down at the bottle dangling from my fingers.

He coughed a laugh and slapped his hand lightly against the table.

"What the fuck does that have to do with the price of rice in China?" he asked.

I lifted the bottle toward my lips, paused, and allowed it to dangle beside in front of my mouth.

"Come on, Ax. We ain't sitting here Slice and Otis. This is Steve and Axton from back in the day - the same two motherfuckers who used to walk to school together every day and have rock kicking contests on the way. Do you love her?" I asked over the top of the bottle.

"That's a good question. I ought to come back and ask you to define love, but…" he paused as he began to rock back and forth in his chair.

"I *do* love her. May not be in the same way you love you mother and father, but it's love, that's for sure. Hard for me to explain, brother," he sighed.

As I exhaled and leaned forward, he raised his index finger in the air to stop me from speaking.

"Here's the deal. I can't fucking imagine, no matter how hard I try – and believe me, I've tried – living life without her in it. This stays right here," he said as he pointed his finger back and forth between us.

"No shit?" I chuckled.

He clasped his hands behind his head and leaned back in his chair. As his mouth curled into the first smile I'd seen on his face in quite some time, he began to speak.

"Just making sure we were on the same page. But I'll tell ya, if that girl ever left me? Shit. Not only would I be done with women, I'm afraid I'd be done living life altogether. Just watching her walk around the house satisfies the absolute fuck out of me. I keep waiting for her to do *something* stupid, and the day never comes. She keeps me young, keeps me happy, and makes me think twice about most of the decisions I'd have never even thought about a year ago. It's love for sure, but it's hard to explain, brother. Hard to explain."

"Well, you just did a pretty good job of it. Makes sense to *me*, anyway. I never really talked about how *I* felt, except you know how I *used* to feel. Far as I can figure, I never fell out of love with Sam. You know, you and I been single for fucking *ever* until now. Most 1%ers have half a dozen bitches they're fucking. You and me? Shit, for the last ten years we ain't had one bitch on our arm. Been telling you and even telling myself I couldn't trust 'em. Well, being honest about it, I'd compared every bitch who even looked at me to Sam. Nobody measured up. And now? Come to find out she's been single for the last ten years or so, and she's felt the same way. It's like destiny or some shit," I shrugged.

He raised one eyebrow and forced a cough, "Destiny?"

I finished my beer, opened the second bottle and took a sip. I cupped my hands around the cold glass, hesitated, and then raised my cool hands to my cheeks.

"Yeah. Destiny," I grinned.

"You goofy son-of-a-bitch. You're in love like a fucking teenager. Look at you. God damn, never thought I'd see it," he chuckled as he leaned forward.

I lowered my hands from my cheeks, realized what I had done, and shrugged my shoulders.

"You know, about you two being apart for so long," he paused and raised his right hand to his chin.

As he rubbed his chin in his palm, he continued, "Being inseparable doesn't define true love. Being separated and having nothing change between you, however, does."

I nodded my head and thought for a long moment without responding. I truly liked what he had said, and I felt it applied to Sam and me without question.

"Hell, there's nothing wrong with being in love. The *right* woman will make a man a better person. *Finding* her is the tough part. In this case, you didn't have to *find* her. Nothing changed between you two and all you had to do was admit it," he said as he turned his palms upward.

"Something like that. I really wanted to make sure you were okay with everything, me being tied down with an Ol' Lady and all," I said under my breath.

He laughed out loud for a second and nodded his head.

"I'm fine with it, brother. Like I said, the right woman will make you better. For you, finding the right one would have been extra tough. It ain't every woman who'll let a man fuck her in in-school detention when there are three other kids in there," he said with a laugh.

I narrowed my gaze and wrinkled my nose slightly, "You remembered that?"

He shook his head as his eyes rolled back slightly, "Remember it? Hell Otis, for us normal motherfuckers, it's hard to forget shit like that. Yeah, I remembered it. Every kid in school probably does too. I'm guessing she's still that way?"

I thought of the night in the botanical gardens and began to laugh.

"Just between you and me?" I asked.

"In your own words, *no shit*," he laughed as he crossed his arms in front of his chest.

"Fucked her in Botanica the other night. Got some kid who was wandering around to come hold her down on a concrete bench while I fucked her," I said as I slapped the tips of my fingers against the table.

"You're fucking shittin' me?" he gasped.

I shook my head, "Nope."

"God damn, Otis. Just some fucking weirdo wandering through the fucking flower garden? You walk up to him and tell this poor fucker you need him to hold your Ol' Lady down so you can pork her? Jesus H

Christ," he chuckled.

"Kind of, yeah. Had to threaten him with an ass whippin' to get him to do it," I shrugged.

"God damn. Well, how'd it pan out? Did she like it?" he asked he shook his head in disbelief.

"Loved it. Hell, she can't quit talking about it," I responded.

"Well, there you go. Like I said, it's love. Fuck, you may be right brother, it's probably that fucking thing you call destiny," he said as he widened his eyes.

"Might be," I sighed as I stood from my seat.

"So what did we learn from all this?" he asked as he stood.

"Just wanting to let you know she's going to be around, and make sure you were alright with it all," I said as I lifted the bottle of beer to my mouth.

"And if I wasn't?" he asked.

I drank the remaining beer, reached for the other empty, and walked to the door. As I reached for the handle, I glanced over my shoulder.

"You probably don't want to know," I responded.

He crossed his arms and swallowed heavily.

"I think I already do," he nodded.

I opened the door and stepped into the hallway. As I tossed the bottles into the trash, the sound of Axton's distant voice filtered out into the shop.

"Tell her I said hello…"

Will do, Axton.

Will do.

SAM

Making life altering decisions without the assistance of or reassurance from others is difficult. Coping with the fallout of a tough decision is always easier if someone close to you helped you make it. The majority of my choices in adulthood were made while talking to my mother over the phone. No longer having that luxury forced me to look elsewhere for support, and luckily I didn't have to look far. Having Sydney and Avery as friends was something I was truly grateful for, and the time had come for me to test their ability to stand up with me in the most trying of times.

"Just let me finish before you guys start," I said through my shaking lower lip.

I felt surprisingly calm considering how I'd felt earlier. Feeling as if I was either far more comfortable with the decision that I expected myself to be, or I was simply in shock, I inhaled a shallow breath, clutched my purse, and exhaled.

"I'm pregnant, and…"

"Oh my God, congratulations!" Avery shouted.

"This is so exciting," Sydney said as she clapped her hands together, "Cambio and I have been talking and he was wanting to…"

I raised my right hand in the air to stop them from continuing, and began to sob. After what seemed like several minutes of sobbing, I wiped my face free of the tears and attempted to catch my breath.

"Sorry, I thought I was done crying," I muttered as I glanced up.

They both sat staring at me as if not knowing for sure what to say or why I was crying. It was obvious to me, and probably pretty obvious to them the tears were not tears of joy, but ugly tears.

"This conversation stays here," I said flatly.

Both women grinned and shrugged their shoulders.

"Okay?"

"Yeah. No problem," Sydney grinned.

"I'm waiting," Avery said as she turned her palms up.

"I'm just going to cut right to it," I sighed.

Talk fast, Sam. Just say it.

I bit the edge of my lower lip and spoke through my teeth, "I need to get an abortion."

As I expected, both women's eyes widened. Avery gasped no differently than if she'd witnessed a murder. Sydney covered her face with her hands and attempted to hide her feelings, but nothing could disguise them. Her face clearly said what her mouth did not.

"Why?" Avery asked under her breath, "An abortion?"

I nodded my head, "It's the only answer."

I clutched my purse and continued, "I don't know if you know it or not, but the entire reason we broke up before was over me wanting kids. He didn't. He enjoys the freedom of being *free*. I do too. It doesn't matter, if he finds out, he'll either kill me or leave me. I *know* Otis. I can't lose him. Not again."

"He doesn't know?" Avery hissed as she folded her arms in front of her chest and thrust herself into the rear of the booth.

I shook my head, "This isn't easy. It really…"

"Tell him," Avery demanded.

I pulled my purse to my chest and held it close, "I can't. You don't understand."

"You owe it to him," she snapped back.

I glanced at Sydney. With her face still contorted, clearly expressing horrific shock and sorrow, she attempted to cover it with her hands while she listened. I shifted my eyes toward Avery.

"I need...I need him in my...in my life. I can't live without...him. I love him," I said as I fought back tears.

"If you love him, tell him," she begged, "You might be surprised."

"*You* might be surprised. If he didn't kill me, he'd leave me for sure. He left me over the mere mention of kids. An actual child would send him running. Hell, you'd probably never see him again," I explained.

"You were what, twenty-one years old?" she asked.

I nodded my head as I continued to hug my purse.

"Sixteen years ago. People mature, things change. Tell him," she said as she leaned forward, resting her arms on the edge of the table.

"His mind hasn't changed. I assure you. I'm sorry, I don't want to argue. I just need support right now," I said under my breath.

Avery crossed her arms and settled against the back of the booth. I shifted my eyes to Sydney, who had finally uncovered her face and was wiping tears from her face.

"Uhhm, I could talk to...I was..." she muttered.

She shook her head and cleared her throat as she wiped her eyes against the heels of her palms.

"I think Cambio and I would be willing to adopt the baby. I'd have to talk to him, but let's just go with it's a yes, at least for now. I mean if you don't want it for sure," she murmured.

I pushed my purse onto the edge of the table and shook my head, "We're going the wrong direction. I'm not keeping this baby."

"Don't kill it," Sydney cried.

"It's not killing *anything*, Sydney. Really, it isn't even a baby yet," I snapped.

She nodded her head as she began to cry. As she worked herself into a full blown sob, she covered her face with her hands and spoke through the gaps in her fingers.

"Yes it is…" she blubbered.

"It's part of you…"

"And it's part of…him."

She slid her hands against her face and attempted to wipe the tears away, "How about waiting?"

I couldn't believe my ears. I expected them to provide support - maybe not both of them - but at least one. I went into the bar with visions of one of them taking me to the abortion clinic, and holding my hand through it all, making me feel better about the decision. Afterward, it would be a secret the three of us shared, and took to our graves. Otis and I living happily ever after would stand as proof that the decision we made was the right choice, and the three of us would be reminded of it every day that he and I lived in our state of true love.

I stood from my seat. Avery continued to sit in the booth, arms crossed, glaring at me.

"So no support from either of you on this?" I asked as I clutched my purse tightly.

Sydney stood.

Avery glared.

And I began to cry.

OTIS

I hadn't spoken with Sam in over twenty-four hours, and I had not seen her in person since the patch in party. Two trips to her mother's house since the party produced nothing, and now she wasn't answering texts or calls. I considered the death of Cash, and how it may have had an effect on her. Although she seemed to take the loss of her mother very well, Cash's death may have been enough to cause her to go into a recession of sorts. Frustrated beyond compare and feeling quite helpless, I sat on bench in her mother's back yard and waited.

We had spent many a night in the backyard, and I always enjoyed the smell of the flowers. After Sam and I parted, the smell of any type of flowers always seemed to bring thoughts of her back to the forefront of my mind. Now, sitting amidst the very yard we grew up enjoying, I was feeling empty and heartbroken.

Other than her going back to St. Louis and possibly having second thoughts of us remaining together, I could come up with no reason for her to be gone. As I glanced around the yard and made note of the changes her mother had made since I'd seen it last, I began to consider other possibilities.

Kidnapping.

Murder.

Car wreck.

Another relationship.

Marriage.

My mind began to spin in circles. I wondered if it was possible that the ATF had her in for questioning, but had no idea of how to find out if they did. After much thought, I decided I'd drive to wherever Gunner was and threaten him until he told me everything he knew.

I gazed beyond the flowers, shrubbery and trees into the corner of the yard. The small yellow building her mother housed her tools in was still in the corner of the yard. As kids, we used to hide in the little shack and make out, often kissing for hours and hours, not necessarily knowing - or being afraid to go forward – with what the next step was.

I cherished those days. The innocence of us both. Kissing until our jaws were tired, riding my bike home afterward, filled with a feeling that nothing or no one provided me since. After I'd get home, I'd lie in bed and rub my lips as I counted the hours until we'd be able to kiss her again.

Loving Sam wasn't a decision I made, it was something that simply happened. Even before I kissed her the first time, I knew. The affection I felt for her was even more apparent every time we were apart, as I would ache for her to return. When we were together, the pain would disappear, only to return again as soon as we separated.

After our first kiss nothing changed - except the level of pain I felt when we were apart. Being away from her after the first time we made love was nothing short of impossible, and we quickly became inseparable following the memorable event. We remained at each other's sides until the end.

I shifted my eyes from the shack to the yard and glanced around at the flowers as I stood. The yard was where we began our relationship, had our first kiss, and also where the relationship ended. As I stared blankly at the mixture of colors and the contrast of it all, I felt the irony in my standing in the yard once again, feeling as if something changed between us.

Although I had no idea what caused the change, it hurt, and it hurt deeply. Loving someone has the ability to provide the greatest degree of pleasure or the deepest feeling of indescribable pain. Which you receive is determined by whether or not the same level of love you're giving is returned.

And right now, I was receiving nothing in return.

SAM

The thought of losing Otis weighed heavy on my heart. My decision to have an abortion had been made, and I felt there was no other way to proceed living life without going through with it. Doing it without the support of someone else - as much as hated admitting it - was more difficult than I would have ever expected.

I sat with my head in my hands and cried, knowing I was going to go through the pain, feelings of emptiness, and second guessing the decision entirely for the rest of my life.

Alone.

Being with Otis again provided me with the greatest gift I could have ever expected. Loving him, and not wondering if I was being loved in return – but knowing – elevated me onto a platform I had never had the previous luxury of being upon. From there I felt as if I looked down upon the other women in the world, knowing they would never have what I was so fortunate to possess.

A man who naturally and without any effort – loved them in return – for the love they provided him.

I wiped my eyes and gazed out the window with unfocused eyes. As my side on the console of the car sat the only other option I felt I had.

A butcher knife.

In the four days since I found out I was pregnant something in me changed. As much as I wanted to remain with Otis for the rest of my life, the thought of having the baby that was growing inside of me eliminated what was becoming more and more difficult to accept as being the *right* choice. If I wanted to stay with Otis, I knew it was the only choice, but it didn't necessarily make it the right choice.

Committing suicide initially seemed to be a far-fetched answer to a desperate cry for help. As time passed and the pain worsened, I felt it was a little more viable of an option. If I could develop the courage to do so, it would allow me to leave this world with my baby, with Otis still loving me, and me without a doubt continuing to love him.

I wondered when they found me what they would think. If Avery and Sydney, after it was all over, would tell Otis what had happened, or if they would refrain from telling him, causing him to wonder if it was something he did, said, or didn't do or say. Causing him pain wasn't anything I wanted to do, but the pain I was feeling wasn't anything I could continue to live with.

Not for much longer.

I closed my eyes and clutched my chest. The pain was almost unbearable.

Continuing to live with the level of pain I was feeling would be impossible. I needed to do something, and I needed to do it fast. The pain was smothering me.

I closed my eyes and wished Otis was holding me in his arms. To feel his arms around me again would soothe the pain, and make everything better. I swallowed heavily, pressed my clenched fists against my chest, and clutched my purse. After a few minutes of rocking back and forth in the seat, nothing changed.

I opened my eyes, glanced out the window, shifted my eyes to the console, and turned toward the window again. The pain continued to worsen.

I glanced at the console and closed my eyes. For a long moment I allowed myself to drift off to a land where Otis and I ran through a field of flowers, holding our child's hands in ours, laughing and loving each other as the flowers beat against our wrists.

I inhaled a shallow breath through my nose. The unmistakable scent of lilac filled my nostrils.

I opened my eyes and gazed at the knife.

My decision was made.

OTIS

"It could be a lot of things, brother. Don't jump to conclusions. You know what I say about the word *assume* don't you? Makes an ass of you and me," Axton said as he turned toward the kitchen.

"When's she going to be here?" I huffed as I glanced at my watch.

"Her and Toad's Ol' Lady are on their way back now. There probably at that little stretch of highway between Wichita and here where there's no service. She'll be here in a bit. Want one of her beers?" he asked as he opened the refrigerator.

"Sure," I sighed as I sat down.

"Good news about Gunner though," Axton said as he handed me a bottle of *Red's Apple Ale*.

I gazed at the bottle and shook my head, "Yeah. Hard to believe he's going to spend thirteen months in the joint. Good for the club though."

"What's hard to believe is that it happened so fast," Axton said as he sat down across from me.

I took a drink of the beer, winced from the taste, and stared down at the bottle. As I looked up, I began to explain what Gunner had told me.

"He said he refused to testify, and they had a special hearing with a magistrate. In the hearing he said he'd misplaced a few crucial reports. He didn't tell *them* they were crucial, but he said they would implicate us in a few things. Anyway, after the missing reports and his statement of no wrong doings on our part while under oath, they asked him to reconsider and gave him a few days to change his story. He went back in for the second hearing," I paused and took another drink of the sweet ale.

"And after he said the same thing, they threatened him with obstruction of justice and tampering with evidence. He waived his right to a jury trial, plead guilty, and they sentenced him the next day at what he called a bench trial as an example to other ATF agents. He said he's got to surrender to US Marshals in about 30 days."

"And you say he showed you all of this on the computer?" Axton shrugged.

I nodded my head, "On the US Attorney's official website. They list all crimes and sentencing there as a deterrent. Yeah, it's right there. Lost his job, pension, everything…"

"I guess everybody has a job to do, just wish his job didn't include fucking with us," Axton said as he lifted the bottle of water to his mouth.

I felt nervous and sick. It had been two days since we had spoken and four days since I'd seen her. No matter what was behind this, nothing good could come of it. No differently than any other Sinner, I refused to talk to anyone about my problems other than Axton. Admitting to the other men that I had a problem or that I was in pain, especially as a result of a woman, would make me appear weak and incapable.

I drank the remaining beer and pushed the bottle between my thighs. Going to Axton's house wasn't something I normally did, and for whatever reason, I had always perceived his home as being off limits. To him, it was a sacred place, and I realized that about him. Our discussions generally went on in the shop or office at the clubhouse, or some other remote location. Sitting in his chair and talking to him was another reminder of the fact that my life was in shambles. I felt like I was at a funeral of an uncle I didn't know, and in a house I was unfamiliar and uncomfortable with.

"Yeah," I sighed.as I stood.

"Where you want this?" I asked as I held the bottle at arms; length.

"Garage," he said as he pointed to the garage door.

As I opened the door to the garage, the unmistakable sound of a car in the driveway caught my attention. I tossed the bottle in the trash, walked to the kitchen, and grabbed another beer from the fridge. Eager to take my search to the next step, and hoping for a miracle, I walked into the living room and sat down.

"Got another beer," I said as I raised the bottle.

Axton shook his head, "Take as many as you want, brother."

Avery walked in through the front door, and although she could clearly see my bike in the driveway, did little to disguise her shock of seeing me in the living room. It was obvious to me either Axton had said something to her about my concerns – which I seriously doubted – or she knew something about Sam's disappearance.

As I anxiously waited for her to sit down, Axton stood and spoke.

"Otis has some concerns about Sam. Want to come in and talk?" he asked.

"Sure, Uhhm. Let me get a beer," she responded.

After getting a beer from the fridge, she came in the living room and sat cross-legged on the floor beside Axton's chair. After taking a few sips from my beer as I studied her, I proceeded with caution.

"When was the last time you talked to Sam?" I asked.

"Been a few days, I suppose," she shrugged.

"Do you remember the exact day?" I asked.

She took a drink of beer, gazing at me over the top of the bottle as she did so. After lowering the bottle to her lap, she inhaled, exhaled, and took another drink.

"Day before yesterday," she sighed.

"Really? What time of day was it?" I asked.

She shrugged her shoulders, "I don't know. Evening time. We all had a drink at the bar, her and Syd and me."

"Evening, huh? You sure it was the day before yesterday?" I asked as I tried to piece together a timeline.

It would have been the day after I talked to Sam last, and if Avery's recollection was correct, the fact Sam talked to her after talking to me - and had not talked to me since - bothered me.

She stared blankly beyond me for a moment, shifted her focus to me, and responded.

"Yeah, I'm sure," she sighed.

"What was going on?" I asked.

"I don't know," she shrugged, "We were just having a drink."

I rolled my eyes, feeling as if I was Jack's attorney attempting to pry information from the ATF agent in court. After taking half of the bottle of beer in one gulp, I stood and began pacing the room.

"Did she call you and want to get together?" I asked.

"Yeah, she did," she responded.

I turned around, frustrated by the lack of information Avery was providing. As I stood and glared at her, I realized I hadn't really explained the nature of my question asking session. After draining the remaining beer from the bottle, I sighed and continued.

"Look, Sam's missing. Nobody knows her more than I do, *nobody*, and this isn't like her at all. You were the last one to talk to her, and anything you can say that'll help me, I'd appreciate. What'd you guys talk about?" I asked.

She uncrossed her legs and stood. Still holding the bottle in her hand, she crossed her arms and studied me.

"Look, she talked about a lot of things. I can't really say," she said flatly.

"What do you mean you *can't say*? She's missing, Avery. *Missing*. I need to find her. Help me out," I said through my teeth.

"Look," she said as she turned toward Axton.

She shifted her eyes to meet mine and sighed, "If anyone knows and respects it, it should be you two. She asked me not to say, and I'm not saying."

Axton stood from his seat and turned to face her, placing his arm on her shoulder as he did.

"Anything you can say might help, anything at all," he said.

As she began to speak, her voice filled with emotion and began to falter, "And I *can't* say anything. It's no different...no different than either of you not...uhhm...not discussing club business with...you know...just anyone. You're sworn to...uhhm...secrecy. Well, respect the fact...that I am too."

"Avery," I began to beg.

She waved her arms in front of her chest, sloshing beer onto the carpet as she did so, "*No!* Answer this, Otis. Did you tell anyone about me shooting those guys that night we got robbed in Mexican town?"

I shook my head, clearly seeing where she was headed, "Nope."

"Alright then. And you didn't because you're sworn to secrecy. I told her I wouldn't..."

And she lost her composure and began to cry. As the lifted her hand to her face and began to wipe the tears, she turned away. Axton reached for her shoulder just as she stomped her foot.

"God fucking damn you, Otis," she shouted as her foot hit the floor.

"God fuckin damn you," she repeated as he turned around.

I clasped my palms together as if praying, "What? Did *I* do something? Come on, Avery."

She caught her breath, inhaled, and after a few seconds, exhaled loudly. As she nodded her head, my heart sank and the pit of my stomach felt like a stone had been dropped into it.

"I can't tell you where she is," she said as she exhaled again.

"Because I don't know. And I uhhm…I can't tell you what she said," she paused and handed Axton her bottle of beer.

As she rubbed her hands against the thighs of her jeans, she continued, "Because I said I wouldn't."

"But if you know her like you say you do, maybe you'll find her. If you were her," she paused and inhaled sharply.

"And you had a decision to make that no woman ever wants to have to fucking make," she began to cry again, and covered her face as she did.

She removed her hands from her face and talked through the tears and sobbing, "And that decision, Otis, that fucking decision…"

"It's got to do…it's got to do with both of you. And she's…she's scared, Otis. She's scared you'll uhhm…scared you'll leave her if you find out," she blubbered.

My mind raced in a million different directions. Confused and sick and tired of the games, lack of information, and angry with the fact Avery wouldn't simply tell me what I needed to know, I searched my, mind for answers while she attempted to catch her breath.

"Because you already…" she cried.

"Left her once for it…"

And I knew.

"Motherfucker!" I shouted as I turned and stomped toward the door.

"*Otis,*" Axton sighed loudly from behind me.

As I rode through the yard, over the curb, and into the street, I saw Axton hop on his bike. It didn't matter, he had no idea where I was going, and there was no way he could ever catch me to find out.

OTIS

I pulled my bike to the edge of the road and stopped, knowing it would never make it down the hill and to where I needed to go. The rest of the trip would be on foot. Although it was out of my view, I felt certain I was where I needed to be.

I stepped over the seat of the bike, reached in my pocket, and grabbed my keys. As I stuck the key into the ignition and locked the bike, the brass keychain Ripp had given me in Austin hung from the key ring.

His favorite saying inscribed on the brass disc, the words were something I had always felt, but hadn't composed into the exact phrase he'd so carefully stamped into to the charm. I clenched it between my thumb and forefingers and rubbed my thumb against the center. After a quick prayer, I looked at the words, and hoped Ripp's phrase was applicable today of all days.

I Got This.

Brother Ripp, I hope you're right.

I opened my saddle bag, pulled the bag from the inside, and placed the items in the two side pockets of my cut. After inhaling a nervous breath, I sighed, turned toward the hill, and began jogging down the path I had spent so many weekend nights walking along as a teen.

When I reached the corner of the path that turned and led down to the river, I saw her car parked along the edge narrow dirt drive. Seeing it provided me hope and filled me with worry at the same time. I glanced toward the tree, and could see her slumped at the base.

I inhaled a choppy breath, swallowed heavily, and exhaled. As I jumped over the edge and began running down the hill, three words continued to rattle around in my head.

I. Got. This.

SAM

I sat at the base of the tree with the butcher knife in my hand, praying for the strength to make the right decision. As much as I realized suicide wasn't the most practical decision or the best for everyone with a similar circumstance, I felt it was *my* most logical choice. After having spent several hours attempting to develop the courage to proceed, I sat exhausted, clenching the knife.

As time passed I became weary. Lacking sleep for several days, I knew if I could stay awake a little longer I may not develop the courage, but I would be able to proceed from lack of will to continue to fight myself.

As I drifted off into an almost dream like state, I heard a motorcycle in the distance. Thoughts of Otis filled my mind. The sound seemed to grow closer and closer. Certain I was losing what little logic I had left, I smiled and glanced up toward the top of the hill.

The sound stopped.

Disappointed, I gazed at the top of the hill as I clutched the knife. After a period of time I was incapable of measuring, a figure appeared at the top of the hill. I stared, feeling as if it truly was a dream, and the figure was an angel – the answer to my problems hanging on her lips – sure to come as soon as she reached the bottom of the hill.

I blinked.

The figure began to come down the hill. As it grew closer, I realized it was either Otis, or I was losing my mind. As the distance narrowed, I *knew* it was either Otis or I had gone completely batty. Using what little strength I had left, I reached up and tossed the knife over my shoulder and into the tall weeds behind me.

"Sam," his voice was soft and soothing.

I blinked my eyes and smiled.

"Sam, are you alright?" he asked.

I nodded my head and tried to stand. As I stood, my weak legs shook, almost causing me to fall. I realized as he reached out to support me I had been sitting for hours and my legs had fallen asleep.

"Did you take something, Sam? Are you on anything?" he asked.

I shook my head, "Legs fell asleep."

"What's going on, Sam? Is there something you need to tell me?" he asked.

I shrugged my shoulders, not knowing what to say. I loved him more than anything, and losing him was more than I could bear to imagine.

"Sam. I love you. Whatever it is, no matter *what* it is, you and I will be fine. You need to *know* that. I mean it. No matter what," he assured me as he held my shoulders in his hands.

"But," I sighed.

I wanted to tell him. I desperately wanted to, but I couldn't muster the courage. After studying him for a few moments, I pulled away, bent down, and picked up my purse. Clutching it tightly and holding it to my chest, I glanced up and I nodded my head.

"Just say it, Sam. Whatever it is that's got you worried," he breathed.

"I'm pregnant," the words escaped my lips before I had a chance to stop them.

Fearful, embarrassed, and waiting for the wrath of God to come down upon me, I clutched my purse and waited.

"You sure?" he asked.

I held my purse to my chest and nodded my head.

"Good," he said, "That's what I was hoping."

I glanced up, and as hard as I tried, couldn't fight back the tears.

"You're not…mad?" I sobbed.

He shook his head as he reached into the side pockets of his cut, "Mad? No Sam, I'm not mad. I love you."

I sighed and continued to clutch my purse.

As he dug in his pockets, he continued, "I'm not proud of it, but as a Sinner, I've played a part – a first-hand part – in seeing many lives leave this earth. Death has become a part of who I am, Sam. To think I could share something as special as bringing a life into this earth, and doing it with you?"

He pulled two pieces of cloth from his cut. As he straightened the fabric and let it hang from his fingers, it was clear what they were. Standing in front of me, holding two rompers – one blue and one pink – he began to softly cry.

"I didn't know what color to get, so I got one of each," he shrugged.

I released my grasp from my purse, reached inside, and pulled out the pregnancy test. As I held it up for him to see, he grinned.

"This just says I'm pregnant, it doesn't give a sex," I grinned as I began to cry again.

"Either way, as long as you two are both healthy, I'll be happy as fuck," he said as he turned his head and wiped his tears on his shoulder.

"How'd you know?" I blubbered.

"I didn't. I just hoped," he responded.

"So you want this?" I asked, wanting as much confirmation as possible.

"More than anything," he nodded.

"How'd you know where I was?"

"Really Sam? You lost your virginity at this tree. Damned thing's been here as the biggest tree in the state for over a hundred years. We used to spend a lot of time here. This was our sacred tree. *Meet me at the big tree.* How many times did you hear that?" he asked.

"Not near enough," I sobbed as I put the pregnancy test back into my purse.

He dropped the rompers beside where he stood and opened his arms. And, as the happiest woman in the world, I dropped my purse, embraced him in a hug, and held him in my arms. As we stood under our sacred tree and held each other, my heart filled with gratitude for Otis and for everything we shared as a couple.

I guess the Sinners are right.

The devil looks after his own.

EPILOGUE

The small room, fitted with two chairs, one medical examination bed, and an Aplio 500 ultrasound machine had three occupants. A pregnant woman, lying on the examination bed, had her gown lifted to the bottom of her swollen breasts. The man, seated beside her and holding her hand in his, stared anxiously at the display screen.

The Physician's Assistant moved the wand carefully along the woman's stomach as she gazed at the screen.

"There's the head," she said as she touched a button on the keyboard, taking a still photo of the image.

"And the legs. Hold on a minute and we'll see if…" she said as she moved the wand up and down slightly.

"This will be cold," she said as she squirted lubricant onto the woman's stomach.

After repositioning the wand, pressing it into the bottom of the woman's stomach, she gazed at the screen.

"If you don't want to know the sex, don't look," she grinned.

"We do, Mrs. Buckly," the woman responded as she glanced at the man as he nodded his head eagerly.

"Call me Debi," she said.

"We do Debi," they said in unison.

"Well, see this?" she said as she motioned to the screen with her free hand.

The man and woman nodded their heads.

"Hips," Debi said.

"And *this,*" she sighed, "His penis."

"Boy?" the man said as he shifted his eyes from the screen to his wife.

"He's definitely a boy. No two ways about it," Debi chuckled as she pressed the button to take another still image of the screen.

"Sam?" the man sighed as he wiped tears from his eyes.

"We're having a little boy," he said, "I can't wait to tell my parents."

His wife nodded her head as she gazed at three dimensional depiction of her son on the screen.

Down the hallway, on the other side of the entrance to the small clinic, four men stood anxiously talking. Dressed in jeans, boots, and leather vests adorned with the patch of the motorcycle club they represented, they stood out in clear contrast amongst the women in the lobby. After a few moments the large man with a beard turned, grasped the door handle, and opened the door slightly.

"Can we come in?" he asked the receptionist seated a fifteen feet away at the admissions desk.

After a moment with no response from the receptionist, he cleared his throat and repeated the question.

"Hey *you.* Behind the desk. Can we come in?" he asked.

She shook her head and forced a smile, "I'm sorry. The ultrasound area is reserved for the husband, wife, and the immediate family," she explained.

He turned toward the other three men, "Family only."

The tall muscular man with olive colored skin shrugged his shoulders,

"Well open the fucking door, Biscuit. We're her brothers."

The bearded man opened the door enough to fit his head between the door and the frame.

"We're her brothers," he whispered.

The receptionist peered through the opening and shook her head in disbelief. The three men, other than sharing the same taste in clothes, appeared to be from four different regions of the world. As she studied the men, the bearded man opened the door a little more, giving her an unobstructed view of the men standing behind him.

She tapped her pencil against the desk as she studied the four men, "Brothers?"

"And the name of your sister?" she asked.

The bearded man turned around and consulted with his friends for a moment. After a short discussion, he turned toward the receptionist.

"Steve and Sam Milner," he responded.

The receptionist shook her head, "I don't know. We're forced to adhere to the policy. Family only."

"Otis!" the bearded man screamed into the vacant corridor.

After a few seconds he screamed again, "Otis!"

The man, still seated beside his wife, turned his head away from the monitor.

"Did you hear someone scream my name?" he asked.

His wife nodded and tilted her head toward the door.

The man stood and opened the door slightly, peering through the crack and down the hallway as he did so.

"What are we havin'?" the bearded man screamed.

"Boy," the man whispered in response.

"What?" the bearded man shouted again.

"Boy!" the man responded in a more distinct tone.

"A fucking boy? Did you say we're havin' a boy?" the bearded man hollered excitedly.

"Yes," the man whispered in response through the opening.

The bearded man turned to face the other three men.

"Pay up motherfuckers. We've got us a boy," he grinned.

As the bearded man turned toward the door once again, he opened it entirely and stood in the opening. The three men behind him each reached for their wallets.

"We all wanna see him. Gal here won't let us come down there. Tell her it's okay," he shouted.

The man extended his raised index finger and turned to face the exam room.

"Fellas are down there. They want to come in and see our baby boy," he grinned toward his wife.

Debi turned to face the man as she furrowed her brow slightly.

"I'm sorry, we can only allow family," she sighed.

The woman glanced up from the exam table and gazed at her leather vest hanging on the hook beside the door. On the back, a Selected Sinners patch with two ribbons, clearly stating her designation with the club.

Property of Otis.

"They're my brothers," the woman stated.

"How many?" Debi asked.

"Here? Four," the woman grinned in response.

Debi nodded her head, "Have them come down. I'll call the desk."

The man peered through the door and waved his arm toward the bearded man, "Come on down."

The bearded man swung the door open and waved toward the men standing anxiously behind him, "Come on fellas, uncle Biscuit's having him a baby boy."

As the men stormed down the hallway, Debi gazed over her shoulder toward the pregnant woman.

"So you have four brothers?" Debi asked.

The pregnant woman glanced up at her leather vest and shook her head.

"No," she responded.

"I have thirty three."

www.ingramcontent.com/pod-product-compliance
Lightning Source LLC
Chambersburg PA
CBHW050715180626
46814CB00002B/447